# RUINSONG

Also by
## JULIA EMBER

*The Seafarer's Kiss*

*The Navigator's Touch*

# RUINSONG

## JULIA EMBER

SQUARE
FISH

New York

SQUARE
FISH

An imprint of Macmillan Publishing Group, LLC
120 Broadway, New York, NY 10271
fiercereads.com

Square Fish and the Square Fish logo are trademarks of Macmillan and
are used by Farrar Straus Giroux under license from Macmillan.

Our books may be purchased in bulk for promotional, educational,
or business use. Please contact your local bookseller or the Macmillan
Corporate and Premium Sales Department at (800) 221-7945 ext. 5442 or
by email at MacmillanSpecialMarkets@macmillan.com.

Library of Congress Control Number: 2019060198

Originally published in the United States by Farrar Straus Giroux
First Square Fish edition, 2021
Book designed by Cassie Gonzales
Square Fish logo designed by Filomena Tuosto
Printed in the United States of America

ISBN 978-1-250-80267-5 (paperback)
1  2  3  4  5  6  7  8  9  10

*For Sophie*

"Underground rebellions, bardic magic, and ruthless tyrannical queens make this a book you don't want to miss."
—HYPABLE

"A darkly shining jewel of a story set in a fascinating new world. This queer romantic fantasy will replay itself in your mind long after you've finished, like an unforgettable melody."
—SARAH GLENN MARSH, author of the Reign of the Fallen series

"*Ruinsong* is a symphony of my favorite things: powerful girls, glittering gowns, and falling in love across a divide. Julia Ember's masterful storytelling immerses you in a world of ruthless magic and court politics. Utterly bewitching and emotionally devastating in all the best ways, *Ruinsong* is a queer fantasy that will captivate the heart and inspire the soul."
—C. B. LEE, author of *Not Your Sidekick*

"An engaging fantasy novel that will push readers to draw parallels between the narrative and contemporary events and conflicts and, hopefully, empower them to use their own voices to stand up for what they believe in."
—SCHOOL LIBRARY JOURNAL

"Ember's prose is smooth and efficient, and her viewpoint characters are believable, compelling individuals . . . I read it in a single three-hour sitting, and I do look forward to seeing more of Ember's work in future."
—TOR.COM

There is some music that is so terrible that it consumes all those who approach it.

—Gaston Leroux, *The Phantom of the Opera*

# RUINSONG

# PRELUDE

# CADENCE

I SIT IN THE CORRIDOR with my dog in my lap, singing him to sleep. My throat stings with magic as the words of the spellsong tumble from my lips. The puppy nuzzles closer, sleeping breath caressing the back of my hand as he snores. His russet ears are as soft as velvet, and he's small enough that his warm body fits in the crook of my knee. His paws twitch, and I lower the key of my song, the way Madam has shown me, and coax him into gentler dreams.

Footsteps approach. I look up, hoping to see my friend Remi racing toward me. The sun is starting to dim, its low rays painting Cavalia's white stone walls in brilliant shades of mulberry and vermillion. Remi's lessons are usually finished by now, and if she doesn't hurry, we'll miss the winter daylight altogether.

She hasn't come in a few days, but this is our alcove—our place—and I'll wait for her until the sun sets.

Instead, my singing tutor marches down the hall, her arms full of books and music sheets. I kneel and hurriedly adjust my skirt so it covers my legs. I'm not on the streets anymore, and it isn't proper for a singer to show her ankles in public. Madam Guillard is strict about such things.

Madam stops in front of me and clicks her tongue at my dog. She sets her books on the bench beside the wall and bends down to scratch Nip's white belly before taking him from my arms. One of his ears twitches, but he sleeps on, snug and sweetly oblivious under the blanket of my spell.

"You shouldn't play with him in your nice clothes. You're to meet the queen, and you'll be all wrinkled," Madam scolds.

Her golden hair, streaked with gray, is bound tightly in a coiled bun. She wears a brocade gown, the same shade of singer's emerald as my skirt, though much more fine. It's strange to see my tutor wear any color other than black. She never made such efforts for the old queen.

"Yes, Madam," I murmur, and smooth my hand over the crumpled fabric of my skirt. My face reddens with shame as I try to brush away the short, white puppy hairs that cling to the taffeta.

As an orphan, my tuition at the mages' academy is paid by

the crown. If she likes me, the new queen could take me away from the school to live with her in the palace down the hill, with servants, a room to myself, and my own bathroom. I've never had such luxuries. But if she doesn't, Queen Elene could have me expelled without a copper to my name.

Before I came to the academy, I lived at the city children's home: a sunless warren infested with rats and fleas. I still have scars on my calves from bites picked raw. The new queen is a mage herself, young and eager to recruit new singers. In her household, I could earn a permanent place. I would never have to fear hunger or fleas again.

And in the palace, I'd be closer to Remi. Her mother, the Countess of Bordelain, has apartments in the eastern wing near the queen's own. I could seek Remi out after her lessons, instead of always waiting, hoping that she will have time to come by. She's not a mage, but she's the best friend I've made since I came here.

I stand and put a bit more effort into brushing myself off.

"You'll do fine," Madam soothes. "Just do exactly as the queen asks and remember our practice."

I trace the square of the divine quartet on my chest and touch the prayer stone around my neck for luck. The stone is the only thing of my ma's I have: a blue lapis, chipped and unfinished, just like my fading memories of her.

Madam extends her hand, and I grasp it, folding my small hand into hers. She leads me down the corridor to our little replica of the great Opera Hall in Cannis. Inside, someone has lit the chandelier. The crystal light illuminates the stage and casts the rest of the room in shadow, golden muses glittering above. They're usually covered in dust, but someone scrubbed them for the queen's visit.

Our new queen sits in the front row of stalls. A footman perches beside her on the floor. She is a white woman who wears her raven hair piled atop her head and styled with silver pins. In place of a crown, she has painted a musical scale in gold dust, with notes depicting the first chords of a storm song. She wears a red velvet dress, trimmed with singer's green along the hem.

My heart swells. She is a mage, Bordea's first singer queen, and she proclaims it with such pride. She smiles at me, as if inviting me to be proud, too. I can't help returning her grin with one of my own.

An opera mask of fine silver adorns her face, welded to look like lace. It covers her nose and most of her ivory cheeks, almost reminiscent of portraits I've seen of Odetta, the goddess of spring and renewal. Though I am sure she wears it only for fashion, since as mages we all serve Adela, the goddess of summer and song.

I saw the old queen a handful of times at ceremonies, dances, and court banquets when the whole academy was invited to sing as an ensemble. And once, up close, when Remi dragged me along to play in the audience chamber, and we were forced to hide under the skirting of a clerk's table when the court began its session. Queen Celeste had been frail and soft-spoken, with translucent pearl skin as thin as tracing paper. Not like a queen at all.

The footman stands and evaluates me with a hard gaze. I clutch Madam's hand as he circles. His billowing black robes flutter like wings.

"She's very small," he says doubtfully. He pats my cheek as I shrink back behind my tutor.

"She's only eight," Madam Guillard says. "But her skill is unequaled. And as Your Majesty knows, we have only three novice corporeal chantrixes at present."

The footman raises a skeptical eyebrow. "Still, she is very young. Her Majesty was hoping to take on a pupil who would be ready to perform in a few years. The uprisings in the north are already getting out of hand. The queen wishes to begin the demonstrations as soon as possible. Dame Ava is up to the task for now, but she is pushing seventy."

In a panic, I look at the queen again. If I don't live up to her expectations, would she hesitate to get rid of me? Madam will not say much about the queen's history in my presence, but I have heard the older students whisper about her. I know that she did not inherit the throne from Queen Celeste, like all our other queens before.

And I know that mages who displease her have started to disappear.

"I promise you," says Madam, "she has been very well taught."

"We'll test her," the queen says. Her voice is deeper than I expected, and raspy. But her words have a singer's lilt and rhythm. She smiles at me again and flashes perfect teeth, straightened with magic and buffed to a porcelain white.

Queen Elene pivots and snaps her fingers at a guard half-hidden behind one of the chamber's pillars. The guard wears a mask as well, tapered gold to match the queen's emblem on his chest. He drags a young white boy from behind him into the light. Skinny and shaking, with smudges of dirt staining his cheeks, the boy stares at me with wide, frightened eyes.

Madam crouches beside me and brings her lips to my ear. In her arms, Nip's eyes open a fraction. I hum a few bars of the sleeping song. He licks my cheek before slumping again.

"You know the heating song we practiced? With the bone stock?" Madam asks. "Her Majesty wants you to sing it for her."

I glance around the chamber for a bowl of milk or duck's

blood. I can't heat air or water. My magic doesn't extend to the elements. I can only affect things that are alive, or have been: plants, animals, or . . .

"You will use him," Madam says, pointing at the boy. Her hand trembles slightly in the air. "And you must not stop until the queen commands you to."

"But you told me not to practice on other children," I protest. Remi asks me all the time for demonstrations, but I have almost always obeyed Madam and refused.

"That's right. You must never practice on other children when you are alone. But this is different. This isn't practice. You are performing for Her Majesty."

"Is he cold?" I ask.

"Very," Madam whispers.

The boy starts to thrash in the guard's hold. The idea of magic terrifies some. They've never been taught or exposed to it. They don't understand that magic can help them. I remember as much from before I came to Cavalia.

But it's midwinter, and I remember the damp walls of the city home, too, the frosty nights when we all huddled together under shared, threadbare blankets and listened to the rats chatter under the floor. I still get cold here, when I forget my cloak or when the snow falls. But at the orphanage it was another kind of cold: a chill that permeated all the way to my bones and clung to my ribs. When the palace officials came for me, after learning of my summer birthday, I hadn't been able to bring any of my friends. Sometimes, when I sit beside my fire in the room I share with Carinda, a bowl of warm stew cradled in my lap, I still think of them.

I can help this boy. For a time, I can make him feel as safe and comfortable as Nip, who dozes against Madam's shoulder. I can give him the memory of warmth.

I climb onto the stage and stand in the center circle, right beneath the chandelier as I have been taught. I straighten my spine and look out into the space where the queen sits, though I can't see her beyond the glare of the lights.

As soon as I begin to hum, magic lifts my senses. I don't need to see the boy to sing for him. I can hear his breathing and the wild hammering of his heart. I feel the pull of his life calling to Adela's magic inside me. He doesn't have to be scared. I clear my throat and begin my warm-up.

"Well, at least she sounds like an angel," says the footman, as I ascend through the scales. "But is her magic strong? We don't need a beautiful voice. We need power."

"Give her a chance," the queen urges, her smoky, regal voice cutting through the darkness.

I abandon the scales and begin the heat ballad. My song

starts as a whisper. Madam and I have practiced this. I know that the temperature of a living boy is a delicate thing. If I sing too loudly, if I lose track of the melody, he will develop a fever or burns on his skin. I remember the bowl of milk Madam placed on her studio floor the first day she worked with me on the heat song. I bellowed out the words, and the liquid boiled to froth, spilling over the edges of the bowl like sea foam.

"Louder, dear, we can't hear you," the queen calls.

Madam Guillard steps onto the stage beside me and takes my hand. "You must do as your queen desires." The corners of her mouth twitch down, and she winces as if in pain. She hums a low song and the chandelier dims, its fire quelled by her command. As a chantrix of elements, my tutor can direct the air. "Maybe Her Majesty will hear you better if she can see your lips."

Spots of light dance in my vision. The queen and her footman flicker back into view. The guard stands beside the stage, holding the urchin with both arms. The boy does not look sleepy or comfortable. Hot tears mark tracks down his dirty cheeks. Scratches cover the guard's burly forearms.

My chin starts to wobble.

"You will sing until Her Majesty begs you to stop. Else you will sing for your little dog instead," the footman snaps.

I look at the boy with his tattered clothes, his skinny limbs and sorrowful eyes, then at my puppy, now awake and whimpering under the crook of Madam's free arm. Nip's small brown ears perk, and he wags his tail at me.

If I had been born without magic, if I had stayed at the city home, a lone orphan among many, it could have been me in this boy's place. If I fail the queen's test, if I am expelled, I might still share his fate.

Tears pool in my eyes, and dread curdles in my stomach, because I know what the right thing to do is, and I can't do it.

I start to sing again. The queen sits back in her chair and smiles. I sing and sing as the boy screams and buckles to his knees, as his skin cracks and blisters, as boiling blood begins to stream from his nostrils, from his sweet, round mouth and too-large ears. I don't look away. My voice does not waver.

After all, I have been well taught.

# CHAPTER 1
# CADENCE

**I LIGHT THE CANDLES** and hum as the prayer chimes begin. The heat from each candle propels a tiny wooden fan connected to an individual music box. The bronze bells inside the boxes each emit one note, played over and over. The ringing metal blends in a mechanical harmony. I close my eyes and lose myself in the simple, familiar tune. The incense tickles my nose with lavender.

The prayer songs are meant to be performed a cappella and in an ensemble beneath the open sky, where Adela can witness, but most of us perform them alone now. Elene doesn't prohibit prayer to Adela, but such public displays of piety and shared song have fallen out of fashion now that our queen worships another.

The double doors to my suite fly open behind me, but I

don't turn around or open my eyes. Today is a day for chaos, for pain, and I will cherish this peace for as long as I can. I've been preparing for this day all year, and still, it's come far too soon.

"It's time to go." Lacerde's voice cuts through the melody. My maid leans over my shoulder and blows out the first of the candles. The propeller stops, and one of the shrill voices dies. The melody falters, incomplete.

She blows out the other candles, but I hum the rest of the song anyway. She begins styling my hair while I'm still on my knees. Her deft, wrinkled fingers sweep through my hair and braid a small section into a crown.

"Your dress is waiting for you at the Opera Hall," she says, dabbing my cheeks with white powder. "There is a carriage waiting for us outside."

I nod and rise slowly to my feet. My legs are numb from holding the position for so long, and despite the prayer, my soul feels heavy, too. Lacerde helps me into a black traveling cloak and ties the hood so it covers most of my face.

She bustles me down the hallway and out into the palace courtyard, where a black carriage stands. The horses are plain brown palfreys, not the showy white stallions Elene usually favors. Today I must pass through Cannis unnoticed. The sight of me, before the event, could provoke a riot.

The driver helps Lacerde into the carriage, but I ignore the hand he holds out for me. The echo of the prayer bells still chimes in my head, and I want to hold on to the song for as long as I can. As a corporeal mage, it's hard for me to focus on the ethereal prayers. My magic yearns for life, and if I touch something alive now, after connecting with the goddess, it will well up of its own accord, eager.

Hopping back up into his seat, the driver clicks his tongue, and the palfreys set off at a canter. We pass through the rear gates of Cavalia, and the guards pause their game of Tam to salute us.

"Are you warm enough?" Lacerde asks. Without waiting for me to respond, she drapes a fur over my lap. The cold autumn air seeps through the gaps in the carriage door, making the small hairs of my arms stand up.

I give her a little smile, even though I'm dizzy with nerves.

I expect the driver to veer right at the fork, onto the main road that leads to the city. Instead, he takes the left route that winds to the outer gates of Cannis and the farmlands beyond. I open the window and lean out. "This is not the route," I call to him. "We're to go straight to the hall."

"No, Principal," he says. "I have direct instructions from Her Majesty to take you this way."

My stomach curls into a knot. There is only one place

Elene would send me along the western wall. I sit back in my seat and look pleadingly at Lacerde. "Why are we going there?"

Lacerde reaches across and clasps my hand. Her fingers are clammy with sweat. She's been my maid for three years now, the longest any of them have ever lasted, and she understands me better than anyone. "We're not stopping, but I think the queen wanted you to see it. That's what the chief justicar told me, anyway."

"I've seen it before."

"She wants you to remember." She winces in sympathy, gaze focused on her lap.

The palfreys keep a steady pace, but I refuse to look out the window now. Beyond the majestic hunting park that flanks the palace's rear gates lies the settlement of the Expelled: a swampy labyrinth of small alleys, ramshackle houses, and disease. The place I will end up if I disobey the queen.

The smells of human waste, sweat, grasses, and livestock blow into the carriage as we roll through the lush farmlands and pastures. I grew up on the lower streets of Cannis. I'm no stranger to the perfumes of life, in all their many varieties, but as we enter the settlement, the scent changes. Here, misery and loss cling to everything, their smells like burned hair and vinegar. Detectable only to a corporeal singer, they are the worst odors of all.

I pull my cloak up over my nose, trying to block them out, but after years of training with magic, my senses are over-tuned.

The carriage rattles to a halt. I pound on the side of the cab with my fist. Lacerde looks out the window and grimaces.

"I'm to stop here until you look out." The driver's voice trembles. He turns to face us, but he won't meet my eyes.

He's afraid of me, I realize. But not enough to go against Elene's wishes.

I take a deep breath. Elene *would* be specific with her orders, especially today. I lean forward in my seat and glance out the window.

A group of elderly men huddle beside the crumbling western wall. They hold their hands out to the carriage but make no sound. Farther on, a town of broken buildings unfolds before us: houses made from scrap wood and metal, with holes in the roofs, all of them small, barely big enough to fit a horse inside. There is a shop selling rotten fruit, and a legion of barefoot, skinny women who trace their stories in the mud with sticks. They wear shirts so old and tattered they almost fall from their wearer's bones. All of them bear the telltale, silver incision scar across their throats.

They are all ankle deep in mud. Elene sends a group of elementals to the settlement once a week to saturate the ground with so much rain it never dries. The fragile houses are continuously washing away in the floods.

No one may trade in the settlement. No one can hire an Expelled worker in Cannis. No one can offer them land to settle elsewhere or even a free room for the night. Those who have tried have ended up in prison, or dead. The inhabitants can leave, to beg in the city or take their chances foraging in the forest among the wolves and bears, but they have no other home to go to and no hope of finding one in Bordea.

A short, white woman with long silver hair points toward the carriage. The scars on her cheeks and across her throat are new, and I recognize her by the shape of her jaw and her fierce amber eyes. A bolt of fear courses through me. Once, Francine Trevale was one of the country's most powerful corporeal mages. She had the ear of the old queen and was famed throughout Bordea for her abilities in war and healing. But she refused to bow to Elene's wishes, and now she is here.

In the academy, they whisper that Francine's strength was such that Elene did not dare have her arrested outright. Instead, they say that the queen sent Francine a chest of jewels to lull the mage into a sense of safety, to make her believe that Elene had chosen to listen to her point of view. Then Elene hired an assassin to sneak into Francine's bedchamber and sever her vocal cords as she slept.

If I refuse what Elene has planned today, she will kill me—if she is feeling merciful. If she isn't, she will exile me here.

"She's seen it," Lacerde growls. "Now drive on."

A group of children dart past the carriage, making the palfreys shy. They sign excitedly to one another in the new language they've created and toss a dried sheep's bladder among them as a ball. They hold a small, precious spark of joy that even Elene for all her cruelty hasn't stamped out. Lacerde smiles at them, and I see her fingers twitch toward her purse.

A small ginger-haired girl misses her catch, and the makeshift ball sails over her head. Our driver snatches it from the air. He digs his nails into the thin, fragile leather until the ball bursts and goes flat. He stuffs it beneath his feet and flicks the reins at the horses to drive on, leaving the children with nothing.

Shuddering, I close the window with a snap.

My dressing room is beneath the main stage of the Opera Hall. It has been decorated to suit me, with fine furnishings in the soft periwinkle Lacerde knows I like. I know better than to think Elene had anything to do with its selection, though she'll probably claim credit later.

The theater servants have left a tray with juice, tea, and fresh pastries on the sofa. I don't touch it.

I allow Lacerde to dress me without turning to examine myself in the mirror. I don't want to see how I look, how they've fashioned me. In my mind, I already see stains of blood on the muslin fabric of my skirt, dotting the white leather of my gloves. Lacerde adjusts my skirt and smooths my hair. Then, with a grunt, she bends down and buffs my new shoes to a gleam.

She opens the door for me so I don't get my gloves dirty and leads me down the dark corridor. My dressing room is the only one in use. All the others are boarded up, so that no one will use them to hide.

I imagine what the Opera Hall must have been like years ago, when so many singers performed here together for more willing audiences. The corridors would have been filled with the sounds of laughter, rustling taffeta costumes, and a chorus of warm-up scales. Above, the audience would be straining to get inside the house, clinking glasses together at the theater bar, speculating on the wonders to come.

If I strain my ears, I can still hear the echo of their merriment in the walls, obscured by the more recent cacophony of despair and pain. The smell of thousands of spellsongs, layered atop one another for centuries, lingers in the musty air. It's been eight years since this place functioned as a real theater, but the Opera Hall remembers.

We climb the stairs up onto the stage. Elene and Lord Durand, her newly elevated pet footman, stand together on the edge, shouting instructions down to the conductor in the orchestra pit.

Elene glances up and nods to Lacerde, who positions me at center stage without releasing me. It's as if they think I will run, even though there is nowhere to go.

No one has dimmed the gas lamps that line the theater's aisles yet, so I have a full view. The theater is much grander than our replica at the academy. The ceiling bears a centuries-old mural of Adela gifting the first mage with magic. The singer kneels beside the sacred pool, and the goddess rises from the water, her mouth open with song and her arms spread wide. Musical notes surround them, each flecked with real gold leaf.

Portraits of the three other goddesses border the mural. Odetta, goddess of spring and renewal, wearing a silver mask that covers her eyes and cheeks and holding a sparrow's skeleton in her cupped hands. Karina, goddess of justice and winter, thin and draped in a linen sheath, with her arms wide. Marena, the autumn goddess of war, chin lifted proudly, staring down with her hypnotic purple eyes, bejeweled with human teeth.

Beneath, row upon row of tightly packed red velvet seats stretch back to the imposing black doors at the rear of the theater. They're made from mageglass, a material designed by the elementals: sand spun, dyed, and hardened so that not even diamond bullets could shatter it. Hundreds of people will fill the house tonight. Dame Ava, the queen's former principal, told me that sometimes there are so many that folk have to stand along the walls.

My knees shake at the sight. My mouth goes dry.

In the second row, a maid kneels between the seats. She scrubs the floor vigorously with a brown cloth, and the sickly scent of lemon wafts up to the stage.

All these seats. All these people. My unshed tears blur the rows of red seats together, like a smear of blood.

"I can't," I whisper.

"You will," Elene says.

# CHAPTER 2

# REMI

**I WALK DOWN THE** theater aisle, still holding the handwritten invitation card they made us present at the door, scanning rows until I find my place. The seat is so small I can barely wedge my hips between the wooden armrests. The queen really packs us together. We're like fruit in a lower-city merchant's cart, ready to be jostled and bruised.

Mama says the theater used to be luxurious, until the queen had the interior redesigned so all the nobles of her broken court could fit inside at once. Our comfort isn't important. The queen won't even let us sit beside our family members for solace. We might sit in the stalls and boxes, but we aren't here to be the audience. We're the puppets in a show for someone else.

A black gentleman in a frayed overcoat squeezes into the

seat beside me. With his long legs, he can't sit straight in the narrow row, and he steps on my foot trying to find space to put his knees.

He grimaces. "Forgive me. Lovely to see they've given us more room this year."

I snort and cover my mouth with my hand.

The gentleman removes his coat and slings it over his lap. Like me, he wears formal but old clothes, his ensemble cobbled together from seasons past. His burgundy waistcoat is missing a button, and his collar is stained yellow. My sky-blue tea dress has puffed sleeves that were the height of fashion two summers ago. My chest spills over the bodice, which barely laces. On any other occasion, Mama would never have allowed me to wear it out of the house.

On his lapel, the gentleman wears the crest of Château Foutain: two doves circling a stone tower. I frown in sympathy. Foutain, like so many noble houses in Bordea, was all but obliterated in the brief war that followed Queen Elene's ascension. The château had gathered an army to protest the queen's border laws and the terrifying spells she uses to keep us all contained. And they paid for it. This must be Gregor, Baron of Foutain, the only member of the house still alive. His wife, two sons, daughter, and grandchildren all preceded him to the grave.

The queen has spared him only to keep the memory of his house's destruction fresh.

In another life, in another time, he and Papa were friends.

"First Performing?" the baron asks.

I shake my head. I shouldn't have to attend the Performing, as I only turned sixteen this year. The law doesn't require attendance until we turn twenty, but with Mama's illness, someone has to go in her place. The census records our family with two living adults, so two of us must attend the Performing each year. There are no exceptions. The queen doesn't care that I am underage, so long as our family pays in noble blood.

"My second," I say.

The baron frowns. "You don't look old enough."

"I'm not."

I don't elaborate, and the baron pulls a cloth from his pocket to wipe a trail of sweat from his brow. "What delights will she have in store for us this year, eh?"

I've tried my best not to think about what is coming. Before the courier arrived with our invitations, it was easy to pretend that this was the year the queen would finally relent.

Papa says that the Performing gets worse each time, as the queen and Lord Durand seek to surpass themselves. Last year, Dame Ava, the queen's torturer-soprano, performed a drowning spell. Our lungs filled with fluid, and people tried to claw open their own throats until she released us.

The lights dim, and the stewards close the doors at the rear of the theater. Everyone goes silent. A slim conductor dressed in the queen's red livery makes his way through the audience to the gilded podium at the base of the stage. He wears a lightning-bolt pin on his breast. I can't remember if it's the mark of the elemental or the maker school. Either way, he's a mage—and probably on the queen's side.

From my seat near the front, I can see the orchestra pit beneath the stage, where a host of common musicians wait with their instruments resting on their laps. Even though they are not mages, the musicians are expected to play their role in this, too. At the conductor's cue, they lift their instruments.

A burly justicar, wearing the red heart pin of a corporeal singer, stands in front of the door that leads out of the pit, blocking any hope of escape for the orchestra. A gold opera mask covers most of his face and shadows his eyes. The queen and many close to her wear it to show allegiance to the goddess Odetta.

I used to pray to Odetta, patron of spring, the season of my birth, when I was a little girl. The goddess was popular with the court, as most of us are born in spring, and so the queen has claimed her, just to show she can.

Back then, Odetta's followers worshipped in a joyful, carefree style. We plaited crowns of lilies and feasted beneath each new moon. But since Queen Elene took the throne, worship of Odetta has changed, sobered. Now we all remember that the harshest winters come before a vibrant spring, that renewal is born out of death.

Papa says that to choose your own goddess and abandon the deity who destined the time of your conception and birth is heresy of the worst kind. Mages are all summer children, blessed with song magic in exchange for their devoted, lifelong service to Adela. The queen is a heretic. She has profaned all the old ways by forsaking the goddess of her birth and claiming Odetta's patronage instead.

I don't pray anymore.

Perhaps that makes me a heretic, too.

I reach under my skirt. I've secured a little pouch filled with lemon drops to my leg. The sourness of the candy helps with Mama's headaches, and I hope it will keep me breathing through whatever pain is to come. Concealing lemon drops under my dress isn't much of a rebellion, but it makes my heart race with daring. If Papa found out, he'd be furious.

I remove two pieces of the candy from the pouch, pop one into my mouth. I nudge the baron with my elbow. When he glances at me, I take his hand and close his fingers around the other piece of candy before anyone else can see.

"Bless you," he whispers, and slips the lemon drop into his mouth.

The velvet curtain lifts, revealing two figures standing on the stage. One of them is Lord Durand, the queen's confidant. I recognize him from last year. Papa says Durand is the architect of the Performings. The queen wanted vengeance on us, but it was he who proposed the method and honed it. As a reward, he was given a lordship and an estate, making him the only noble exempt from the horrors of the Opera Hall.

The second figure, a girl, surprises me. The queen has always employed the same chantrix for the Performing: a fire-haired mage named Ava who wore her advancing age like a carefully chosen accessory. This girl looks much younger, and she stands hunched, wringing her hands. She presses against the rear curtain as if looking for the first chance to run. She stares into the crowd with wide eyes that never stop moving.

"She looks ready to faint," Baron Foutain whispers. "Do you think that if the principal were to expire onstage, they'd just forget the whole thing and send us home?"

"Maybe we can sneak out in the shuffle," I say. "Climb the balcony, steal the mage pins off some of those stewards, and bribe our way to freedom."

"I like it." The baron nods, his hazel eyes twinkling. He

weighs his purse in his hand. "I've got a few coins to throw at this endeavor."

Lord Durand takes center stage and clears his throat. "Esteemed guests, on behalf of Her Majesty, I am humbled to present a new talent to you this evening. Our most gifted corporeal singer, and a delightful, exuberant mezzo-soprano."

He sweeps a low bow, but when he lifts his head, he's smirking. The theatrics of all this make me sick. I fish another lemon drop out of my pouch.

Still, the audience applauds politely. The queen will be here somewhere, watching the proceedings from behind the stage or concealed in one of the dark private viewing boxes above us. No one wants to be seen resisting.

Though we know she watches us, the queen remains out of sight. There have been too many assassination attempts. A few years ago, a knight came into the theater armed with a musket. Just last year, a group of commoners tried to break down the rear doors to free a sobbing violinist who hadn't wanted to be part of the Performing.

The queen executed all of them.

Durand beckons the new singer forward, and she creeps to him like a timid barn cat. There's something I recognize about the shape of her nose, the curve of her pink rosebud mouth.

She's pretty, but in a fragile way, like a pressed flower petal in the pages of a book. She's thin and white, with ivory skin and long blond hair styled into a sort of tiara. A green gown clings to her frame, her waist cinched by a shimmering corset inlaid with emeralds.

I'm sure that I've seen her before, though I can't think where. We haven't been near the mages' academy or the palace for years.

Durand pushes the singer into the light. "Chantrix Cadence de la Roix," he says, and I nearly choke on the lemon drop. "The jewel of Her Majesty's academy, ready for her first season."

I start to cough, but the baron isn't paying attention to me anymore. Cadence de la Roix. I *know* that name.

When Queen Celeste ruled, my parents often took me to court. While they met with the ministers and dined with the queen, I wandered the palace halls alone. Back then, neither of my parents ever worried about my safety. The palace swarmed with guards and mages, and at the time, no one suspected that they might turn on us.

On one of my adventures to the mages' wing, I met a girl. We soon became best friends, inseparable. We played games in the empty studios, ran through the palace's vast gardens, and stayed up late almost every night, whispering stories by the fireplace in the great library.

I remember sitting with her above the gallery during one of the old queen's lavish balls. Queen Celeste was making an address to the attendees as Cadence stared down at the party, at my parents and all their friends, with a mixture of wonder and envy. Once she passed her exams, her position would be secure, but even then, her life would belong to the crown. She had nothing, and in the old queen's days, even fully trained mages were poor civil servants. Cadence would never earn enough to dress in silks and dance beneath the starlit glass ceiling of the ballroom. We were told that this was the order, the hierarchy the goddesses demanded when they destined our births.

As we watched the party below us, I squeezed her clammy fingers and promised her that when I became a lady, we would go to balls together. I imagined us out on the floor, dancing and laughing, the envy of everyone.

I thought it would be so simple to ask a girl to dance.

Year after year, I found her when we visited the court, until one day, she simply vanished, as if swallowed up by the palace's labyrinthine halls. I cried my eyes out, but Mama told me to be happy for her. Without a patron, Cadence would be bound by debt to the academy, forced to pay the school from her earnings over her lifetime.

We never returned to the palace after that season. Right after Cadence disappeared, the new queen dismissed her old ministers, ended the banquets, dances, and functions of the court, and the war began.

In the years since, I've thought about her all the time. I've wondered if she was safe, if someone else was sneaking her sugarplums and almond cakes from the confectioners, if she was happy.

Lord Durand leans over and whispers something in Cadence's ear. Her face flushes. She looks ready to scream. But as Lord Durand steps back, she gulps down a breath, and her expression relaxes. She dips her head and curtsies to the audience.

The baron reaches over and pats my arm, but I can't tear my eyes away from Cadence's face. Is she really going to do this? She used to be a good person. I remember her kneeling in a bed of snowdrops, her eyes bright and her cheeks pink with cold. Her dog had gotten a thorn stuck in his paw as we'd chased each other through the gardens. She'd hummed a healing song for him, so soft I could hardly hear, and cradled him against her chest. Then she begged me to tell no one, lest her tutors find out she was practicing magic out of class.

She needn't have asked. Back then, I never would have betrayed her secrets. I'd have done anything for her.

I've always imagined her living at a quiet country hospital somewhere, nurturing the sick—far away from the war and

Cannis. And all this time, she's been here, training to become a monster.

My hands curl into fists in my lap.

Cadence lifts her chin and begins her song. We all brace ourselves against the enchanting, beguiling sound. Dame Ava was a powerful singer, but her voice wasn't beautiful. Not like this. The sound seems to fill the entire Opera Hall, and at first, I feel nothing but the soaring beauty of the notes and a deep, aching sadness for the girl who sings them.

Then my feet start to burn.

It's as if the wooden floor has caught fire. Screams begin all around me. I let go of the baron's hand, lift my feet and claw off my shoes. Clear blisters form on my soles, bursting, and still the heat intensifies. My heels crack and start to bleed. Panic seizes me. My skin is going to dissolve; it will melt clean away and leave nothing but exposed sinew and bone behind.

People in the rows around me scramble, trying to flee on their hands and knees. They climb over seats and rush toward the doors. I need to get out. The doors from the hall will be barred from the outside, but if we all push together, surely, even mageglass can't hold.

Where is Papa? If I escape, I can't leave him behind.

But before I can run, the song ends.

The screams do not.

Onstage, Cadence falls to her knees. From exhaustion or regret, it's impossible to know. The pain in my feet makes my head swim. A small whimper escapes my lips.

I hate her for her terrible strength.

I hate her for her weakness.

Above the moans and sobs, Lord Durand projects his voice. "Due to the power of today's chantrix, Her Majesty is pleased to offer you a second demonstration."

Beside me, Baron Gregor vomits into his lap. A second song? No. None of us will survive it.

But maybe this truly is the end, and at last, the queen has decided to execute us. Her force of justicars and militia grows stronger by the day. Maybe she doesn't need us anymore to govern the provinces and smooth over trade deals. I scan the rows more urgently for Papa. If we're to die, I have to say goodbye.

From her knees, Cadence begins another song: a soft tune, instead of belted soprano notes. I can barely hear her over the panicked voices, but the pain in my feet abruptly stops. As I stare at my soles, the blood seeps back into my pores, the blisters heal and then fade entirely. My skin turns pink and plump once more.

But the pain in my heart lingers, beyond the reach of any song.

The baron sobs into his arms. He rocks back and forth as

his back shakes. "Thank you, thank you," he repeats over and over again.

Others around us begin to chant their thanks as well. *Praise be to our most gracious, merciful queen, who has healed us, who has reminded us once again of our place, who keeps our country safe.* I pull my crumpled riding cloak from under my seat and wrap it around my shoulders. How can they thank her? The queen is a monster, with a menagerie of torturers at her beck and call.

I bite my lip. I won't say those words. I will never, ever say them.

# CHAPTER 3

# CADENCE

**WHEN I RETURN TO** my dressing room, there are so many flowers piled up that I can't see the floor. Brilliant topaz orchids, tulips of every shade, and roses red as blood create a lush, living carpet. With such a display, I can almost trick myself into believing that tonight was an ordinary concert. Almost.

I sink into the chair in front of my dresser and cradle a bouquet of fresh roses against my chest. Flowers can't make up for the sounds I heard from the stage, the smells that filled the air. In my head, the screams and the scrambling of feet echo, so loud, even over the music the orchestra played to drown them out. I sniff the bouquet. It has a strange aroma—a little bit too sweet, a little bit too perfect—magic grown.

I thrust the flowers aside and scoop Nip up from his make-shift bed of lilies. He didn't ride in the carriage with us, so

Lacerde must have fetched him during the Performing, knowing I would need him after. He whines as I lift him, but a gentle cantabile has him fully alert with his tail wagging. Even full grown, he's small enough to fit easily on my lap.

Sometimes I feel guilty about singing to him. Nip is the only family I have left, and I sing to him so often, it's hard to know which of his reactions are genuine. I stroke his fur, and he licks the back of my hand.

Someone knocks on the door, and then Lacerde sweeps into the room, shoving the flowers hastily aside with her foot.

"The queen is very pleased. She says how magnificent you were tonight. Beautiful and elegant and terrible," Lacerde says, her voice flat and tired. Her skin is ash gray and her eyes rimmed with red.

She pulls a stool from the corner of the room and sits behind me to take the pins from my hair. Now that I see myself in a mirror, I don't think I look beautiful or elegant. Terrible is more accurate. My eyes water with barely constrained tears. My blond hair is plastered to the edges of my face with sweat. My skirt is covered with dust from when I fell to my knees onstage.

But beauty was not the purpose of tonight. I practiced the healing song endlessly, spending hours with the choirmaster in the library, mastering its rhythms so I could erase every trace of the magic burns. Every note had been faultless, the rhythm syncopated to precision, but I doubt anyone in the audience really cared about that. No one had limped back to their seats, and that was applause enough.

Lacerde takes Nip and places him back on his little bed. She half lifts me out of the chair by my hips. I stand and brace myself against the wall. The corset is so tight my entire torso feels numb. Lacerde grunts and clucks as she undoes the laces. I suck in deep, fragrant breaths as my stomach muscles relax into their new space.

I raise my arms, and she lifts my heavy dress over my head. The shock of the room's cold air makes me shiver in my simple linen shift, but Lacerde quickly swathes me in a thick velvet dressing gown. She'll never allow me to get too cold. If I become ill and can't sing, Elene will blame her. We both know how that will end.

"The queen wants to visit with you tonight. She's having a meal prepared in the Opera kitchens. She thought you might be tired after this afternoon and would like to eat something before returning to the palace. She and Dame Ava always used to feast together on Performing days," Lacerde says.

"Shall I go over?"

"Her Majesty will fetch you."

She begins bustling around the room, transferring the flowers into neat piles so that they will be out of the way for the queen's arrival. I hum the coda of a heat song. The bundle of roses in Lacerde's arms glows and then turns to ash.

A laugh rises almost like a sob in my throat. It feels good to use my magic for fun, even if I can only do it here, with only Lacerde to witness.

"Goddess's bones!" she curses, but her eyes dance. "Take it back!"

I shrug, even though a small smile tugs at my lips. "I can't. Not enough life matter left."

It's a lie. Even though Elene doesn't allow me to devote a lot of time to practicing with plants, I can manage a simple rejuvenation spell. But despite how long we've been together, Lacerde has never taken an interest in the limits of my magic.

She rolls her eyes. "You're impossible."

Another soft knock at the door. Lacerde brushes past me, stepping on my toes. I yelp and fix her with a glare. She's not even subtle about her revenge.

She opens the door and drops into a low curtsy. I stay put in my chair as Elene enters, though my legs bounce nervously under the dressing table. Elene is carrying a white kitten against her bosom. A pink satin bow circles its neck, meant to be endearing, but all I can think of is a pretty hangman's noose. Her gaze falls on me, and her lips press together. I swallow and sink off my chair into a curtsy.

Elene thrusts the kitten into my arms. It meows plaintively and swats at a tendril of my hair with its tiny, white paw. It's all I can do not to push it away, and I force myself to murmur thanks.

She never gives me true presents. Elene will use this creature as she did the last—as a motivator for my obedience. A few years ago, she had my calico drowned when I refused to sing a heart song outside the home of a minister who had dared to question her. In the end, he met an ugly death at the hands of a singer less skilled and more vicious as Elene made me watch. It would have been a mercy if I had obeyed and made him pass peacefully in his sleep, his heart simply frozen in his chest.

Afterward, she took me for a drive and brought me to the Expelled settlement for the first time. Elene didn't threaten me directly—she never does—but she didn't need to. Elene always gets what she wants. Refuse her, and she will find a way to make things worse.

I'm valuable to her, but even I will only get so many chances.

Elene scowls when she sees the pile of ash. "What happened here?"

"Just a little accident," Lacerde murmurs, and I feel guilty for putting her in the path of Elene's ire.

But as Elene's frown deepens, cold fear tightens like a gar-rote around my throat. The ease I'd felt just a moment ago, alone with Lacerde, vanishes. "I'm sorry," I whisper. "I'll clean it up."

Elene holds up her free hand for silence. Each of her nails is painted to match her mask, with a singer's-green base and tiny purple gemstones. She sings a line from a song I know well. Her voice is dissonant and hoarse, but there is still magic in the discord of notes.

As she sings, the ash gathers in a cyclone, the little tornado spitting petals, stems, and thorns. Lacerde gasps as a pile of fresh roses falls at her feet.

Elene steps around her creation and extends her hand to me. "Shall we dine, pet?" she asks, her voice a low, dangerous purr.

The Opera kitchens have prepared a feast for us, but my appe-tite withers under Elene's stare. The table is dressed in the old court style with more forks and knives than we can possibly use, napkins folded to look like peacocks to match Elene's gown. I wonder how long the Opera Hall staff have been planning every detail of this day. Even though they only open a few days of the year now, the theater still employs a full complement of attendants and servants.

I select the smallest spoon so my bites will look bigger, and dip it into the coriander soup. I make a show of each mouthful, nodding and forcing myself to smile, even though the soup leaves a bitter film on my tongue.

But when the steward brings out the second course, a juicy fillet of roasted duck with dark, red plum sauce, I gag. The smell of burning human flesh is seared into my memory, all too similar to the crisp skin of the duck breast.

Elene takes a few bites, then waves the steward away. She shakes her head at me. "I shouldn't have put the Opera Hall through all this trouble. It's wasted on you. Dame Ava loved our meals together."

I take a half-hearted sip of wine, hoping it might console her. Then I imagine the Opera chefs scraping the plates after we have left, consigning our lavish meal to the trash. Fine kitchens like this never give the scraps to the beggars outside, since doing so would only encourage them to come back. So much waste when there are so many hungry in Cannis. I bring the spoon to my lips again, but as I open my mouth, my stomach heaves. I push the bowl aside.

"This was meant to be a treat." Elene frowns and points to

the door. "Go, then. You don't appreciate it, and your sourness will spoil the food. I will dine alone."

Without waiting to be told again, I leap up and bolt.

A new carriage waits for me behind the Opera Hall. Our driver from before is nowhere to be seen, and my usual coachman, Lacerde's gangly nephew Thomas, holds the door open. He takes my hand to help me up the step.

When I sit down, I find Lacerde already inside, darning one of my stockings. She barely glances up from her needle as I enter. "You didn't eat, did you?"

"I wasn't hungry. And she doesn't listen to me. There was duck for the second course."

As a corporeal singer, my senses are attuned to things that have been alive. Even on days when I haven't just Performed, when a meat dish is put in front of me, all I can think about is what it once was. If the animal died scared or in pain, I can sense it by the texture and smell of the meat. As a mage, Elene ought to understand.

Lacerde heaves a sigh. She sets her sewing aside and reaches over to pat my hand. "You did what you had to tonight. Refusing outright wouldn't have helped anyone."

She's right, in a way. While Dame Ava has a flair for showmanship, her magic isn't strong enough to perform two songs in succession on so many people. Had Ava sung the burning song, she wouldn't have been able to heal the audience afterward.

I turn my face to the window, tears blurring my vision. Knowing that doesn't make what I had to do any better.

Thomas clucks his tongue at the horses, and they spring into a lively trot.

Via the direct road, the palace is a short drive from the Opera Hall. I would prefer to walk, to bask in the night air, blissfully alone, but I'm still wearing my dressing gown, and the wind outside is bitter. Besides, too many noble folk will stay the night in Cannis before traveling home. I could feel their hatred through my songs. If they could, they would have tossed it at me like a set of throwing knives.

I don't know how to dispel or subdue a crowd like the justicars do. Elene hasn't made it part of my training. I need time and stillness to concentrate, and I'm so used to scripted rehearsals that if ten people were to run at me, my voice might get trapped in my throat. They could rip me apart like a doll. I may be a mage, but I'm only one person.

The horses break into a canter, and we rattle down the boulevard. Merchant carts and stalls stand outside the Opera Hall, stationed to lure the nobles leaving the Performing. I think that they probably won't make much profit today. Folk won't want to linger in the theater's shadow.

Catching sight of the white horses and the queen's insignia on the carriage door, the merchants drop to their knees in the street, caps in hand. I draw my dressing gown tighter around my shoulders. If they knew that Elene's new principal singer rode in the carriage, instead of the queen herself, would they still show so much respect?

Whatever they think about Elene in the secret recesses of their hearts, no one dares express it for fear of her spies. But what folk say about Dame Ava, I know. They call her a torturer, a demoness. They say that Adela will turn her back on Ava because she's made a mockery of her divine gift. Will they whisper the same things about me now?

A white woman jogs up to the carriage, a toddler balanced on her hip. A tattered red dress hangs askance on her shoulders, exposing alabaster skin pimpled with cold. She smells very faintly of orange blossoms; magic that still clings to her skin, like an old friend convinced of an impossible reunion. I'm surprised by her daring, but she must smell my magic as well and know that I am not the queen, or she wouldn't approach this carriage. To the trained nose, the scent of our magic is a signature we cannot hide, no matter how much perfume we wear.

She says nothing but raises the child so we can get a better look. His arms are so slender.

Lacerde cranks open the window as Thomas slows the

carriage. I nod to her, then shrink back, out of the beam of light cast by the streetlamps. She deposits a farthing coin—the largest amount we can give to any Expelled under the law—into the woman's outstretched fingers. The light is dim, but I could swear that the woman slips a piece of paper into Lacerde's fingers in return. But without missing a stitch, my maid returns to her sewing.

"There," she breathes after a moment, and holds up my stocking. "Good as new."

She doesn't have to fix them. Elene pays her a handsome wage and gives her an extra allowance to buy items for me. But we're the same: Both of us are from the streets, and neither of us sees the sense in paying good coin to replace something that can so easily be repaired.

When we reach the palace, the guards wave us through the gates with barely a glance. Thomas pulls up in the courtyard. Lacerde stuffs her sewing kit and my stockings into a leather satchel, then wrenches open the carriage door. We jump down and head inside.

"Shall I bring some porridge and tea to your room?" she asks. "I haven't eaten yet, either."

"No," I say, and feel a stab of guilt at the disappointment in her eyes. I enjoy our quiet time together, too. We can spend a whole evening eating apple porridge and reading together. "Sister Elizabeta is expecting me."

A few nights a week, I work in the public hospital run by the nuns of Saint Izelea. Helping Cannis's poor with my song is a kind of penance, time I give back to Adela to atone for the way I befoul her magic in the queen's name.

The hospitals aren't allowed to admit folk out of favor with the queen, so although Elene doesn't understand my reasons, she doesn't care that I go, as long as I don't strain my voice. The public hospitals are often overcrowded and smell of rot and blood. Most of the magic I perform there is tedious and routine: setting bones, delivering babies, the monotony occasionally broken by more difficult cases that are outside their usual singer's ability.

"Do you think it's a good idea for you to go tonight?" Lacerde asks. "You've used so much magic today already. Her Majesty lets you go because it doesn't interfere with your work, but if she visits you tomorrow and you've strained your voice or gotten sick . . ."

"I have to. I'm on the schedule. They'll be expecting me."

She sighs. "At least have something to eat before you go. And remember to make your report to the chief justicar in the morning."

I sigh but incline my head. Elene requires me to make a report when I visit Saint Izelea's. She's convinced that the hospitals are secret breeding grounds for trouble. If I spot a hooded noble lady slipping coins to the orderlies or treat any injury inflicted by magic, I'm to inform the chief justicar immediately. Ren is a bloodhound—he can sniff out the smallest irregularity in a person's tale as easily as I smell magic. No one ever lies to him and gets away with it. I have seen the room he calls his Parlor of Delights, where he interrogates suspects.

But Sister Elizabeta doesn't have anything to hide. Maybe hospitals outside of Cannis act more rebelliously, but Saint Izelea's is only a stone's throw from Cavalia. Elene can practically see the nuns from her balcony. It would be foolish for them to act against the crown.

"I always do," I say.

Lacerde squeezes my shoulder. Her touch lingers, and relief shivers down my back. The tears I have tried to hold back all day flow freely. For just a moment, I feel the childish impulse to throw myself into her arms. I wrap my arms around my chest instead.

"I'll fetch you some broth and lay out your clothes," she says.

# CHAPTER 4

# REMI

**AFTER THE HEALING SONG** ends, Lord Durand helps Cadence to her feet. She stumbles from the stage, bracing herself on his offered arm. The baron gives me a clean handkerchief to wipe the sweat and tears from my face.

With the magical Performing over, the orchestra delivers a full program, each song beautiful and entirely devoid of magic. I barely listen, taking the hour to fix my hair and dab red paint on my lips instead.

I can't let Papa see me with snot dripping from my nose. He feels guilty enough already, just knowing that I had to attend before my time. Maybe I'll tell him that the song was weaker in my section of the theater. That we could hardly hear. It *is* Cadence's first season, so maybe he'll even believe me.

When it's finally over, and the queen's stewards unseal the

theater doors, Papa waits for me in the atrium. He's so tall that I can see the back of his ginger head easily over the crowd. He wears a black waistcoat that despite its age still fits elegantly. The rest of the audience scrambles past us as he looks me up and down, then wraps me in a one-armed hug.

His hand trembles on my back. "I'm sorry, Remi."

"For what?" I ask, and bury my face in the warmth of his chest.

Papa scowls. "You shouldn't have to go through this—none of us should! It's an—"

I tug on his arm and steer him out of the Opera Hall. If he gets too worked up, Papa may say things neither of us wants the queen or her guards to overhear. Where my safety is concerned, he doesn't always filter his words. I may take a few risks myself, but I can't bear the thought of Papa getting arrested.

I look through the open doors of the Opera Hall. Stewards are already moving between the rows, cleaning up. I want to get as far away as possible. If we linger, we might see Cadence again. The sooner I can start to forget that I was tortured by my childhood friend, the better. I can't help but wonder, though: If she recognized me, would she even be sorry? Or has she been so completely transformed by the queen that she wouldn't feel even a touch of remorse?

We make our way through the lobby and onto the busy

streets of Cannis. The city avenues are wide, bustling with carriages and people. The buildings have been redesigned in recent years, their facades done up in the fashionable pink stone the queen likes. I've heard most of their interiors are crumbling, but the queen only pays for the parts of the city she can see from the palace up on the hill.

All around us, dozens of nobles clamber into hackney cabs. The lineup of carriages extends around the corner and as far as I can see down the street. Beggars swarm, hands outstretched, brandishing malnourished babies and buckets for coins.

I look away, but Papa thrusts a crumpled franc note at a woman with two skinny, dirty children at her feet.

"Don't look away," he says gently, after the woman moves on. "We all did that for too long. It's why we're in this mess now."

I bite the inside of my cheek. Papa likes to say that in the old queen's days, the court was too inward-looking, too focused on ourselves to understand what was happening in the rest of the country. The mages resented us and the commoners hated us, so they didn't come to our aid when Queen Elene murdered her way to the throne and cast us all aside. By the time the commoners were ready to help us, the queen and her mages had already defeated our armies and cemented their hold on Cannis. It was too late.

"I told Rook to park the carriage down the lane. I need to

51

visit the dressmaker. Your mother wants us to pick something up," Papa says, shaking his head with a forced laugh. "It's only a few blocks. You don't mind the walk, do you?"

I glance down at my shoes: delicate satin heels with green bows and white trim. They were the only nice, new thing I wore today, and ironically, the most endangered during the Performing. But after what we've endured, it feels indulgent, even seditious, to walk. I nod.

Together, we stride down the lane. Papa exchanges terse glances with a few people I recognize but doesn't stop to greet them. Now that we're outside, in the brisk, fresh air, he's remembering to be cautious. Right after a Performing, the queen's spies will be everywhere on the boulevard, listening for any hint of rebellion. The simplest greeting can be interpreted a hundred different ways, twisted until it's incriminating.

I won't mention the little pouch of lemon drops to him right now.

As we walk, I don't bother to avoid the puddles that dot the streets. The water soaks through my shoes and stockings, deliciously cold against the tender new skin on my soles. Papa rolls his eyes when I crash through a particularly deep pool, drenching the hem of my dress.

I want to get home, away from this city, away from our murderer queen and Cadence, but we don't come to Cannis often.

Mama has been one of Master Dupois's patrons since she was a girl, and she trusts no one else with our dinner clothes and evening dresses. And while Mama can travel, it requires preparation and a route with inns to stop at along the way, so she does not often make short trips to buy clothes. She submits her orders by courier, and Papa dutifully picks them up whenever he visits the city on business errands, or on Performing days.

Once we go a few blocks, the street starts to quiet. Merchants loiter outside their shops, and skinny dogs bask in the sun. A flower girl approaches us and thrusts a nosegay into Papa's hand in exchange for a copper. He pins the bouquet to my lapel.

The dressmaker's shop is located down a long alley. The street was once lined with fashionable exotic-fruit stalls and jewelers, but now Dupois's shop is the only business. Our carriage is parked in front of the shop already, partially obscuring its chipped blue facade. Papa's driver, Rook, lies across the carriage bench, sleeping, while our two black carriage horses chew daffodils from the window box.

The manikin in the window displays the same beautiful, pearl-inlaid, gold chiffon dress that was in the shop a few months ago, when I accompanied Papa into the city to meet the son of one of his endless acquaintances. Master Dupois sits beside it, idly looking at a bronze pocket watch. He's a small, bald white man, with nervous, active fingers that keep reaching out to pluck threads from the already perfect dress.

"Dupois!" Papa calls, his voice friendly but tired.

Hearing us, the shopkeeper scurries outside. He bows to Papa, then heartily wrings both of our hands. "A pleasure, Viscount, as always."

Formality isn't required by law anymore, but many shopkeepers keep it up, hoping to sweeten their noble patrons and put them in a generous mood. Dupois ushers us inside. I look around while Papa waits by the counter for Mama's order. There are fewer spools of luxurious fabric than I remember, and the shelves, which once held hats and purses of every style, are nearly empty.

Dupois's lone assistant sits on a stool, stitching a corset with glass beads. He's a gangly boy, all legs, with golden brown eyes and a little cut over his left eye. The corset reminds me of the garment Cadence wore onstage, and I hastily turn away.

I unwind a lavender silk scarf and brush off the film of dust covering it. The scarf is impossibly soft, embroidered with delicate green and pink blossoms.

"I will give you an excellent price for that," Master Dupois calls. He pushes a carefully wrapped package across the counter to Papa.

"Are you moving your premises?" I ask. "There isn't much merchandise here."

Dupois and Papa exchange a look.

"No." Dupois swallows. "The queen normally uses her own tailors for the palace. She prefers to train mages of the maker school who can direct the fibers in the thread, rather than employing more traditional craft. These last years have been hard. My shop had a reputation, and now . . ."

He trails off, but I understand. Cannis is no longer home to Bordea's decadent court. A talented dressmaker like Dupois would once have had endless work. Now most of the nobles only come to the city when summoned for Performings and long ago employed new tailors closer to home. We raise doux goats on our estate and have to ship their cashmere abroad for better prices, since most houses can't afford it anymore. If not for Papa's business, we would probably avoid the city, too, and Mama would have to shop closer to home. I wonder why Dupois doesn't choose to leave the capital and set up his shop elsewhere.

I go back to admiring the scarf, but out of the corner of my eye, I see Dupois slip another, smaller package across the table to Papa. I raise an eyebrow.

"A gift for your nameday," Papa says with a wink when he

catches my expression. He tucks the package into his coat and takes out his purse. He counts twelve gold coins and slides them across the counter to Dupois.

"Viscount, this is too much! Your wife and I agreed on six!" splutters the shopkeeper.

"We'll take the scarf, too," Papa says. He slips Mama's parcel under his broad arm and steers me toward the door. "Remi should have something nice." He snorts a laugh, one that sounds a little more genuine than before. "And to replace your pretty window flowers, for I fear my driver has been lax, and our horses have eaten their fill."

"Thank you, my lord." Dupois bows low and doesn't lift his head until we exit the shop.

Rook wakes with a start when Papa clicks his tongue at him. The youth hastily sits up and takes the reins. A lone yellow flower sticks out of the side of one of the mares' muzzles. I pluck it from her mouth before Papa can see, and Rook shoots me a grateful smile.

Papa helps me into the carriage. Inside, I melt into the familiar red leather seats with a sigh. He sits beside me and secures the carriage door. His shoulders slump with relief. Rook snaps the reins, and the two horses take off at a trot, bearing us down the alley, toward home.

I pull the curtains across the carriage window. Today, I have no more desire to look on Cannis. I tuck a flannel blanket over my legs and skirt. It's a four-hour journey back to our château, and all I plan to do is sleep.

I remember the year when the Performings began. I was about ten and furious at being left behind when my parents made the trip to the city. The new queen had been on the throne for two years, and we hadn't gone back to our apartments in Cannis since her ascension, though no one would tell me why.

I missed my room overlooking the palace's winter garden, the thrill and bustle of the court. I missed Cadence and worried about her. I didn't understand why Mama wouldn't allow me to write to her, or at least to her new patron, to request permission to visit. I believed that the Performing my parents spoke about in hushed whispers must be the grandest party of all. Why else would the queen be planning to gather all her nobles together on the anniversary of her coronation? Why else would all of Mama's friends start to talk about it as soon as they thought I'd gone to bed?

On the day my parents were due back from Cannis, I sat by

my bedroom window and watched the long, grassy drive that stretched from our front gate, beyond the orchard, to the cobblestone courtyard. I imagined them cantering up the drive, dismounting in a flourish of silk and velvet, and laughing their way back inside the house, the way they always did after a visit to the city, when their spirits were high.

When I saw the carriage pass through the wrought-iron gate, I pressed my face and hands to the glass. I waited for my parents to ride in behind it, jubilant and out of breath from a gallop. They loved to race each other on the last stretch home. But when I noticed how slowly the carriage moved, I knew immediately that something was wrong.

I hoisted myself up so quickly that I ripped the lace hem of my new skirt. I ran down the steps and flung open the heavy brass doors that led to the courtyard. Papa's footman chased after me, but I was like water, flowing through his outstretched fingers. I lost both of my shoes as I sprinted down the drive.

The carriage had stopped. Papa climbed out when I reached it. He braced his back as he hobbled toward me, legs shaking with each step. Usually when Papa walked, he stood tall and proud. His green eyes were strangely red, and the skin around them was puffy.

Still, he lifted me off the ground and twirled me in a half-hearted arc. Mama pushed the black curtains on the carriage window aside, hand trembling, and peered out at us.

"Why are you out here, sweetheart?" Papa asked. He helped me up into the carriage. "Where are your shoes?"

Inside, Mama slumped against the wall, a blanket drawn up to her chin. Papa closed the carriage door behind us. The driver clicked his tongue at the horses. They burst into a lively trot, spurred on by the promise of food and a warm stable. Mama winced in pain.

"What's wrong?" I slid into her lap and pressed close to her.

She stroked my hair and pressed her forehead against mine. "Nothing. Don't you worry about it."

Papa reached over me and squeezed her shoulder. Our carriage rattled up the drive.

Later that night, after they had tucked me into bed, I heard them yelling. Back then, they never argued. I hid beneath my blanket, afraid of what their anger at each other might mean.

Everybody had always said my parents had a fairy-tale love story. Papa had been a boisterous young gentleman, a third son, studying law in the city. Mama had been one of the old queen's ladies-in-waiting. When Papa had gone to the palace to sit his exams, Mama had spotted him in the long line of waiting students, glasses askew and riding cloak disheveled. She'd purposely bumped into him and stolen his pen case, so she could burst into the examination hall and give it back under the pretense of having found it on the floor. She'd dressed in her best and had stolen his heart as well.

Downstairs, the screaming continued. Their voices rose louder and louder. The dining room was directly beneath my bedroom, and I couldn't escape the noise. I climbed out of bed and perched beside the empty fireplace to listen.

"You're being hysterical," Papa shouted. "This won't last forever. It can't last. No one will stand for it to happen again. You'll see. By next year, the witch will be off the throne."

"You don't know that, Claude," Mama snapped back. "You have no way of knowing that."

"I hope it," Papa said, his voice gentler. "We all do. If we all keep hoping—"

"Hope isn't going to fix this! We have to fight it! But in the meantime, we cannot have more children. Not now. Not when they might have to face this."

"You want Remi to grow up alone?"

"With how things are, I don't want Remi to grow up at all," Mama growled. Then she broke into sobs. "If she grows up, then she'll . . . we'll have to bring . . ."

"This is a blessing," Papa insisted. "We have tried for so long."

"A blessing or an omen?" Mama asked. "They'd be born in the autumn. You know how rare it is for Marena to bless those of our blood with conception at this time of year. The baby would have a war gift. What would that mean for a child at a time like this? Would the queen even let them live?"

"I always hoped we'd have another. A sibling for her." Papa's voice sounded distant and sad. "Can't you think about this? For another week, at least?"

Mama sniffled. "Maybe someday. When this is over. But, Claude, not until then. We can't afford to put this off. I'll start to show soon, and then what will we do? You know the laws the queen wants to bring in. I'll send for the mage tomorrow."

"It is your decision," Papa said, his voice clogged with tears.

I wandered back to my bed, hugging my chest. I'd always dreamed of having a sister to run with over the estate, to teach to ride and shoot. Sometimes the château was lonely without any other children, and I longed for the liveliness of the court and Cadence's quiet laugh. But whatever had happened in the city had shaken my parents to their core. I'd never heard either of them sound so defeated.

# CHAPTER 5

# CADENCE

I STAND AT THE basin and scrub the stage makeup from my face while Lacerde lays out a black tunic and a pair of wool breeches on my bed. They once belonged to a groom in the stables, but a soft song was all it took to lure her to sleep for long enough that I could snatch these clothes. The tunic is a little too tight, and my mass of blond hair barely fits under the borrowed cap, but at night, I don't think anyone will look too closely. I mask the scent of my magic as best as I can, dabbing cologne behind my ears and on my wrists. It wouldn't trick a palace mage, but it should work to fool folk who don't know me well.

Lacerde passes me an unfamiliar leather satchel. I reach inside, and my fingers curl around something cold. Sighing, I draw out a short, crystal-handled dagger.

What does she think I'm going to do with this? The blade is barely longer than a letter opener. And knives are messy.

"What if you get too scared to make a sound?" she demands, a defensive edge in her tone. My cheeks heat. I don't want to admit that I've imagined the same scenario myself. "What if they put a hand over your mouth or choke you? Tonight's a night for precautions. Just take it."

"Where did you even get this?" I mumble. Weapons are not allowed on the palace grounds. For us mages, our voice is our weapon. Elene says that anyone who should be armed already is. There are ward-songs on the gates that should have made concealing the dagger impossible.

"Try to be back before dawn this time. You need some sleep," Lacerde says, ignoring my question. She opens the double doors that lead from my suite into the hall.

A man waits outside, reclining against the wall. I take in his lean frame, his high, angular cheekbones and bright blue eyes, as dread squeezes my chest. The aroma of cinnamon hovers in the air. He wears a simple singer's-green robe without a pin to mark his school.

"Well hello, my little Quarter Note," Ren exclaims in his melodic, bubbly voice, a direct contrast to his stark gaze boring into me. "Where do you think you're headed at this time of night?"

"To—to the hospital," I stammer. He knows where I go, so why is he here? I look to Lacerde for help. "I'm allowed."

"Is that so?" Ren asks. He folds his arms over his chest and gives me a stern, almost fatherly scowl. "Her Majesty sent me. She tells me you were very good tonight, though she worries about your appetite. Maybe you should rest. You must be very tired."

"I *am* tired," I admit. My fingers travel to the prayer stone at my throat. "But I said I would go."

"Her Majesty says you were . . . hesitant . . . before the opening curtain tonight."

My hands grow clammy with cold sweat. I thought Elene would have let that go, after I sang for her tonight. I draw my cap down over my eyes. Is he here to punish me? It wouldn't be the first time.

"I just want to go to the hospital," I whisper.

"Of course you do," he shoves his hands into the pockets of his robe. "But if I were to have you followed tonight? Would my spies say that's where you went?"

"Where else would I go?"

The chief justicar's eyes sweep over me again, slower this time. They hesitate on the brown satchel, and I almost cringe, imagining what he will do if he discovers the dagger inside.

Ren has used spells on me before. Most of them mild, meant to sting or ache, without really damaging me. Without Elene's express instruction, he can't do lasting damage. But once, he used a breaking spell and snapped my wrist when he thought I'd omitted something in my report.

It was the only time Elene ever stepped in to protect me. When she found out about Ren's spell, she cast him out of the palace and refused to let him return for weeks. Whether her motivation came from anger over how he treated something that belonged to her or a spark of genuine feeling for me, I will never know. But for a few joyful days, I dared to hope that he'd been sent to the Expelled settlement and would never return.

Now that my own magic is more advanced than his, he doesn't try it so often. His voice doesn't have the same raw power that mine does, but he's quick, and what he lacks in ability he makes up for in gruesome creativity. I don't want to test him.

"Well," he says at last, and sweeps me a little bow. "Be sure to stick to the well-lit roads, Chantrix."

Although it isn't far, by the time I arrive at the hospital gates, I'm sweating and out of breath. My magic reserves must be even lower than I thought after the Performing, and exhaustion makes my vision blur at the edges. But I promised to come, and my goddess is watching.

Saint Izelea's is located in an abandoned town house given to the nuns by Elene after its previous occupants fled to the countryside. Like Elene, these nuns, versed in healing arts, are pledged to Odetta, and I think she feels a certain affinity toward them even if she believes the hospitals harbor rebels. This quarter was once the height of fashion, but now many grand homes stand empty, overrun by rats and weeds.

In the first years after Elene took the throne, the Performings happened on her whim. Her hatred of the noble folk is legendary even now, but in those years, she did nothing to hold it back. If a piece of news displeased her, she would have nobles dragged into the performance hall in the mages' wing for a private concert. As a child, I had watched the guards march entire families through the palace gardens from my studio window. Sometimes they emerged alive, though shaken and staggering. Other times I would only see them again when a wagon came to collect their corpses.

I've never dared to ask Elene about it, but Lacerde told me the story behind her hatred for the nobles. When she was a young mage, brimming with potential, she'd fallen in love with a young viscount. The nobleman's family was out of favor and barred from the court, the result of a distant relative's treason.

The old queen would not allow his family to rise again, frustrating all of the viscount's ambitions.

Elene was one of the most gifted students the academy had ever produced. She wanted more than a life of service to the crown.

Together, they plotted to overthrow the old queen. The viscount would rally the support of the upper class. Queen Celeste was thought weak, and her tax policies and expensive wars with Solidad were roundly despised. She did not know how to navigate the growing cultural divide between common folk and the nobles in their estates. Elene would sway the mages, offering them the chance to join the court as equals to the nobles.

But the old queen forgave the nobleman's family. Free once more to pursue roles in government and take his place at the court, the viscount abandoned Elene. He married another: a woman of his own rank. And when Elene refused to just disappear, to put aside months of planning and the promise of a new life, he lured her to his father's estate and locked her in a tower.

Too afraid to ever let her out again, lest she end his life with a song or expose his treason to Queen Celeste, he set fire to the tower. If Elene had died, everyone might have thought it was an accident. A tragic, terrible accident, befalling a promising student. And they would have ached for the viscount, a young man nurturing an impossible love in secret, hoping to hide Elene from his father and his betrothed. The tower was old, with a wooden roof and rotting beams. People would have believed it.

But Elene had lived to ruin him.

After so many years at the palace with Elene, I know her well. She might have forgiven the viscount for abandoning their love, but she could never have forgiven his betrayal of her ambition.

Elene likes to say that when she murdered the old queen in cold blood, mounted the viscount's charred corpse on a pike in the city square, and took the throne, she'd been restoring control to where it rightfully belonged. After all, the divine quartet had given magic to us mages, not the noble folk.

*And surely, if the goddesses had meant for the nobles to rule,* Elene would purr, *they would have given them more than the delusion of power.*

I have faith in the divine quartet and know that we are all instruments of their will, but even I have a hard time believing the goddesses wanted Bordea to become what it is.

I stumble through the overgrown courtyard to the hospital's door. The nuns are too busy with their patients to maintain the garden's former splendor, so weeds grow through the cobblestones, and the fountain is cracked, water pumping directly onto the walkway to create a muddy swamp. A film of algae grows over the front steps. I edge carefully through the garden on tiptoe, trying to keep myself as dry as possible.

When I knock, Sister Elizabeta answers almost immediately. Her face, usually pink and jubilant, is drawn with worry.

"Thank the divine," she says, taking me by the hands and ushering me inside. "We think one of the patients has a tumor. Our chantrix isn't up to it."

Tumors require a special kind of finesse. Often, the singer must compose a new spellsong for each occurrence, and even then, it is not uncommon for the patient to die anyway. Cancers of the blood or bone marrow have no cure, even with magic.

I know the hospital's chantrix from our days together at the academy. Mercedes has never been particularly strong or skilled. In fact, she was almost given a "lesser" classification at our exams, and her healing abilities are mediocre at best. Any form of cancer is way beyond her skills.

I peel off my cap and hang it on the peg beside the door. Sister Elizabeta slings a white hospital robe over my shoulders and places the order's ceremonial white coronet over my hair. I don't have to wear the habit when I'm here—Mercedes never does—but it makes me feel closer to the goddesses, like I am part of something greater.

At the palace, we all compete for Elene's favor. Ren isn't the only mage who resents my position. All the other corporeal singers hate me for being chosen as principal. They think I am too young and unproven, and they despise me for the strength of my magical gift.

It hasn't always been like this. When I was young, all the novices helped one another. We played, took lessons, and ate together. But I watched them grow from carefree children into honed weapons under Elene's instruction.

I haven't been close to another mage since Elene sent Marie to work in the countryside as a lesser cultivator at the royal agricultural estates. Marie was the nearest I've ever come to having a lover, and even our time together was sometimes marred by jealousy. For a time, our relationship was everything to me. We would steal moments alone, concealed by library stacks, our hands and mouths turned explorers. But then we would walk to our classes and examinations and have to face the widening chasm that our exam results slowly carved between us.

When the academy had taken me in, I was too young to keep any contact with my friends at the city home. My only friend outside the mages' school was Remi. But her mother was a countess, and close to the old queen, so her family was one of the first to flee from their apartments in the eastern wing.

Sometimes I still climb up and sit in the palace gallery that overlooks the grand ballroom, where we spent so many hours together. It's always empty now, and covered in dust, but I remember the press of Remi's shoulder on mine, the warmth of her thigh when we would sit there together with fingers entwined, looking down at all the fine ladies. Our friendship was so uncomplicated.

No one ever holds my hand now. No one would dream of it, save maybe Lacerde. And if she knew what I'd become, Remi would probably be disgusted with herself for touching me. At least I can be sure she didn't see me at the Performing, for she's still years too young to sit in the Opera Hall.

Sister Elizabeta doesn't ask me how the Performing went. She knows I'm required to make reports on her, so she never speaks of Elene or events outside the hospital. Here, I am a healer, a penitent who comes to serve the quartet with her song. Here, for a little while at least, I can pretend.

I follow the nun down the dimly lit hall. They use tallow candles to mask the smell of death, but even the scent of burning fat can't drown out the decay. Grand, old carpets are rolled up against the skirting boards. Nail holes dot the walls where picture frames once hung. The nuns decorate with shelves filled with medical books on anatomy and spells, vats of alcohol to sterilize instruments and clean linen. The low, constant murmur of pain accompanies our steps.

Elizabeta leads me up the staircase into a private room at the rear of the old house. A small blond girl lies on a cot near the window wearing only a ragged brown shift. She can't be older than ten. Her skeletal chest rises and falls too slowly. Mercedes sits in the chair next to her, singing softly against the pain, but it doesn't seem to be doing any good. The girl tosses in her bed, twisting the sheets in her small hands.

At first, I balk in the doorway, thinking she might be an Expelled, but there is no telltale cut along her throat. She is simply one of Cannis's many, many poor. Like I once was.

When she notices me, Mercedes stands and offers me her chair. I sit next to the girl and brush a sweaty lock of hair back off her face. She doesn't have a fever. The pain alone is making her sweat.

"Where is it?" I ask Mercedes. Even if she isn't skilled enough to treat the tumor, she should be able to find its location.

"Her head," Mercedes whispers. "Behind her left eye."

I take a deep breath. Precise magic taxes me even more than targeting an entire room. Causing pain is easy. Healing is much harder. Brains are nothing like the soles of feet. Any error, any puncture, and the girl could die. With my healing at the Performing, I could afford not to be perfect. Now I can't be anything else.

"Can you bring me a glass of water?" I ask Sister Elizabeta.

The nun nods and scurries from the room. I tremble all over. When I stood onstage, the light of the Opera Hall chandelier blinded me. My magic developed a picture of the audience's life force, but I couldn't see their faces. I can see this little girl all too clearly.

Skilled corporeal mages used to study anatomy and travel abroad to the great universities in Solidad and Osara, where they learned surgical arts to enhance their magical craft. I don't have any such training. The new university in Cannis, opened by Elene for the common folk, does not teach such things. And even if crossing the border were still possible, Elene would never allow me to travel so far away from her. I'm not skilled or confident enough to cut into the child's head and remove the tumor outright. So I have perfected a different method. I target the cancer and kill its tissues from within, so that it withers and dies. The girl's body will then destroy it in time.

Elizabeta returns with a mug of water. I take a long drink, then put it aside. My empty stomach grumbles.

I start to hum softly, taking a profile of the girl's body. In addition to the nearly fist-sized tumor that grows behind her eye, she has a badly healed fracture along a metatarsal bone in her foot. She couldn't have been walking very well, even before the cancer struck.

The freezing song is difficult to sing and outside my comfortable natural range. I'm better versed in heat songs and binding spells, but cold is easier to control than heat for precise work, and less likely to damage the tissue around the tumor. Human tissue, I learned early at the academy, can freeze for short periods and recover. It isn't always so with heat.

I begin hesitantly, trying to keep the image of the tumor in my mind as I sing. My voice is shaky and unsure—Elene would never allow me to sing like this in public—but the magic works the same. My song wraps its icy tendrils around the tumor and freezes it. The little girl whimpers, her small frame trembling.

For a terrifying moment, I wonder if I have infused my song with too much power. But if I stop now, the incomplete healing might damage her brain. So I sing on. I let myself get lost in the magic and melody of the song. My reserve of power is almost gone, and my throat is on fire. If I'm able to speak at all in the morning, it will be a miracle.

The tumor grows colder than metal left in the snow. My song lifts higher and higher. I feel the cancer contracting, dying.

"I think it's working," Mercedes whispers from the corner.

The little girl watches me with clearer eyes. I stop singing and press my hand to my flaming throat. Mercedes hums a different tune to lull the child to sleep. She will need to rest now so her body can fight.

I smooth a hand over the girl's forehead. The corners of her mouth twitch upward. Something like happiness flutters in my chest. *Thank you*, I think to her as she sleeps, *for letting my song bring more than pain.*

## CHAPTER 6
# REMI

I SPEND MOST OF the next week in the stables, hiding from my parents.

When Papa and I first arrived home, Mama waited in the atrium to hug me, her fingers stained with ink from scribbling in the estate ledgers, but as soon as I disappeared upstairs, my parents started fighting again.

Mama wants to spare me the Opera Hall, to take her place at the Performing again, even if she knows it might kill her. Papa won't allow it. For him, to subject me to the Opera Hall is a grave sacrifice, but the thought of losing Mama is beyond his endurance.

After that first night, Papa sequesters himself in his study on the third floor. Mama embroiders in her parlor, her needle stabbing furiously through the fabric of her sampler.

The barn, with its calming, earthy-sweet smell of hay and leather, is my refuge. I steal sugar from the kitchen, dust my palms with the powder, and wander from stall to stall, letting the horses lick my hands clean. The stable boys sense my mood and make themselves scarce.

I have two horses of my own: a stocky black-and-white cob called Chance, whom I adore, and an elegant, long-limbed chestnut palfrey named Eloise, whom Papa approves of. I purchased Chance myself from a traveling market that set up on the outskirts of our estate. He's built like a small draft horse, with a broad back, a thick mane that hangs to his knees, and sturdy, feathered legs.

Papa told me not to buy him—ladies do not ride cobs—but his expressive, white-rimmed blue eyes captured my heart. I paid for him myself, so he's mine in a way Eloise isn't. He was trained to pull a wagon, not to be ridden, but he's slowly getting better with practice.

I save a whole pocketful of sugar for Chance. I let him delicately lip it from my palm, his long whiskers tickling the skin of my wrist. While he focuses on licking sugar from his teeth, I slide my saddle into place and tighten the girth. Then I lift each of his hooves in turn and carefully pick out the stones.

"Ahem." A cleared throat makes me straighten and look up.

Papa stands outside Chance's stall, holding a black saddlebag in his hands.

"Lunch," he says, raising the pack. "I thought we might ride for the city today." He reaches into the stable to pat Chance's chubby neck. "I'll even let you ride this guy."

My brow wrinkles with suspicion. It's faster to ride than travel by carriage, but it's still at least a three-hour journey to Cannis. It's midday already, so we won't be able to return before nightfall. Papa wouldn't plan such a journey on a whim.

"I have to meet a business contact. There have been problems getting our latest shipment across the border," he says. "I've already informed the steward. He'll follow behind us with a carriage and our things."

"And you want me to come with you?" I try to bite back a smile. The Performing is over, and by now, the queen's justicars will have gone back to their usual posts. We could explore the city. I could go to the ribbon stalls, the horse markets . . .

He looks me up and down, appraising. "I don't think you need to change. You look pretty clean."

Chance butts my shoulder, smearing the sleeve of my dress with horse spit and bits of chewed hay. Papa visibly winces.

I cross my arms and fix him with a glare. Papa has taken me to a few of his business meetings, mostly in towns near our estate. But all too often of late, these "meetings" have turned into awkward presentations of suitors for me. He's desperate to see me married off to a commoner, because if I marry below my station, I will forfeit my title. And in doing so, free myself of the obligation to attend the Performing.

I hate all the posturing, the arranged flirtations, but it's not as if Papa is trying to marry me off for land or money. We have more than enough of those already. He believes it's the only way to keep me safe.

Papa shrugs weakly, but then his brows knit together and a note of urgency enters his voice. "Remi, I know your mother and I have always encouraged you to take your time, but that singer at the Performing . . . she's wasn't like the queen's other mages. I've never seen power like that, and this is just her first season. She will only get stronger. She will break us."

The mention of Cadence twists like a knife in my gut. I've done my best over the past week to forget her. I think back to Baron Foutain and how he had wept with gratitude; the way the audience had chanted their thanks to the queen.

"Most of us already seem pretty broken."

"You know what I mean. I've been to eight Performings now. Eight. Last week was the worst it's ever been. I don't think Dame Ava is capable of a showing like that. The queen always strives to up the ante, so next year it will be even worse." Papa shakes his head and offers his hand for Chance to sniff. "I don't want that for you. I don't want you to endure a life of this."

"I knew her," I blurt out. "The singer. I recognized her when Lord Durand introduced her."

"What?" Papa whispers.

"Remember when I was small, and there was a girl I always used to play with in the mages' wing when we stayed at the palace? That was her," I say, even as anger clogs my voice. "Mama always said she found a patron. I guess she did."

"That sweet blond girl with the little brown-and-white dog?"

I swallow hard. "That's her."

"When we first left the palace, you were so anxious to know where she had gone. You kept asking your mother to forward a letter for months." Papa rubs his forehead, then sighs. "Does it make it better or worse, knowing what happened to her?"

"Worse." The image of her standing onstage, shoulders hunched and forlorn, flits through my memory. I bite the inside of my cheek. We were friends. *Best* friends. And she hurt me. So why do I care that she might be hurting, too?

Papa squeezes my shoulder. "Let's go. I've known Jon for years. He's a good man. Maybe you'll like his boy. I gather Nolan is good-looking, and he's doing very well in his apprenticeship. He will be a master mason someday."

"Maybe." I duck my head and busy myself with adjusting

Chance's throatlatch so Papa won't see the tight press of my mouth.

Nolan very well might be handsome, and the rank of master mason is certainly nothing to sneer at, but I've never been interested in boys. I had a crush of sorts on my friend Elspeth a few years ago, but when I told her, she stopped talking to me. *Our kind of people*, she said, her narrowed eyes and curled lip betraying her disgust, *don't engage in that sort of depravity*. Her words cut me.

Here in Bordea, the mages and commoners love and marry as they please—not caught up in ideas of bloodlines and inheritance. They don't force their children to learn outdated, Sapphire Age ideas about sexuality and gender or arrange marriages for political gain and dowries. But for generations, all the noble families we know have resisted change.

If I had been born a mage, I would be free to flirt with pretty girls, and no one would judge me for it. I've imagined myself sometimes: strolling through the market with a mage's badge pinned to my collar, winking at the shopgirls or seducing a fire-haired tavern wench over a mug of ale. Not that I know anything about seduction.

I've never actually talked to my parents about it. Sometimes I think about telling Mama. When we sit together in her parlor, she talks about the progressive beliefs of the mages, and how, with a different leader, Bordea would be stronger for incorporating them. But then I think about Elspeth, and the look of disgust she gave me. I never want Mama to look at me like that.

I wonder what Elspeth would say if she knew my parents were trying to marry me off to a commoner. It's not done among "our kind of people," either. Maybe someday soon, I'll be able to trust my family with the truth about me.

Just . . . not today.

I plaster a smile on my face and turn to Papa. "I'll be ready to leave in a few minutes."

"Good," Papa says with a nod. "I'll meet you in the yard."

We trot most of the distance to Cannis, stopping only once to relieve ourselves and allow the horses a drink. Papa's mare is tall, with a long, ground-eating stride that forces Chance to break into a canter to keep up with her. By the time we reach the pub where Papa has arranged the meeting, my pony is struggling to pick his feet up. He leans his weight on my hands through the bit, and my shoulders cramp. When I finally dismount, he gives a relieved sigh and doesn't even fidget as I tie him to the post.

"Rook will be along with the carriage soon," Papa says as we turn to go inside. "We're only a few blocks from the hotel. He'll take the horses there. I thought it might be nice to walk."

I nod. The insides of my legs ache. It will be good to stand. Chance has a comfortable, lumbering gait, but his back is so wide that my legs have to stretch to get around him. Eventually, I will train him to go sidesaddle, but for now, while he's green and still spooks at shadows on the road, I ride him astride.

I wonder what Nolan will be like. All of the young men Papa has introduced me to so far have been perfectly *nice*, with good manners and pleasant looks. I can pass an hour in their company easily enough, even if I don't feel anything romantic toward them, but Papa starts each meeting with such hope in his eyes, and I hate the way his expression shifts, disappointed, when I reject another boy and another opportunity to escape.

"Are you excited?" Papa asks.

I roll my eyes and he smiles, mistaking the source of my embarrassment.

"Don't worry," he says. "I have actual business with Jon today as well, so we'll have things to discuss. We won't be eavesdropping on you and Nolan."

We arrive at the pub, and I follow Papa through its jovial outdoor garden. Papa pulls the door open, and a burst of warm air and hickory smoke envelops us. The pub has a practical but cheery atmosphere, with tables made from simple, untreated wood and a bar counter stacked with a row of ale barrels. Its patrons seem to be mostly merchants and craftsmen, who swap loud stories over plates of fried fish and new potatoes. Some of them look up and stare as Papa closes the door behind us. I self-consciously rub at my sleeve, where Chance's slime is still visible.

Standing on his toes, Papa squints over the heads of the other patrons, then tugs me toward a corner table. Two black men recline in the pub's best leather-back chairs, taking small sips from gray mugs. They stand as we approach.

The younger of the two is my age. He has beautiful, smooth umber skin, curly black hair, and impossibly long eyelashes that highlight his hazel eyes. His arms are roped with muscle, and he doesn't try to hide his open, friendly smile. He's by far the best-looking of the suitors Papa has tried to throw at me. Not that his looks affect me beyond an aesthetic appreciation.

Nolan sweeps me a little bow and pulls out the chair beside him.

Papa leans down and whispers in my ear. "Give him a proper chance. For me. Please."

I nod and ease into my chair, forcing a smile.

"Claude," the older man says. He steps forward, balancing on a cane, and takes Papa's hand warmly.

Papa claps him on the back. "Jon. It's been far too long. How are you, my old friend?"

After we all sit, Papa flags a barmaid to our table. She'd been serving a group of craftsmen, but she takes one look at Papa and me with our costly clothes and scurries over. The queen has made us into recluses, living in isolation in our villages and châteaus, but we still have money, and the server knows it. Papa orders a selection of sandwiches for the table. I swallow down disappointment. After such a long ride, I'm craving the ale the craftsmen drink at the bar and a nice steak pie. But Papa will want me to impress this boy, and that's hard to do with gravy on my fingers.

"I had hoped to catch you last week about the shipment," Jon says, then clears his throat. "But under the circumstances . . . the Opera Hall . . ."

At Jon's words, the soles of my feet start to itch in remembrance of the song.

Papa gives him a curt nod. He hates talking about the Performing with his business contacts. Too many of the commoners have mixed opinions of the event: Some who once suffered under their local lords' laws rejoice at the queen's brutal method of control, while others look on it with revulsion. Jon's expression is kind, but if there's anything Papa can't stand from his friends, it's pity.

The barmaid returns bearing a silver plate of dainty finger sandwiches. Nolan grimaces before his father shoots him a severe look across the table. I hide a smile behind my hand. Maybe this will go better than I expected. At least we have something in common.

"Let's just enjoy our food. Remi and I have no desire to relive those horrors," Papa says, and lifts a cucumber sandwich to his mouth.

"M-miss Remi," the young man stammers. He turns to me with so much earnestness in his lovely eyes that I feel sorry for him.

Papa really has gone out of his way to find someone I might like. I can see that this boy is beautiful. When his white teeth flash, I yearn to feel something—that rush of giddiness and heat and shyness that some of my friends describe—but I don't. I am more likely to feel something for Cadence, monster that she is, with her long blond hair, gently curving waist, and timid smile. And even if it will keep me safe, Papa won't let me marry Jon's son unless it will make me happy, too.

My immunity to this boy's sweet charm feels like failure.

"Sir," I say, and offer the boy my hand to kiss. Our fathers turn their chairs to the side and start discussing the price of shipping our latest batch of cashmere.

"My name is Nolan. But you already knew that, I guess."

The boy clears his throat and glances around the pub. "Would you . . . like to take a turn about the room?"

I can't help it. I burst out laughing. The pub is so full of people I can't even see the other side, much less a path to walk. Our fathers stop talking and look at us in alarm.

Nolan bites his lower lip, then starts laughing as well. "My mother told me to say it," he explains. "She said it was something highborn folk ask."

His father sighs and rolls his eyes. I shrug off my overcoat and look over to the bar. After the ride, I want to collapse into my bed beside the fireplace and sleep, but for Papa's sake, I will make this effort. Besides, it might give me the chance to get what I really want.

"Tell you what," I say. "Battle this crowd with me and buy me a steak pie, and we'll take a turn."

Smiling wide, Nolan clambers to his feet and offers me his arm. I take it, and still laughing, we go in search of stiff ale and fresh-baked pies.

# CHAPTER 7

# CADENCE

I SIT CROSS-LEGGED ON the floor of the library, fingers clasped in my lap, trying to feign interest as Anette practices her scales. Madam Guillard has begged a favor, so I'm trapped supervising hopeless third-year students, even though I want to spend the day alone.

Anette is like me: an orphan who came to the mages' academy with nothing but the clothes on her back. Her parents were merchant sailors, though, so her circumstances have not always been as dire as mine. Everything they owned was tied up in their ship. When it sank, Anette was left alone and penniless, condemned to the same city home that raised me.

Elene is considering her. Anette is the only corporeal singer in her class, and Elene likes to recruit a few of us each year. Her justicars are well paid, but it's a dangerous position, and the ranks need yearly replenishment.

The girl's wide green eyes fix on me as she sings, watching my face for any hint of approval. She wears a rich velvet dress of singer's emerald, probably given to her by Elene as an early promise of interest. The garment makes her look like a doll, her tiny nine-year-old frame swamped by folds of fabric. Her brunette curls are meticulously pinned up and styled with green ribbons. I wonder if she did it herself, and how long she spent getting ready for this informal audience with the principal.

I don't have the heart to tell her that I have no influence on Elene's selections.

Anette has a fine timbre and an impressive vocal range for her age, but her magic is weak. She's supposed to be freezing the bowl of chicken stock that rests on the floor next to me. Her song conjures the thinnest film of ice across the top of the broth, nowhere close to freezing it solid.

Elene will be disappointed. I don't want to think what that might mean for Anette's future. Madam Guillard tries to keep the children who disappoint Elene until their exams, but she isn't always successful. Imagining Anette stripped of her fine clothes and forced to return to the city home, to a life of hunger and fleas, makes a lump form in my throat.

Since Anette's a child, Elene may at least let her keep her

voice, so she can make a few coppers selling cheap magic on the streets. But even that's not a guarantee. There are plenty of children in the Expelled settlement, too.

Across the library, two final-year students huddle together at a long table covered by open books. They watch us and giggle. Both wear pins with a ringed copper circle to mark them as novices who have passed their first round of exams. One is an elemental, the other a corporeal singer like me. By their sixth year, most decent students can detect the level of magic in another mage's song. They know Anette isn't strong.

They both have round cheeks and glossy hair, and the carefree look of girls who have never known what it's like to go hungry. Their mockery makes something protective flare up inside me. Anette and I share the same surname, de la Roix, because we both belong to Elene. In a way, it makes us family. I scowl at the students and they blanch, turning hastily back to their books.

Anette finishes her song and sweeps me a deep curtsy.

My legs have long since fallen asleep, but I stagger to my feet and applaud. "Brava!" I say. "Well performed!"

The girl's face flushes with pleasure. She curtsies again, nearly stumbling in her excitement, and murmurs, "Thank you, Principal."

Someday, someone else is going to tell Anette that her voice isn't powerful. Maybe I'm being kind, or maybe just selfish, but I'm not going to be the one who destroys the hopes of this little girl. If she's lucky, and Elene doesn't throw her out, she might achieve a lesser classification and be able to work as a palace guard or a junior healer in some provincial village.

If I could help her be stronger, I would. But while I can give Anette instruction on technique, Adela gives magic on her whim. Her gift only whispers to Anette. It does not fill her, breathing and growing like a second soul, as it does with me. The goddess has not chosen to make Anette powerful, and there's nothing I can change about that.

I wrap my arm around the girl's shoulders. "You sing beautifully. But when you begin the chorus, make sure you're really focusing on the bowl. I think your attention wandered to me a few times. You can't lose focus, even for an instant. Really project your voice. And make sure you light your prayer candles. Every night."

The library doors fly open, and a man strides in, dressed in the canary-yellow livery of the Couriers guild. He clutches a folded letter in his outstretched hands. I wince as he tracks slimy black mud across the polished marble floor. Novice mages maintain the academy. I remember scrubbing these library floors all too well.

"Madam Guillard has gone out for the afternoon," I say,

hurrying toward him so he won't leave any more footprints. "If you have a dispatch for her, you can leave it in her study. I'll show you the way."

The courier flips the letter over and studies the prim handwriting on its face. "No. It's addressed to a Mademoiselle Cadence de la Roix, Principal. I was told to find her here when I inquired at the gate."

I snatch the letter from his hand. The courier's jaw slackens in surprise.

Flushing, I hiss, "*I* am Cadence de la Roix."

The novices crane to see better. Who could possibly be writing to me? I sniff the paper suspiciously, smelling for a hint of unfamiliar or dangerous magic. Outside of the hospital, I have no friends in the city.

"Excellent." The courier rifles through his satchel and produces a ledger. The page displays a row of wax seals, some with signatures beside them. He taps a green crest emblazoned with a treble clef, the mark of the hospital. I suck in a breath and hastily scribble my name beside it.

When the courier has gone, I turn my back to the novices and rip open the letter. Sister Elizabeta never writes to me. We always agree on the timing of my visits in person. I'm not scheduled to go back to Saint Izelea's until the end of the week.

I scan her missive. It's short and direct:

*Cadence,*

*We have received a patient who was in a riding accident.*
*His ribs are crushed, and the flesh of his stomach is turning*
*purple. Mercedes is not up to the task. I fear we will lose*
*him. He is a personal friend. If you are able, please attend*
*us at once.*

*E.*

The hospital loses patients all the time. Even I have been unable to save some of the souls I encounter on my shifts. Some illnesses and injuries are beyond magic's ability to heal. Despite many mages dedicating years to the study, we still have not found the right songs to heal even the common flu. Sequestered inside Saint Izelea's, I doubt Sister Elizabeta has had much chance to make personal friends. I suppose the man could be a relative, someone from her life before she pledged herself to Odetta and a lifetime within the hospital's walls.

I crumple the note and turn to Anette. "I'm sorry, but I'm going to have to cut our practice short."

Anette dips her chin, but her voice trembles as she says, "Of course, Principal. I will practice projecting my voice."

"Tell Madam Guillard that I will practice with you again," I say, and pat her shoulder. "Tomorrow, if your lessons permit."

She gives me a toothy smile, her eyes alight with hope.

Maybe I can persuade Elene to let me keep her until her exams. It's not unusual for singers of my rank to take an apprentice. Lord Durand has already sent a folio of music sheets to my studio, ideas for next year's Performing. If I sing loudly and let Ren's spies hear me practice, there is a chance Elene will allow it.

I walk slowly to the library doors, then, once outside, sprint back to my room. Lacerde is sleeping beside the fire with Nip in her lap. When he hears me, my dog jumps down, tail wagging furiously. I kneel and gather him in my arms.

"I thought you were assisting Madam Guillard this morning," Lacerde says, and opens one eye.

"The student felt unwell," I say with a pang of guilt. "Flu, maybe."

"And you believed that?" Lacerde rolls her eyes. "Look at the weather outside. Did you never fake sickness to go play in the sunshine? At that age?"

"I didn't dare," I mutter. When I was Anette's age, I no longer had the luxury of practicing in the academy library on my own schedule. Elene had already taken a very personal interest in my education. Sick or not, I practiced every day.

Lacerde's gaze falls on the letter in my hand. "What's that?"

"Nothing," I say, and toss the note, seal down, onto my bed. For some reason, the urgency of Sister Elizabeta's missive makes it seem private. I may have to tell Ren about it later, in my report, but I want to hear Sister Elizabeta's story first. It's frowned upon for the nuns to hang on to their family and friends from the outside world, but it's not a crime. My flippant gesture soothes Lacerde's suspicion. She leans back in her chair again.

Nip nuzzles my face. Holding him against my hip with one arm, I pull my heavy wool cloak from the stand. "I'm going to take him out for a while. It *is* a lovely day."

"Was it the child who faked the flu, or you?" Lacerde laughs. "Take it slow, though, and sing him something for pain. His arthritis is bothering him."

She squints at me and taps her throat. "And for goddess's sake, put on a scarf. I know you don't like the other healers tampering with your voice, but you still sound a little croaky from the Performing last week. The queen won't be happy if she hears you."

I deposit Nip on the bed while I put on my cloak and fetch one of Lacerde's hand-knitted scarves from my wardrobe. She's right. I don't trust the other healers in the palace with my voice, not when any one of them would gladly cut my throat for the chance to be principal. Mercedes is incompetent, so I won't let her heal me, either.

I change my shoes from the slippers I wear around the palace to a pair of scuffed work boots, shoes that no one will associate with a palace mage. Then, after making sure Lacerde's eyes have firmly closed again, I snatch up the letter and bury it deep down in the pocket of my cloak. Nip barks excitedly, his whole body jiggling with the force of his wagging tail.

When I reach the hospital, Sister Elizabeta stands at the door. She casts a furtive glance over my shoulder and then ushers me inside, her face chalk white and glimmering with sweat. A novice nun, shrouded head to toe in white linen, scoops up Nip and, at my nod, bustles him away. He will spend the evening being fussed over and fed scraps from the nuns' plates. They usually give him a bath, too, and when I collect him, he'll smell of roses.

"Come on," Sister Elizabeta says. "No time to change today, I'm afraid. He's in the upper bedroom. His breathing is shallow, and he isn't responding."

"Who is this man?" I tug off my cloak and drape it over my arm. The air in the hospital is stiflingly warm. "Who is he to you?"

"A dear friend," Sister Elizabeta murmurs.

I want to ask more, but a thin wail coming from the second

floor makes me race for the staircase. In the back bedroom, a young white man moans on the cot. His overcoat and shift have been cut away. The alabaster flesh of his chest, stomach, and abdomen have all turned dark purple from the blood pooling inside him. His breathing is labored, but when he sees me, he gives a muffled shout of fear.

His clothes are very fine but look as though they were made to fit someone else. He's not a noble. Of that I feel sure. His legs have a slight bow to them, common in folk from the lower city who didn't get enough to eat as children. So how does he know who I am? And why is he afraid?

Mercedes sits in the chair beside him, gripping his hand, not even attempting to sing for him. Two novice nuns stand on either side of the bed, tossing handfuls of ash into the air.

I sniff the air, and my brow creases. The ash is made from pine. I know all the peasant superstitions about magic from my childhood. Some of the folktales suggest that the effect of a song's power can be diluted by throwing pine ash into the air. It's nonsense, of course, but if Mercedes is struggling to heal the young man, why are they throwing ash?

My gaze snaps to Sister Elizabeta. She shifts ever so slightly under my stare, her hands clasped behind her back.

"This wasn't a riding accident, was it?" I ask.

Fear grips my heart. I shouldn't have come.

"I told you we shouldn't have written to her!" Mercedes wails. "Better to let him die than have the queen find out—"

"Hush, child," the old nun admonishes. She lifts her chin and studies me, almost defiantly. "No, Cadence, it wasn't a riding accident."

I bend forward and breathe in the smell of the magic binding the boy's chest. I recognize the Constrictor, a spell designed to gradually tighten until the victim's ribs break and all the air is crushed from their lungs. It can take days. A powerful spell like this, which causes such an agonizing, restrained, and slow death, could only be cast by a strong, experienced corporeal singer.

This magic smells faintly of cinnamon and leaves a metallic taste in the back of my mouth.

I close my eyes. "How did you come to tangle with the chief justicar?"

"The less you know about this, the better," Sister Elizabeta whispers.

I know I should run and leave the patient to his fate. If I treat this man, this boy, Ren may smell his own magic on me when I go to make my report.

But the boy coughs a splatter of blood, and I remain motionless.

As a commoner, he isn't barred from the hospital by birth. Maybe I can convince Elene that I was confused, that I had not recognized the scent of Ren's magic . . . By the time I make my report, the patient could be long on his way. The nuns could plead innocence, too. They are just common folk. They can't be expected to recognize a binding spell.

My mouth feels like I've swallowed sand. I can't lie directly to Ren. He'll see right through me, and if Elene evens suspects that I've omitted something, she'll send me straight to him. But I'm not scheduled to be here. If I'm quick, maybe no one needs to know at all.

The choice of spellsong is typical of Ren. Elene chose him as her justicar for his sadism—Lacerde once remarked that pain sustains Ren like food. No one wants to be brought to the high court to be subjected to his version of justice. There are rumors that Ren ventures out at night, alone, intent on finding new victims on the streets when the city courts don't provide them, though he is smart enough not to let Elene find evidence of that. Maybe this youth was just in the wrong place.

"Is this man a criminal?" I ask.

"No. But even if he were, do you think he deserves this?"

"I didn't even notice the spell at first," the young man wheezes. "I just went on with my day, but it kept getting tighter . . ."

I look over my shoulder at the door. I'm not involved yet. I can still go home, slip back into my rooms. Lacerde thinks I've only gone for a walk, and that timeline still holds . . .

Taking a look isn't a crime, only helping, so I hum the words to a revealing spell. Ren's magic resists, pushing against me, but I raise my voice, and it glimmers into view, stretching around the man's torso in the form of a great, writhing snake. Its forked tongue flicks out, and it tastes the air. One of its green, slitted, reptilian eyes swivels back to stare at me.

I take a deep breath, then say, "I need you to bring me a pair of garden shears."

The novice closest to me just stares down at the gleaming snake encircling her patient's waist. "Sh-shears, Chantrix?" she stammers.

Slowly, I grin. Using shears and blades as visual talismans to focus my song is a trick Madam Guillard taught me a few months ago. My song still does the work, but the shears will give me focus.

The novice flees, and Mercedes comes to stand beside me, watching with rapt attention as I press my cheek against the youth's chest. Pain ricochets through my jaw, but I grit my teeth and begin to hum a healing spell. The youth lets out a scream as my song manipulates a broken rib back into place.

Sister Elizabeta has never put me in this position before. She has never asked me to take a case that violates the law or might put any of us in peril. She's never refused to tell me any details of a patient. Mercedes seems caught between awe at my skill and terror that I might discover the youth's identity. This is her hospital, but I come here every week. Seeing how she looks at me now, like an outsider, stings.

A shiver courses down my back. The nuns are the closet thing I have to friends. Hospitals that break Elene's laws, by treating rebels or noble folk, are at risk of being shut down, their nuns dispersed. The worship of Odetta that the nuns share with Elene won't protect them if the boy is found to be a rebel. As leader of Saint Izelea's, Sister Elizabeta might face prison, or worse. Mercedes could be condemned to join the Expelled. I can't stand the thought of either of them rotting in the dungeons beneath the palace or being given over to Ren.

Sister Elizabeta is right. I don't want to know anything about this boy. I can't tell Ren what I don't know.

Footsteps clatter back up the stairs. Gasping, the novice thrusts a pair of garden shears into my hands. It's obvious they haven't been used in some time. The blades have almost rusted together. At least magic can't get gangrene.

I hold the sheers to my lips and begin a heating song. I sing and sing until the metal blades glow red, ignoring the throbbing pain in my throat. I slide them around the python's neck, and bracing myself as it hisses, I cut down with as much force as I can, severing the creature's head. Ren's magic dissolves. As the pressure slackens, the young man gives a groan of relief.

"Here." I beckon Mercedes. "If you block his pain, I will tend to the worst injuries."

Mercedes nods. She clears her throat and begins the words to a healing song. She has a soft voice, with a high, almost child-like pitch. Her song is pretty enough, but like Anette's, there's no real strength in it. The boy's torso remains purple, his ribs broken, but his eyelids roll, and he sighs as Mercedes lures the worst of his pain away.

"With your permission," I say to the boy, "I'd like to send you to sleep. It will be easier for us to heal you."

The youth gives a small nod. His eyes have started water-ing from the shock and sudden relief. Mercedes stops singing, deferring to me again.

I whisper the words of the sleeping song. The young man drifts into sleep, a peaceful smile twitching on his lips. Then I bend my head and murmur a prayer to Adela. I always thank her after a healing, but this time, I beg for protection as well. For all of our sakes, Elene cannot find out what I did today.

# CHAPTER 8

# REMI

I NURSE A GLASS of mulled wine in the hotel salon, long after Papa has gone up to bed. I think about Nolan and his hopeful, beautiful eyes, then back to the Performing last week. Maybe I could be happy with him. Certainly I wouldn't be the most miserable married woman I know. And Papa's right. If I marry Nolan, in some ways I'll be free. I won't have to bear the sentence of my rank any longer.

But can I bear letting Nolan use my body as we are taught marriage requires? Can I bear him heirs? The idea of doing *that* with a man repulses me. And I don't know if I could stand to watch the hopeful light inside him die when he realizes what a disappointment I'm going to be as a wife. He wants a girl who can love him. He deserves that.

Tilting the glass up, I drain the final dregs of the spicy, hot wine. I never sleep well in the city anymore, with the streetlights and the noise. As a child, in my pink canopy bed in the palace, the murmur of the city lulled me to sleep faster than anything. It was a safe noise. But ever since I attended last year's Performing, the city sounds make my stomach squirm. If I go up to bed, I'll lie awake for hours, just reliving what happened in the Opera Hall.

I pick up my coin purse and consider it. Mama increased my allowance at the start of the year, when I turned sixteen, but because there is nothing to buy in the small villages that border our estate, I've been pretty frugal. I glance out the hotel window. The night sky is cloudless. I could clear my head with a ride, and maybe one of the decadent pastry shops we passed will still be open.

I sling my crumpled riding cloak over my shoulders and leave a small pile of coins for the barman. I check my appearance in the hall mirror and smooth my unruly auburn hair. My alabaster skin has a tan glow from a summer spent outside with the horses; the bridge of freckles over my nose, inherited from Papa, has grown more pronounced. Mama's warm brown eyes and round cheeks stare back at me. I brush at the stain on my sleeve and decide it is useless. Then I make my way to the hotel's stable block.

Chance is stabled right at the rear of the building. His stall has no window, but his hayrack is full. I feel sorry for him, tucked away at the back of the stable. The hotel is the fanciest in Cannis. They probably find Chance ugly and want to keep him out of their other patrons' sight. Piebalds aren't exactly fashionable, and the hotel won't want people to get the wrong impression about the type of guest it attracts.

I sidle into the stall beside him to wrap my arms around his neck. He sniffs my shoulder and nibbles my hair. He smells of fresh grass and home. For a minute, I'm tempted to bed down in the straw beside him and spend the night here, listening to the horses.

Chance pins his ears as I remove his rug and toss it to the side. But he quiets when I pull his tack out of the storage box in front of the stall. At home, he spends most of his day in the paddock with the other horses. His box in our barn is open and airy, with a clear view of the yard. I'm sure he's anxious to leave Cannis, too. I sling his saddle over his back and slip the bit into his mouth. I lead him out of the barn and climb aboard.

At least here in the city, I don't worry about riding out alone. People are afraid of the queen's justicars. Those who break the law tend to disappear, never to return, or turn up dead weeks later bearing the marks of terrible magic. Then there are rumors about the queen's own magic. No one really knows what she's capable of without her band of singers, but people speculate.

Some of Mama's friends say that Queen Elene is the most powerful mage since Arriah the Dissonant in the fifth century, even though she is a heretic.

Even Cadence, with all her monstrous power, looked afraid onstage. I remember the way she lingered next to the stage curtain and how she fell to her knees when her song was over. What does the queen do to her, once the curtains are drawn? Do the justicars spy on her, too? I can't help but wonder what she was feeling when she heard our screams.

The city center is dark and mostly deserted. To my disappointment, most of the shops have closed. The queen enforces strict laws prohibiting gathering at night, but I didn't think even the pubs and food stalls would close so early. We trot past a bakery, and I sigh. Beautiful cakes sit in the window, iced to look like castles and winter landscapes. I can still smell the nutmeg, vanilla, and sugar in the air.

A few drunk pedestrians stagger home, bracing themselves against the buildings. A group of children huddles under the small warmth of the streetlamps. Their shadows make Chance dance sideways.

Chance pulls on the reins. After being shut away in a dark stall all evening, he wants to gallop. The road is pretty clear, so I slacken the reins, and he leaps forward into a canter. His hooves pound the cobblestones, shattering the night's silence and splashing pools of rainwater onto the sidewalks. A few of the drunks shake their fists at me as we fly past.

Both of us are breathing hard when I pull up. I don't recognize the street anymore. We've galloped away from the city's center, into one of Cannis's many abandoned neighborhoods.

The street is lined with decrepit houses. Once, they would all have been as grand as our château in miniature. This neighborhood would have been a flurry of life and parties, filled with Cannis's elite. Now, most of the houses are boarded up, and even the street itself has started to decay, its cobblestones worn flat and weeds growing between them. The palace is just up the hill behind the roofline of the houses.

But one house, near the end of the street, has light coming from the windows. A sign hangs in front of it, depicting a green treble clef. It's a universal sign for hospitals in Bordea. And though I know I shouldn't, I nudge Chance forward with my heels and study the front of the house through its rusting iron gate. With a start, I realize that I recognize this house from my childhood. The Frelene family, now all dead, once lived here.

Underneath the treble clef, the sign reads SISTERS OF SAINT IZELEA.

My hand flies to my mouth. I know of this place. A few years ago, Mama had a seizure the morning of the Performing. She'd been ill for several years, after our local healing mage refused to perform a safe abortion, and she was forced to turn to other methods with the midwife. The herbs they placed in her womb seeped into her blood, leaving her prone to headaches, muscle weakness, and occasional seizures. In desperation, Papa brought her to one of the city's hospitals, which, by law, should have turned them away. But the nuns, despite the danger, had welcomed Mama.

They hadn't been able to cure her, but the magic fortified her body enough that she lived through the pain of the Opera Hall that day.

The fight my parents had when they returned home made all their others pale by comparison.

"Another Performing like that will kill you!" Papa shouted.

"You can't take her," Mama hissed. "I won't let you take her."

"I need you. *We* need you to live," Papa said as his voice cracked with emotion. I heard his footsteps pace the length of the dining room, and when he spoke again, his tone was flat and hard. "If I have to tell the stewards to lock you in this house, I will do it."

Through the fireplace grate, I wasn't able to hear Mama's response, but in the morning, Papa told me that I would take her place the next year.

Since then, things have never been quite the same between

them. Mama sleeps in her dressing room and fills her days writing letters to distant friends to avoid speaking to the husband who sits on the sofa opposite her.

Still, my family owes these nuns a debt. I put my reins in one hand and reach for my coin purse. I can never truly repay them for what they risked for my family, but the old building is in disarray. The front drives, once immaculately kept, have overgrown with nettles. The fountain is stagnant, and moss grows over its lip. Insects buzz across the dirty water.

The facade of the house hasn't fared a lot better. Under Lady Frelene's strict keeping, the marble pillars and gargoyles practically glowed. But after years of neglect, the house's white stone has faded to muted gray. I can make a donation that might ease some of the nuns' burden. I don't even have to give them my name.

I glance over my shoulder at the dark, empty street. I don't hear voices or footsteps, so I don't think that I have been followed. I dismount and lead Chance to an empty, dusty stable in the abandoned coach house. There isn't any hay for me to offer him, but I don't intend to stay long. The pony nudges my shoulder, then glances pointedly at the empty hayrack.

"I'm sorry, boy," I whisper, and stroke his sweaty neck. "I'll steal an apple for you tomorrow at breakfast."

This doesn't seem to placate him. Chance stomps his foot

and butts my shoulder again, harder this time. I sigh and give him a final pat, though his disappointed snort tears at my heart. I secure the stall door and make my way up the hospital's cracked front steps.

A locked bolt stretches across the oak door. It's the only aspect of the house that looks well maintained. The bolt is in the new, magical style that allows the owner to operate it from inside using vocal commands. It's probably a gift to the hospital from the queen, meant to aid the nuns in keeping people like me out. I take a deep breath, then reach for the brass knocker.

Chance nickers at me from across the courtyard. Inside the hospital, I can hear people rattling about and, more distantly, cries of pain.

What if someone recognizes me?

The bolt glows red, then disappears. The door creaks open, and light floods the overgrown garden. It's too late to reconsider. A gaunt-cheeked nun stands on the threshold, an assortment of towels stuffed under her arm. Her eyes sweep over my riding cloak, my dress, and the gold locket at my throat. She presses her lips together and crosses her arms.

"Can I help you?" She shifts so that her body fills the doorway, blocking my path.

"I'm here to see Mercedes," I say, and before she has a chance to react, I push past her into the hall.

The nun peers outside into the courtyard, then slams the door behind me. She plants her hands on her hips, eyes roaming wildly around the empty hall. "You shouldn't be here," she snaps. "You know you shouldn't be here. How do you know Mercedes? Why do you want to see her?" Her gaze travels to my stomach and the slight rounding, visible even under my tight bodice. "If you're pregnant, there's nothing we can do to help you here."

I grind my teeth. I've always been chubby, but never self-conscious about it. I don't even mind being called fat if it's said as a fact, not an insult. But this nun is being deliberately rude. Even if I'm not supposed to be here, I'm not going to tolerate that.

"I'm not pregnant," I growl, biting the inside of my cheek. I pull the purse of coins from my cloak pocket. "I'm here to repay a debt. Mercedes saved my mother's life."

She hesitates, then ushers me down the barren hall into a little office with a desk and two rickety chairs. Gesturing for me to sit, she closes the office door. "What is your mother's name?"

I don't know if I should answer that question. If I give her Mama's name, she'll have a record of me. Maybe this nun is a kind of gatekeeper, sent here by the queen to guard the hospital. Other than my clothes, she has no evidence, yet, of my birth rank.

But if she turns me in, the hospital could lose their singer and their endorsement from the queen. Chantrix Mercedes committed the first crime years ago by agreeing to help Mama at all. Given the state of things here, I don't think they can afford to lose her.

I decide to take a chance. Lifting my chin, I say, "Laurel, Countess of Bordelain."

Her harsh expression softens. "I remember her. I was on shift the night your parents came here. I'm sorry about the way I acted before," she says. "We can't be too careful. Many of the noblewomen who come here are seeking Mercedes's aid with an unwanted pregnancy. We can't get a reputation for helping with that or anything else. I know you understand. The queen . . ."

"Can I see her?"

"She's with a patient now," the nun says. "Wait here, and I'll bring you to her when she's finished."

She bustles back out of the room, dropping one of the towels on her way. I bend down to pick it up, then recoil. The underside of the white towel is covered in thick green mucus and spots of brown blood. I bury my nose in my handkerchief.

I need to pay Mercedes and get out. I don't have the stomach for death and blood. I weigh the coin purse in my hand. I could toss it on the desk and leave. The debt would still get paid. It's the money the hospital needs, not my gratitude.

I put the purse back in my pocket. I've come this far, and I want to speak to the singer. I want to know how she ended up on this path of healing, compassionate despite the queen's laws. I want to know why she can do it when Cadence can't.

The clock on the wall ticks slowly. I lean across the office desk and flip through the ledger. The first page shows a list of patrons and their treatments. Ailments from a wart on the toe to miscarriage to broken bones all sit together on the page. Most of the rows list Mercedes's name as the singer responsible for treatment, along with a flourished signature that makes me smile. But not all of them. There is no signature on several entries, all attached to the most difficult medical cases. Some of the patients are recorded as deceased.

My head jerks up at a sudden surge of song, coming from the room above. It's a gentle song: low and soothing, like a lullaby or a ballad—nothing like the high soaring notes of the Performing—but it makes me shiver nonetheless. I put the ledger aside.

Outside of the Performing, I've never watched a corporeal singer work. Not up close, at least, though I remember seeing them set bones at a distance at sporting tournaments, back when the court still held them. Raw power like they have, which can't be seen, frightens me. I don't like that a small, frail girl like Cadence can bring hundreds of people to their knees with nothing more than a song. Some weaker mages still work outside of Cannis, but their power is nothing compared to what the queen's mages can do.

Before Queen Elene took the throne, Mama used to have lots of friends who were mages. She still insists that most are decent people who are just afraid of the queen, and only obey her in terror. She says their magic has its own beauty. If Mercedes agrees to see me, maybe I can watch her treat a patient up close. Maybe, if I watch another singer perform, on the less auspicious stage of a hospital bed, my fear will ebb away.

Up close, I might learn that they have weaknesses after all. The queen would not like that. I grin and the thrill of committing such an act of rebellion compels me to my feet. I follow the melody's trail up the hospital's dusty mahogany staircase.

The outlines of old portraits, long since removed, cling to the walls like ghosts. The gas lamps flicker. The place really does need a renovation. The hallway smells of mildew, blood, excrement, and a strange sweetness like honey and soap. It smells the way I imagine the sewer under a public bathhouse must be like. I press the handkerchief to my nose again.

The song leads me to a room at the very end of the second-floor hallway. The door hangs partially open already, and I nudge the gap wider with my shoulder. Inside, two figures stand over a plain bed. One is a nun, cloaked in white robes. The second figure must be the singer. She's dressed in purple velvet with immaculately curled, long red hair. She wears gardener's gloves to protect her hands from the sick.

They watch a young man toss in the sheets. I *know* him. It's the same young apprentice I met in Dupois's shop after the Performing. His shirt has been cut open, one of his ribs juts out at an odd angle, and purpling skin stretches over his chest. Has he been run over in the streets? Kicked by a horse?

My instinct is to rush forward, to sit beside him and comfort him, but magic song fills the tiny room. I feel the strength of it, lapping like cool water against my skin, making my bones feel light. But the mage's mouth doesn't seem to move.

I squint into the gloom and catch a glimpse of another mage sitting behind the nun. I can't see her face. She sits with her head bowed as if in prayer, long blond hair falling down over her face.

For a second, the apprentice's eyes flutter open, and he stares straight at me. Recognition flickers in his gaze. His brows knit together in a question, but then Mercedes hums a tune and he drifts to sleep.

The other singer stands, and I can't help the gasp that escapes from my lips. The nun and the two singers turn toward the door. Their eyes fix on me.

# CHAPTER 9
# CADENCE

I FINISH MY HEALING song and look up to see a girl standing in the doorframe watching me. She has striking, deep brown eyes and loose copper curls that frame her round face. A gold locket hangs above her ample chest. She looks much wealthier, and cleaner, than my usual patrons at the hospital.

When she notices my stare, she scrambles back into the darkness of the hallway. Sister Elizabeta runs after her. They exchange angry whispers, but without using more magic, I can't hear what they say.

Mercedes squeezes my arm. My throat, already sore, goes dry. The girl saw me and ran. Is she one of Ren's spies? Will she tell him what I did here? If Ren finds out that I undid his binding curse, if he tells Elene . . .

Something about her is familiar. Her clothes seem to mark

her as nobility. Fear makes me shiver. Was she in the Opera Hall? Has she stalked me here to hurt me?

Sister Elizabeta gently tugs the spy back into the room, her expression grim. I take a sip of water and try to settle my stomach. She's too young, surely, to be a trained assassin. The girl doesn't look any older than me. But where I am thin and white as eggshells—a wraith, as Elene often calls me in her less indulgent moods—she has generous, round curves and slightly pink, sun-kissed skin. Sister Elizabeta steadies her with a hand on her arm.

"She came to pay a debt to Mercedes," Elizabeta says. Her lips press together in a scowl, and wrinkles of annoyance appear on her forehead. "She was told to wait in the office downstairs."

The girl steps forward, shrugging off Elizabeta's hand and ignoring Mercedes. "I know you," she says accusingly.

I take another sip of water, stalling for time. From her clothes, her clipped diction, and the accusing stare she's leveling at me, she has to be a noble. Maybe she's older than I think. Coming face-to-face with one of my victims isn't something I've planned for. At least not like this. I've imagined them cornering me in some dark alley, in a hidden part of Cannis, throwing stones, and shouting. Somehow this is worse.

What can I possibly say now?

And why does she look so familiar?

I glance at Sister Elizabeta for help. "I—"

"And not just from the Performing," the girl continues. "From the palace, when we were children. We used to play together all the time." She spits the memory like venom, poison in her voice.

As she glares at me, moments and memories flood back in a tide of emotion. Her voice has a different timbre than I remember, but the rhythm of her words is the same. Her eyes haven't changed, either. And even though most of my memories are like black-and-white sketches, outlines without color or depth, I remember her.

It can't be. I know *she's* not old enough, at least not for a few years. But the faint, familiar scent of my own magic still clings to her skin like an unwanted perfume. She was there. I look down at her feet and press my hand to my throat as bile threatens to creep up.

There's no escaping what I've done.

"I remember," I whisper, and rise. Part of me wants to embrace her. I've missed her so much. But her expression is drawn and angry. I pull the blanket up over the young man's shoulders instead.

"What happened to you?" she demands. Her shoulders start to shake with barely suppressed rage. "When I couldn't find you at the palace, my mother said you'd probably found a patron out in the countryside. She said I should be happy for you. I hoped you'd gone somewhere nice. I never thought . . ." Her hands curl into fists at her sides, and her voice chills. "I never thought you'd become the queen's monster."

Part of me wants to defend myself. I didn't know she would be in the Opera Hall, and I want to believe that I would never have knowingly hurt her.

But I can't know for sure.

How did she find me here? I glance toward the door, half expecting to see one of Ren's green-robed justicars waiting in the hall. Elene could have sent Remi to test me. She's done it before, offering respite from the Performing to young nobles for a year or two in exchange for their help in catching out a singer she suspects.

"Why are you here?" I ask.

Remi flings a small velvet purse at Mercedes's feet. It clanks when it hits the wooden floor, heavy with coins. "I'm here to repay this hospital for helping my mother. She would have died in the Opera Hall if they hadn't helped a few years ago."

"You've taken her place," I whisper. Elene takes censuses. She knows how many adults are still alive in each noble family, and she requires that number to attend the Performing each year unless someone marries outside their class. Elene doesn't care who attends from each family as long as the number is right and their birth is noble. I've heard of children taking their parents' places before, when the parent falls ill or gets too old to bear the song, or when they rot in Elene's dungeons.

"She wouldn't have made it through another year." Her chin trembles.

I wince and look away.

"Why did you do it?" she whispers. The rage has started to seep out of her, and fear slowly takes its place, flaying my heart raw.

"I had to. If I hadn't done it, someone else would have. And then it would have been worse."

"Worse?" she barks a laugh. "For you, maybe."

"Elene would have brought Dame Ava back. Ava isn't strong enough to sing two songs. The first song was already decided a year ago, so she would have done it and just left you. The effect might not have been as strong, but there would have been no healing. It would have been worse for me if I'd refused, you're right, but if I hadn't, you'd still be in pain!" I snap. "So aren't you glad *I* did it, instead?"

Her eyes brim with unshed tears. "No," she says. "I'm not *glad.*"

The patient stirs in his bed with a groan. Mercedes sings him back to sleep as Sister Elizabeta steps between Remi and me.

"Miss," the nun says, her voice curt and tight. "We allowed you entry to the building on the premise that you were here to briefly visit Chantrix Mercedes. We did not allow you to come in so you could harass one of our other singers."

"She's not one of *your* singers," Remi hisses. Taking a deep breath, she drops into a rigid curtsy and turns to Mercedes. "I'm sorry. I came here to thank you. I didn't expect to find one of the queen's creatures here."

The comment stings. I bite my lip and wrap my arms tightly around my chest.

Mercedes bends down and retrieves the purse from the floor. She weighs it carefully in her hand. "Whatever this is for, I'm sure it's too much."

"Two years ago, my father brought my mother here before the Performing. She was having seizures. If you hadn't treated her, she would have died in the ceremony that day."

Mercedes says nothing. What Remi describes is a violation of one of Elene's dearest held laws. *Magic,* she says, *should belong to the people, not to the thieves who robbed our country for their own gain over centuries.* Knowing how close I am to the queen, and what I've seen here already today, Mercedes probably won't admit to breaking another law if she can help it.

Remi squeezes past Sister Elizabeta. She closes Mercedes's fingers around the purse. "It's yours," she says. "You can keep it or give it to this place. I don't care."

"Okay." Sister Elizabeta takes Remi by both shoulders and

steers her toward the door. "You've done what you came for. I think it's best if you leave now."

"No," I cut in. I'd given up hope of seeing Remi again, but now I can't just let her walk away, hating me. For so long, I've held on to the idea that somewhere in Bordea there is a person who still thinks well of me. I'm not ready to let that go. "Let her stay. I want . . . to talk to her."

Remi snorts.

"I'm not sure that's wise," Sister Elizabeta says, and Mercedes nods her head in agreement. "She's not even supposed to be here. She should leave before anyone else sees, and you should get back to the palace."

"You want to repay them?" I demand, ignoring the nun and glaring at Remi through the stinging tears that threaten to spill down my cheeks. "I'm going to stay. The hospital is overflowing, and there are three nuns out spreading alms tonight. You can assist me. That is, if you actually mean what you say about wanting to thank them, and aren't just throwing them money it's clear you don't need."

The anger I feel isn't fair—I'm the one who hurt her—but it burns inside me. Even if it has been years, she should know that I would never sing for Elene because I want to. I should leave before Ren or any of his spies realize I'm gone, but I can't walk away now.

"Fine," Remi says. Her eyes narrow, and she rolls up the sleeves of her gown. "Let's get to work."

The silence between us hovers like a foul smoke, but I can't deny that Remi is a good worker. I saw her gag when we walked past a patient with a gangrenous hand. As the daughter of a fine lady, I suppose she's not accustomed to things like that. But it's either pure stubbornness or an iron sense of duty that compels her, because we've worked for over an hour and she hasn't tried to run. But other than short responses to my medical instructions, she hasn't tried to talk to me, either. Even in the crowded public ward, the nuns give us a wide berth.

We sit beside a patient who complains of chest pains so strong he feels them in his lower back. In cases like this, it's hard to know if the source of pain comes from the chest at all or from the back. Remi holds him upright as he babbles to me about his symptoms.

Even though I could diagnose him without listening to all his chatter, I've learned to be patient. It's not just the noble folk who fear the strength of my magic. People don't want to believe that I can learn everything about the way their body works in the space of a few whispered notes. It relaxes them to let them tell me their problems, as if I were a surgeon instead of a mage. It saves me time in the end.

"I can feel it here," the man groans, pressing a place at the top of his rib cage with a dirty hand. "Can't hardly walk or sit up."

"How's your breathing?" I ask. "Shallow?"

He shakes his head. "No, it's fine."

It sounds like a disk slip, rather than anything wrong with his heart. I turn my head away and hum under my breath to verify, so softly he won't hear me. My song forms a hazy picture of his spine and the muscles around it.

"Turn him over," I say to Remi. "I don't think it's his chest."

"I've just said it's me chest," the man splutters, wincing as he tries to rise on his own without Remi's help. "What's got you thinking elsewise?"

"A lot of the muscles in your chest stretch right around your body," I say, and pat his shoulder. "Everything is connected. It's anatomy, not magic. Just science."

"Aye, science." The patient nods, satisfied that he is safe as long as science, not magic, guides my hand. He leans back into Remi's arms. She unbuttons his shirt with strong fingers, then turns him over onto his stomach.

The memory of her pudgy child's hands rubbing Nip's belly

comes unbidden, and my eyes sting again. I wonder if Nip would recognize her.

Those child's fingers used to stumble over the simplest of pianofortes. When did they become so strong, so graceful? I glance at her face out of the corner of my eye. Remi is fully focused on the patient, rubbing his back for comfort. She's a little bit beautiful like this: intent, biting her full, soft lip between her bright white teeth.

I swallow hard and look down at the patient. After what I did to Remi, it's not my place to have thoughts like those.

"You're going to feel a lot of heat," I say to the man. Beside me, Remi stiffens.

I run my fingers along the exposed channel of his spine. He tenses, but when I start to sing, his muscles obey my command to relax. My voice comes out as a hoarse rasp, which makes me wince. The sound isn't lovely, but that doesn't matter.

The patient lets out a little moan of pleasure and sags into the mattress. My song unwinds the muscles that have tightened around his spine and realigns the slipped disk.

"Aye," he says as his eyes roll back. "That's the spot."

"What does it feel like?" Remi asks suddenly, breaking my concentration. "This type of magic?"

The patient raises a floppy arm. "Shh. Don't interrupt her. It feels nice."

"Do you want to go to sleep?" I ask.

When my patients are not in critical condition, I always ask them. To take away their consciousness without consent seems like a violation. He gives me a half-dazed nod, and I ease him into slumber.

"What does it feel like?" Remi repeats.

"I've healed you before," I say quietly. "It feels more or less the same as that."

"I was distracted—you know, by the overwhelming pain?"

Wincing at her words, I focus the same healing song on Remi. She jumps when the magic seeps into her, then goes limp in her chair, as if all her bones have softened into butter. Her head lolls, and a curl of hair falls across her face. On impulse, I reach out and brush it back.

She flinches away, alert again in a second, despite the lull of my song.

"You can't just do this," she says, gesturing around the open hospital ward, "and think it cancels everything else out."

"I didn't want to Perform," I hiss, turning in my chair to face her. "I don't want to do any of it. But I've been very close to Elene for years. If you try to resist her, everything gets *worse*. She makes sure of it."

"But you have *magic*! Surely you could—"

"Elene has magic, too. No one knows how much for sure." I

reach for a clean towel and angrily fold it into a ball. "And she has an army of justicars who *like* having a mage on Bordea's throne. I have been trained for one purpose only. I don't know how to fight an army. If I resist her, I'll end up in the slums with the rest of the Expelled. I could end up dead."

Remi crosses her arms. "Better to be dead than complicit."

"Easy for you to say that," I snap. "When in your life have you ever struggled?"

Her eyes blaze. "You have the nerve to say that to me, after what you did to us at the Performing?"

"I answer to Elene every day. Every day is another chance for me to displease her and end up on the streets again or dead. Have you ever been hungry? Have you ever slept in a bed infested by fleas, not sure if you're going to wake up in the morning because it's so cold? You suffer once a year, and then you go back to your châteaus, your fancy estates. I *live* here. Your yearly nightmare is my *every day*."

My voice rises, and everyone in the ward, nun and patient alike, turns to stare. I cover my mouth with my hand and hiss. "I have seen children dragged into an auditorium and come out as corpses, their bodies tossed onto wagons like garbage. I have seen powerful mages reduced to sobs, unable to ever sing again, and then cast out to live in squalor. You don't understand a *thing*—and yet you're judging me."

"Have you ever even tried to stand up to her?"

"When I can. In my own way."

"*Directly.* Not some silly compromise."

"Once," I whisper. "I stood up to her once. She wanted me to kill one of her ministers while he slept. And I should have just done it, because in the end, he suffered. He died in agony at another's hands."

Finally, Remi looks away. "I could tell you were afraid. On the stage."

A blush of shame lights my cheeks. "Yes."

Whatever she may think of me, it feels good to admit it to someone. I'm always too afraid to act. And after tonight, I have every reason in the world to be scared. I've aided a potential fugitive. I've spent the evening in the company of an enemy of the crown.

I reek of forbidden magic.

But then Remi gives me the tiniest of smiles, and I realize that, in this moment, I'm not afraid at all.

We're interrupted by Sister Elizabeta. The nun thrusts two mugs of steaming tea into our hands and points to the window. Early-morning orange sun filters through it, bathing the hospital floor in warmth and light. Remi sets the tea aside and jumps to her feet.

"My pony will be angry," she jokes, and tugs on one of her

curls. "I left him through the night without any hay. And my father will expect me back."

"Well, we wouldn't want your pony to be angry," I murmur. "I need to head back myself, before everyone wakes up."

She tosses her borrowed apron onto the linen pile and sprints for the door. I want to ask her where she's staying, to see if we can meet again. But the goodbye freezes on my cowardly lips.

# CHAPTER 10

# CADENCE

I BARELY MAKE IT back to the palace and into my bed before two servants throw open the double doors to my suite, each holding a silver tray balanced atop a white-gloved hand. My stomach sinks. It's unusual for breakfast to appear before I call for it, which can only mean that Elene is planning to visit me.

I sit up and press a hand to my throat. It's so sore I can't even manage the croakiest of thank-yous. Even my ears hurt, but I have to pretend that I'm fine. Elene can't know about my visit to the hospital yesterday, or she'll send me straight to Ren to make my report.

The servants place their trays on the side table and lift the lids with a flourish. I breathe in the scents of fresh bread, warm butter, and an array of cheeses and fruits. At least Elene decided not to torture me with meat dishes today. She must be in a good mood. Both servants bow and back out of the room, closing the doors behind them.

I wrap my dressing gown around me and shuffle to the table. My knees wobble and threaten to give way. After all the energy I used at the hospital, my magic reserves are entirely gone. I couldn't heal a paper cut.

If Elene visits now, she's going to know there's something wrong with me. I lift my arm to my nose and sniff. The faintest trace of cinnamon spice still clings to my skin. Ren's magic has left its mark on me.

I sink into the carved golden chair beside my table with a groan. I whistle for Nip, and he trots to my side. Wincing, I hum a few bars of a pain-soothing song for his arthritis. After a day spent with the nuns—being fed cakes and sweetmeats, no doubt—he seems pretty spry this morning, but the only way to purge Ren's stink from my skin is to overlay it with magic of my own. My spell is weak and ghosts over Nip's fur with no effect. He whines, cocking his head to one side.

I should have ignored Sister Elizabeta's note. But if I had, the boy would surely have died. And I'd never have seen Remi again.

My heart beats a little faster just thinking her name. The gap-toothed girl with bony knees I knew as a child is long gone. When she smiled at me, my soul lifted. For just a minute, I felt less like a monster.

Nip nudges my calf with his head. He peers up at me, eyes glued to the untouched food on the table. I can't resist his soulful, brown eyes. With a sigh, I rip off a chunk of bread and toss it to him. The new white kitten peeks out at us from behind my bed. I throw the last morsel of cheese at her, but she refuses to come closer. The bowl of food Lacerde placed on the floor for her lays untouched.

I finish what's left of my breakfast, then go to the window to let some air into the room. The fire roars in the hearth. Lacerde keeps it lit day and night, summer and winter so I won't get sick. I'm more likely to slowly roast to death than catch a true cold. I fling the window open, and a breeze rushes in. The air outside is crisp and smells of damp stone and rose petals.

I throw off my dressing gown and change into a simple white linen tunic and a pair of cream breeches. A glance in the wall mirror reveals that the white garments make me look even more ghostly than usual.

Protocol demands that I dress respectably when I make public appearances, but Elene doesn't care how I dress inside the palace. She knows as well as I do that the tight bodices of fine, fashionable dresses restrict our breathing and make singing more difficult. Some of the older mages even speculate that the fashion was designed by jealous nobles for exactly that reason.

My throat feels as though I've swallowed a pine cone whole. Everyone expects me to go to my studio to practice today. Even a small deviation from my usual routine might be enough to arouse Elene's suspicions, so I sigh and collect my music folio from the desk by the window.

Pushing open the doors to my room, I find two servant girls waiting for me. Both are white and wear matching blue skirts, their long blond hair swept back into braids. One clutches a jug of water, the other a tray of cheeses and sweet breads. They will follow me to my studio to lay out the feast. Elene makes no secret of her desire to see me fattened up.

*It won't do,* I heard Elene whisper once to Lacerde, *for my principal chantrix to look like she has one foot in the grave.* Singers should look strong and robust—the picture of health and power. She probably wishes I looked more like Remi. In her prime, Dame Ava possessed lavish, voluptuous curves and straight, proud posture. She hadn't been a cowering wraith onstage. And I am sure she never once gagged at a private feast with the queen.

Part of me has always been tempted to work a little spellsong on myself. Just a simple one, to bring color to my cheeks and brighten my eyes, add some flesh to my hips. But the consequences of self-singing can be dire. We're taught that from our first days at the academy. It's too difficult to maintain concentration when you start to feel the magic's effects on your own body. Sing a note too high or too fast, and you can end up freezing yourself alive.

A few centuries ago, when there were more of us, the hospitals and asylums were full of corporeal singers who had tried to change themselves.

I run my fingers over the bones that jut from my collar. The danger in it doesn't make any of my longing go away.

The servants follow me down the hall to my practice studio at the end of the corridor. My space is small and bright, with large bay windows that look out over the palace courtyard. It's mostly unfurnished, to allow me enough space to move as I practice, but a small pianoforte sits in one corner, and a huge oak bookshelf dominates the back wall. A bouquet of ever-bloom daisies rests atop the pianoforte, grown by skilled mages to stay fresh for years. The servants place the water and the tray of food down on the pianoforte, then wait expectantly.

"You can leave," I say, pointing toward the door. My voice cracks as I speak. One of the girls winces.

I've never asked them to stay, not in all my years at the palace, yet they always wait to be dismissed. But even when they can tell I'm in pain, they never speak to me, either. At first, I wondered if Elene had invited two Expelled girls back into the palace to work, but I've since heard them in the hall giggling together, when they think I am out of earshot. So it must be fear that keeps them so silent and vigilant. They drop low curt-sies and scurry out into the hall, heads bowed.

Now alone, I select a book from the wooden shelf and sit down with my back against the wall. The outside cover is a volume of music theory—composition—but I've cut out the interior and stashed a novel inside instead. Sister Elizabeta buys them for me at the market sometimes and gives them to me at the hospital.

It's not that Elene prohibits me from buying them. But anything that distracts me from my practice would displease her, so I keep them hidden, lest she order me to get rid of them. I treasure the little windows into what a full life might look like. I know that real life, even for people who live outside Elene's domain, rarely follows these perfect trajectories, but the books make me smile all the same.

I love the novels with sword fights and mechanical guns best. What would it be like to fight with a weapon instead of a song? I imagine my fingers wrapped around cold steel, my lips pressed in concentration. What would it be like to have someone willing to fight over me?

But warriors with swords and happy endings, like the ones shown in the books, are for sweet, demure ladies who cross-stitch and ride horses down fragrant park lanes. They are not for creatures who torture people with their songs.

I hug the book against my chest and stare up at the ceiling.

Someone knocks on the door. I scowl, hastily shoving the smaller romance volume back into its textbook casing. I sniff the air. The aroma of Elene's magic drifts under the door. My stomach drops, but I school my face into a wooden smile.

She can't suspect anything. If she does, everyone at the hospital, Remi, and I will all be in danger.

I ease myself onto the pianoforte bench and pour myself a glass of water. I take a sip, then rasp out, "Come in."

I cringe at the sound of my voice.

Two henchmen push the door open and step into my little sanctuary. They stand on either side of the door to salute me, rigid and at attention. The queen sweeps in after them, dressed in an ivory gown and a mask of white lace and swan feathers.

I curtsy and bow my head. The sight of her makes me simmer with anger. She's left me alone in the week since the Performing, but I haven't forgotten what she made me do. Nor the detour she forced the driver to take before I got to the Opera Hall.

Elene embraces me tightly and then pushes me back to kiss both of my cheeks. I allow it, but even for the sake of my ruse, I can't bring myself to return her warmth.

Behind the mask, her eyes narrow, but she gushes, "I just can't get over how fabulous you were last week."

A third servant appears at the door, carrying a golden chair with velvet cushions. He places it in the center of the room, and Elene settles onto it like a cat.

"Just perfect," she continues. "I know I told you at dinner afterward, but you were so tired and out of sorts that I thought you needed a few days to yourself. I'm glad to see you're back to your practice. Has Durand sent the new music sheets up?"

I nod, keeping my eyes glued to the floor. If I speak, she'll notice the hoarseness in my voice. The sooner she leaves, the better.

But Elene's gaze sharpens, and her mouth quirks up at the corners. My confidence sinks like a stone in a bucket.

"Let's hear a few scales," she says, smile widening. "Your songs at the Performing were very beautiful, but not as technically perfect as they might have been. Maybe I can help you?"

Nudging the music theory volume with my foot, I croak, "I'm reading up."

She leans toward me and presses her hand to her mouth in concern. "Cadence, you sound terrible. Is your singing voice this bad? Show me."

I cough out a few bars, which does little to relax her.

"Did Lacerde forget to wrap you up? It's been so bitterly cold outside. I know how you love to walk that dog. If that maid let you get sick—"

"She didn't."

"I swear, if you're ill because she neglected you, I'll have her thrown straight out."

"I'm just tired."

"Are the nuns wearing you out at the hospital?"

"I haven't been there in days." It's the first outright lie I've ever told her.

Elene stands up and paces around the room before coming to stand behind me. She lifts my chin with one hand and braces my stomach with the other. "You must look up when you sing," she says. "Project your voice. You're always looking at your feet. Try again. A high note."

Closing my eyes against the pain, I project my voice as high as I can. Her effort isn't worth much. I'm not some novice; there is nothing wrong with my position. My song emerges as a squeak. My hand flies to my throat.

I glare at Elene. She could heal me, rather than putting both of us through this charade. But she won't risk showing off the range of her abilities in front of anyone—least of all me—and I would never ask another singer. Elene is the only mage here who is not my competition, and the others would try anything to take my position.

I am worthless to Elene without my voice. And it scares me to think of another mage tampering with it.

Elene heaves an exaggerated sigh. "This won't do at all.

Have you been like this all week? I did wonder if two songs was a good idea." She sits down in her chair again and smooths her ivory skirt. "Maybe we should have skipped the healing song. Performing two magic songs on that many people is a lot for anyone. Next year, we'll plan for just one."

I think back to the Performing, to the screams as I sang, to the way people scrambled over seats and each other to get away from me, only to be trapped by the mageglass doors. My song burned their skin away. If we'd skipped the healing song, their wounds could have become infected. Some would never have walked again.

And now that I know Remi was among them, it's a hundred times worse.

Rage stiffens my spine. How does Elene expect me to live with myself?

No other singer in her employ is capable of the magic I worked at the Performing. No one else could have managed two songs on so many people at once—not even Ren. I cannot refuse to obey her outright, but I have enough power to bargain.

I look Elene in the eye and say, "If you make me Perform again, I will heal them all, no matter what you say about it."

One of the henchmen gasps. "What you say is treason."

My blood pounds so hard I can feel it in my ears. I square my shoulders, waiting for Elene to have me thrown in the dungeon or use some of her infamous magic on me at last. Other than that haunting night outside the minister's mansion, I have never stood up to her. But I can still hear Remi's accusing words echoing in my mind: *Better to be dead than complicit.*

But Elene doesn't react. She merely steeples her fingers together and says quietly, "I'm glad you're finally realizing that you're a mage, and not a mouse." She gathers her skirt to stand, motioning for one of her servants to take the chair. "Just remember that all magic has limits. Be careful when you push yours."

"I was thinking I might take an apprentice." I brace myself for her refusal, but in this moment, I have the advantage. It won't last, so I must ask while I can.

"Oh?" Elene smiles. "I'm glad to hear you're taking more of an interest in grooming a protégé. Do you have someone in mind?"

It's hard to imagine Anette as my protégé. Certainly, she will never stand on the stage of the Opera Hall and devastate with her song. But if I take her on, she will be safe long enough to take her exams. Maybe Sister Elizabeta will let her work at Saint Izelea's after that. She can carry towels and empty bedpans, even if her magic never grows strong enough to heal.

"There's a third-year I think might suit," I say. "Madam Guillard asked me to tutor her. I think she has potential."

"Splendid," Elene says. "I'll make the arrangements."

She snaps her fingers at the two henchmen. After casting

me a dirty look, the one who accused me of treason opens the door. Elene walks into the hall, then turns back. "And let's plan to have dinner later this week. I'll give Lacerde the time."

When the door closes again, I sink slowly to my knees and pick up my book. I hold it so tightly that I rip the corner of its frayed cover. It's hard to know, with Elene, if I just won our battle or lost it in some way I have yet to feel.

The palace servants will expect me to spend the whole day in my studio, but I can't focus on the novel. Any singing practice is out of the question, since I need my voice to heal.

I pull a few real theory volumes from my shelves. When I came to the academy, my natural aptitude meant that I was never a true novice in the way Anette is, but a few of my old books might still help her technique. I can cobble together a lesson plan, and we can practice the specific songs she'll need to pass the exams.

She might never be strong, but with enough practice and time, she could achieve a secondary pass. I'm surprised by the flutter of excitement I feel. Teaching might be fun, and even if I can only save this one child from the consequences of Elene's disappointment, it's something.

With an armful of books, I sit in a patch of sunlight filtering in from the window and allow myself to smile.

# CHAPTER 11

# CADENCE

I RETURN TO MY room in the afternoon, the theory volume tucked under my arm. It's risky, taking my hollowed-out book back to my room where the servants will move it about as they clean, but all I want to do with my evening is read in bed with Nip curled in my lap. Maybe I'll make friends with the new kitten, too, if I can finally lure her from her hiding place.

When I push the doors to my room open, the little kitten scampers right up to me. I'm used to Nip greeting me, but he's nowhere to be seen.

I bend down to scoop the kitten up, and she purrs against my cheek. Her left paw is covered in sticky red blood. As she struggles, I push back her fur to take a look at the pad. It doesn't appear cut or injured, and she doesn't flinch when I give it a little squeeze.

A laundry maid changes the sheets on my bed. She doesn't meet my eyes when I say hello. Something is wrong. My hands clench. I flush hot and cold with dread.

"Nip?" I call into the room.

"Come on, lazy," I say, heart in my throat, as I walk over to his sleeping place. "I missed you."

Nip lies in his bed drenched in blood. I stumble back, gagging. The sickly sweetness of the blood and the cinnamon magic in the air around him linger like smoke from an extinguished candle.

"I'm sorry," the laundry maid wails. She tosses my sheets to the side. "Principal, he said I couldn't tell you before you saw. He said he'd know if I—"

She doesn't have to say who. I press my hand to my stomach and vomit on the carpet. Nip. The only family I had left. This is Ren's handiwork, but I know where the order came from. Was this what Elene meant by limits?

The maid steps forward. She takes hold of my arm and helps me to sit down. Pointing at the mess, she whispers, "I'll clean it all up. Why don't you go down to the kitchens? Someone will fix you a cup of tea."

The kitten squirms in my hold, meowing. Unconsciously, my grip had tightened until I was squeezing her. I thrust her into the maid's hands. "I'll clean it up. Take her. Take her home and never let me or the queen see her again."

"But miss—"

"*Do it!*" I scream.

She drops into a curtsy and stumbles out of my room.

I stare down at Nip's body. His lips are pulled back, revealing red-stained teeth. The blood continues to flow from his mouth, thick like syrup. This was recent. Elene didn't want anyone to have the chance to clean it up before I found him. If I'd hurried back from my studio, I might have caught Ren in time.

Burying my face in my hands, I start to sing. The pain builds in my throat, but I push through it. Slowly the blood reverses its course, flowing backward into my little dog until there is no sign of his death on the floor. I clutch my mother's necklace. When my spell is complete, he almost looks alive again, but there is no spark inside him. I whisper his name, but he doesn't move.

I sit on the floor beside him, then bring my knees up to my chest and start to cry. I can fix his broken body, but I can't bring him back.

I should have known Elene would do something, that she would never let what I said to her go. I should have come straight back to my room. I should have been here to protect him.

Outside my window, I hear angry voices and the crunch of something being dragged over gravel. A child's scream cuts across the garden: thin and sharp and scared.

My legs shake, and another wave of nausea crashes through me. I can't stand up.

The scream sounds again, more desperate this time and farther away. Slowly, I push myself to my feet, gripping the desk chair for support. I fling open the windows. The low evening sun stings my wet eyes as I look down into the garden.

Two guards wearing the red livery of Elene's personal battalion drag a small figure down the path that leads to the academy performance hall. The child is cloaked head to toe in black, a sack pulled over their head.

I've seen this happen so many times before that, at first, my impulse is to shut the window. I don't know who the child is, only that their life at the palace is over. When they emerge from the performance hall again, they will be thrown onto a wagon, voiceless and bound for the settlement.

But today, I'm not going to let that happen. Angry tears forge burning rivers down my cheeks. Elene took a life from me. I'm going to save one from her.

I lean out the window as far as I can, scraping my elbows on the rough shingles of the roof below.

"Stop!" My hoarse voice barely rises above a whisper. I clear my throat and shout, "Stop!"

One of the guards glances over his shoulder, up at my window. His brow creases in confusion, but then he shrugs and keeps walking, pulling the child with him.

I try to sing, to summon the vines that creep up the performance hall's facade, to make them block the door. But as the first note of the song leaves my lips, the guards wrench open the doors of the hall and shove their prisoner inside.

I sink back down onto my knees.

I'm too late.

I'm always too late.

# CHAPTER 12

# REMI

**"YOU LOOK LIKE HELL,"** Papa says as he sits down at the breakfast table beside me. "Late night? Was your room okay?"

"Couldn't sleep," I mumble as I spread jam on my toast. If I'd wanted to, I could have slept for a few hours before breakfast, but my mind was too busy churning over what had happened at the hospital.

"Thinking about Nolan?" Papa asks, a little too enthusiastically.

"No—gross." I roll my eyes, then ball up a little piece of bread and throw it at him.

He holds up his hands in mock surrender, but a grin tugs at his lips. "Okay, okay. I'm prying. I get it. But the two of you seemed to be getting along yesterday."

"He was nice," I say. "And he bought me a steak pie."

"A catch, then," Papa jokes. "Maybe I could invite Jon to the château. It might be helpful for you and Nolan to have some time to get to know each other away from Cannis."

I nod with as much enthusiasm as I can manage.

I wish I could tell him how I feel about men, but I worry that he will look at me with the same disgust that showed on Elspeth's face. I'm his only child. I don't want to be a disappointment. Besides, it's obvious Papa thinks I'm completely infatuated with Nolan. I don't have the heart to take that away from him. Not yet.

I crack open my egg with the edge of my spoon. It's been a few hours, but I can still feel the glow of Cadence's healing song inside me. My chest flutters, and my body feels strangely light, like I'm floating in water. Even though I haven't slept and have bags under my eyes, I feel like I could outrun a horse. No wonder the queen doesn't let us have access to magic. With this much energy, *anyone* could start a rebellion.

I can't stop thinking about how Cadence tried to touch me. I pulled away, but part of me wanted to feel the caress of her fingers against my cheek. I yearn to know what it's like to be touched by a girl, creature of the queen or not. And despite her incredible power, there's still something sweet, almost innocent, about her. Something I don't want to shatter.

"Shall we get on the road? Your mother will be glad to have

us home, I expect," Papa says. He dabs the corner of his mouth with a napkin, then pushes his plate aside. "And I'll be glad to get away from this city. I hate Cannis."

When I was small, the season in Cannis had been Papa's favorite time of the year. He loved the balls, masquerades, and banquets; the carousel of diplomats and state affairs. He and Mama would chatter like two robins in the back of the carriage, excitedly planning a full calendar of engagements.

I squeeze his hand. "Maybe one day you'll love it again."

He sighs and pushes the handle down on the little coffee press. "Maybe. If I knew for certain you would be safe."

I reach for the press and pour myself a steaming cup of coffee. "I don't know how I could live with myself if I just abandoned you and Mama."

"We brought you into this," he says forcefully. "If we had been more aware . . . if we had understood how the people we ruled were suffering, how the mages resented us . . . maybe none of this would be happening. We should never have allowed a murderer to be crowned. You were a child. None of this is your fault."

"It's not yours, either. You couldn't have known what Queen Elene would turn out to be."

He glances around the hotel bar. It's nearly empty save for us and an elderly black gentleman sitting alone at a table in the corner of the room. He whispers, "Don't say things like that here. When we're at home, miles away, then it's safer, but in Cannis . . . many of the people here love the queen. They won't keep our secrets."

I shrug my shoulder toward the old man, who obliviously munches his way through an entire basket of bread, his eyes closed with pleasure. "Do you think he's a spy? He looks like a justicar to me," I chuckle.

Papa laughs so hard he nearly spits out his coffee. We finish our breakfast in happy silence; then he gets up to pay our hotel tab. I tug my riding cloak around my shoulders, even though the window reveals a bright autumn morning.

I think about what Cadence told me about Queen Elene's power. She was right. Not knowing what the queen is capable of *does* make it worse. If we don't know how her magic works or how strong it is, how can we ever fight back?

I meet Papa at the hotel bar. The porter already stands beside the door with our bags, waiting to take them to our carriage.

"Do you have an extra farthing for the cleaning maid?" Papa asks, rummaging through his coin purse.

My hands fly to the pocket of my cloak before I remember that I gave my whole purse to Mercedes. "Sorry, I think I packed my purse away."

"Typical." Papa rolls his eyes. He places two gold coins

on the desk. The porter's eyes widen, and the barman's fingers twitch toward the coins. Papa shakes his head at them. "Share this with all of the staff."

Our carriage waits in the hotel courtyard. It arrived in the city last night, and my clothes were waiting, unpacked in my room, when I'd stumbled in during the small hours of the morning. Rook is half-asleep again in the driver's seat, but when he hears us coming, he straightens and takes the reins.

Chance is tied to the rear of the carriage with a long tether, alongside Papa's chestnut mare. He chews the rope so intently I worry he will get free before we arrive home. Some horses would continue to follow the carriage anyway, but Chance isn't one of them. He would run straight into some poor farmer's grain shed, and we would find him eating his way through their entire crop of corn.

Papa climbs into the carriage, but I go to Chance and tie a double knot in the rope. He nips my arm when I pat his neck. He hasn't forgiven me for leaving him in a stall all night without food.

As I turn to board the carriage, a group of riders gallops into the courtyard. They wear the queen's livery with her mask insignia emblazoned on their chests. Their horses are frothing at the mouth, coats streaked with sweat and dust. The riders form a semicircle around our carriage. I step into Chance's shadow and peer at them over his neck.

But their leader looks right at Chance, and me, as he dismounts. He wears a silver armband that marks him as a captain in the royal army. My uncle used to wear such, before nobles were banned from serving. The captain gestures toward my pony, and one of his men jumps down to grab Chance by the bridle. Two others bang on Papa's carriage door, then drag him out into the courtyard.

"What is the meaning of this?" Papa asks, tone soft. He spreads his arms wide, so they can see he isn't reaching for a weapon. If the queen has sent for us, the best thing we can do is go quietly. "What grounds do you have for arrest?"

The riders ignore his questions. The man nearest to me works Chance's lead free, takes hold of my arm, and hauls me before their leader. A crawling sensation creeps down my back. Someone must have seen me at the hospital. It's the only explanation. But I was so careful . . .

The captain takes a swig from a flask at his hip. His soldiers force Papa to kneel on the cobblestones. Papa grimaces in pain. His left kneecap was broken in a hunting accident years ago, and he still struggles to bend it. My hands curl into fists. How dare they?

I wrench my arm free from my captor's hold. "Don't touch me! Let go of him!" I know that I should be quiet, should be meek, but I can't just watch them treat Papa like that. Not when this is all my fault.

"Remi," my father hisses, but I ignore his warning.

"Tell me what's going on." I meet the captain's hard stare, even though he towers over me. "It is my legal right to know the charges against me."

"That pony," the captain says, jabbing his finger at Chance, "was spotted outside the hospital of Saint Izelea last night. The informant said it arrived late in the evening and did not leave again until morning. Your father is a suspected member of the resistance. We've had our eyes on him for a while, but we didn't think he'd be brazen enough to try anything in the city."

Even though I left the laces of my corset loose for travel, it suddenly feels too small. I take a staggered breath. I knew this could happen, but I thought that if anyone betrayed my where-abouts, it would be someone inside the hospital who had seen me with Cadence. Not that my strange-looking pony would give me away before I even stepped inside.

And Papa? A member of the resistance? If that is true, he's never confided in me. I shoot a glance at him, but his eyes remain glued to the cobblestones, a muscle tensing in his jaw.

He has meetings in Cannis almost every fortnight, and he usually comes to the city alone. I remember the mystery parcel he took from Dupois right after the Performing. He said it was a present for my nameday, but now . . .

How much does Mama know?

"That's impossible." I keep my voice as steady as I can while my heart races. "My father and I were here all of last night. We met a few friends at the pub on the Rue Railletée. We have been here since then."

"This horse has a distinctive coat," the captain snaps. "And the informant told us it was not a large animal, being ridden at speed by a person wearing an expensive velvet cloak. He looks down at Papa. "He said the rider was alone. From your father's height, it seems unlikely he would ride such a beast. I think you may have passed a message on for him."

"You have no proof of that."

"You are of noble rank. Saint Izelea's employs a corporeal singer. You are barred from entry by law. Our suspicions are enough to bring you to the palace." His lips curl into a sneer. "As for proof, I leave that to the justicars."

I won't confess to them. Chance's piebald coloring is unusual, especially as a noble's mount, but not unique. The charge he is levying against me of visiting the hospital is bad enough. But being a member of the resistance is treason. My chin juts forward. "You can hardly expect me to believe that this is the only piebald horse in the city of Cannis."

The captain glares at me, then shrugs. "We sent a dispatch to the hospital as well. We are bringing in a few of the nuns and their singer for questioning. If you are innocent, you've nothing to fear."

"When it comes to Queen Elene, there is always something to fear," Papa says.

The captain gestures toward a riderless horse and nods to his men. The two soldiers haul Papa roughly to his feet. Another rider joins them, and together, they hoist Papa over the horse's back like a sack of flour.

I look away, tears stinging my eyes. I can't watch this humiliation. They will parade him through the streets like a common criminal, and it's all my fault.

The captain motions to the soldier holding me. "We'll not treat a woman thus. Pass her up to me."

The guard lifts me, and I'm satisfied to hear a little grunt of effort emit from his lips. I'm pleased that my weight allows me to be passively inconvenient to him. I don't make any move to wrap my arms around the guard's neck to support myself. I let my body go as limp as a doll's. Let him struggle.

"Really?" the captain growls.

He takes hold of my arm and swings me up into the saddle

behind him. Then I feel a sickening sort of gratitude toward him as I look at Papa, slung facedown over his horse. I take a deep breath. I can't arrive at the palace rattled. I need to keep my wits if we're going to get out of this.

If Papa really is a member of the resistance, then he's avoided arrest for years. What if I've ruined all his work? I must fix this.

Who will they bring to testify against us?

I don't want to believe that Cadence would betray me, but I hardly know the person she's become. She may have asked me to stay and work with her in order to entrap me.

"Wrap your arms around my waist," the captain instructs. I can't disobey his direct order. Scowling, I do as he bids. Jumping down isn't an option. If I run, they will hunt me down like an animal in the streets.

Our rank has no dignity anymore. In the queen's eyes, we are less than nothing.

It doesn't take long to reach the palace, but by the time we clatter up the paved drive through the queen's orchard, I am close to vomiting. I can't imagine how Papa must feel, hanging like luggage while the horse churns stones and dust into his face. I wish I had never gone to the hospital at all. Whatever Mercedes did for Mama, repaying her wasn't worth our lives. If the queen finds us guilty of aiding the resistance, she'll surely have us put to death.

Our little entourage stops in front of the palace's intricate wrought-iron gate. Through the bars, I catch a glimpse of Cavalia, the royal palace, for the first time since I was a child. It looks different than I remember. Under the old queen, the white stone palace always looked cheery, alive with colorful banners hanging from its parapets, and yellow and purple flowers in boxes outside every window. Now it looks like an ice sculpture: perfectly chiseled and immaculate, but cold and dead.

The captain shouts a greeting. A gangly boy in a guard's uniform rises from his stool and stumbles over to the gate.

"Business?" he asks, peering around the captain's bulk at me.

"Bringing these two to the dungeon." The captain waves a dismissive hand toward Papa. "Suspected of engaging with one of the queen's singers . . . and treason."

I bite my lip. They can't be relying on the word of a merchant who saw my horse late at night.

Mercedes isn't one of the queen's singers, but Cadence is. What the captain says confirms it. She's turned me in; reported me to the justicars. I can still feel her magic in my bones, and her betrayal penetrates almost as deep.

"Who?" the boy asks. He wrings his hands and straightens his uniform. "I was on duty last night at the academy. I didn't see anyone leave or come in late."

"That's none of your business, boy," the captain snaps. He rummages in his saddlebags and pulls out a signed document. "Now let us pass. These two have an appointment with the chief justicar. I'm sure he'll get to the bottom of everything."

After a quick glance at the captain's document, the guard signals someone on top of the wall, and the iron gate creaks open. He salutes the cavalcade, and we enter the hellmouth.

The soldiers dismount as soon as we get inside the palace walls. They remove their swords and muskets and toss them into a chest beside the gate. Then they unstrap Papa from his horse to pull him down. Spots of bright red blood dot his cheeks, and dirt cakes his lips.

I swallow down a sob. Just like in the Opera Hall, I have to be strong for him. We have to make it home.

"Take him to the lower dungeons with the criminals," the captain shouts. "Let him mill around with the lowlifes of the city for a few hours before the chief justicar gets to him. Might loosen his tongue up a little bit. Not that the justicar isn't capable." He chuckles, and a few of his men join him. They start to drag Papa toward a wooden door beneath the palace wall.

"Wait!" I yell, and jump down from the captain's horse. "Don't. Don't take him anywhere. You have everything all wrong. He has nothing to do with any of this. I went out for a ride last night, and my horse stumbled. I went into the hospital to see if they had any bandages. I swear, I didn't meet with any singers."

The men holding Papa's arms pause. My father looks at me in shock, green eyes wide. "Remi? What? Why didn't you tell me?"

"I meant to, but I didn't want you to worry. I didn't think it would matter," I babble. I don't know if my lies will serve, but I will say anything to make them release us. I can't imagine—won't imagine—Papa in a dank cell, surrounded by cutthroats and thieves.

The captain shrugs. "Take him. I'll bring this one to the justicar myself."

"Take him where?" I scream as two of the guards drag Papa to a cellar beneath the wall and out of sight. "Tell me what you're doing with him! I told you, I went alone. He has nothing to do with any of this!"

"He's still wanted for treason. We've had him in our sight for a while, as I said. Just because he isn't involved in whatever happened last night doesn't mean he's innocent." The captain flashes me a yellow smile. "This gave us an excuse to bring him in."

As I scramble for words, he nods to one of his men. "Take her to the upper cells. We don't want her harmed before the chief justicar has his way. You know that Ren likes them fresh."

One of the soldiers lifts me, but this time I fight. I scramble and kick and claw at his eyes, even as three more men rush forward to help. But in the end, it doesn't matter. They drag me into the dungeons and seal me in the dark.

# CHAPTER 13
# CADENCE

**THE DOOR CRACKS OPEN,** and someone hurriedly pushes a covered tray inside. It joins the collection of untouched, spoiling food that litters the floor. I could have kept the food fresh if I'd wanted to—not that I would have eaten it—but I'm more interested in using my magic to keep Nip's corpse from rotting. The smell of the spoiling food combines with the incense I've lit for prayers to create a pungent smoke. I wrap my duvet tighter around myself and lean back into the mess of pillows on my bed.

I don't want to see anyone. I've shut myself away for nearly a week. And not even Lacerde dares to enter my room now.

A scuffling noise comes from the hall, followed by Durand's loud voice. "This is getting ridiculous. How long is this going to go on? Have any of you even been inside to check that she's eating, drinking?"

"You tell me!" Lacerde shouts back. "When is Her Majesty going to intervene? I'm not going in there again."

She tried to speak to me at the start of my isolation. A few hours after I found Nip's body, Lacerde came to my room with a bowl of hot soup. She brushed my hair and spoke softly, and at first, I soaked up the comfort of her touch.

But then I started imagining her in Nip's place on the floor, her eyes glazed with death, blood seeping from her open mouth. If Elene came to believe that Lacerde was my friend and not just a servant, her life would be in danger, too.

I screamed at her to get out, and when she refused, I sang the words of a choking spell that left her gasping for breath and scrambling for the door.

"This is getting out of hand. Get a hold of yourself. She's a teenage girl. What are you afraid of?" Durand snaps.

"A teenage girl," Lacerde echoes. "Well. Why don't you go in there and see how harmless she is?"

Durand lets out a little squawk of indignation. But he starts fumbling with the lock, then pushes both double doors open and steps inside. He surveys the mess on the floor. His eyes roam over Nip's perfectly preserved body, and I watch the color drain slowly from his ruddy face.

He braces shaking hands on his stomach. "Come now, Cadence. You must be starving."

I sit up in bed, still cocooned in the white duvet. Durand stoops down to pick up today's tray. He holds out his free hand to me and speaks as if I'm a toddler . . . or a *dog*. "There's a good girl. Doesn't this look good? The chefs have been making your favorites . . ."

The last time I saw Durand, he was pushing me forward into the light of the Opera Hall chandelier, making me Perform. I decide to give him a little taste of the song he was so excited to hear. Despite the emotional energy it takes to maintain Nip, a few days in bed have done wonders for my magical reserves. I can feel Adela's gift coursing through my veins.

I begin the heat song. At the first note, Durand lets out a high-pitched shriek and runs for the door. He recognizes the tune, as well he should, since he listened to me practice it often enough in the days leading up to the Performing.

But running doesn't help him. He falls a few feet from the door. He screams and clutches at his shoes, knocking the trays of decaying food across the floor.

I can't help the smile that twitches at my lips. This is justice. And maybe this is what I need to do in order to fix everything, instead of playing nurse at the hospital. Remi was right. I can't hide at Saint Izelea's, working my small magics, and think that cancels out everything that I do in the queen's name. Watching Durand writhe makes me feel more alive than I have in days. He crawls forward on his hands, and I sing until he tumbles into the hallway. I do not begin a healing song.

When the door snaps shut again, I rise from my bed and pick up the freshest tray of food. I sit cross-legged on the floor and remove the silver top from the dish. Ignoring the fork and knife at the side of the tray, I lift a fried potato to my lips. A line of grease drips down my chin.

As I finish the last morsel of potato, the doors fly open again, and Elene strides into the room unannounced, flanked by six of her guards. Durand limps in her shadow.

She moves with a furious, staccato stride, stepping over my discarded trays, until she stands over me. She looks angrier than I've ever seen her, her hands curled into fists at her sides, her brow furrowed above her mask.

For all my anger is justified, I feel like a disobedient child, caught in some naughty act. From this angle, Elene seems all too vast in her hooped skirt and long train. She towers over the guards behind her, who watch me with fear in their eyes.

Elene sinks into the chair beside my writing table, arranging her blood-red skirt so it falls gracefully around her.

"So, Cadence," she says, voice disturbingly friendly, at odds with the cold, angry expression on her face. "What do you want? We need you to get back to your practice, to normalcy."

Considering what she did to Nip after the last time I argued with her, I never expected negotiation. I stare up at her, then cock my eyebrow in a mirror image of hers. "I want my dog back."

"You know full well that's impossible," Elene snaps. "But we'll get you another one."

"No."

She grinds her teeth. "You can't stay in here forever. What do you want? What will get you to come out of your room and stop sulking like a child?"

"*Sulking?*" I demand, rising up onto my knees. "You killed Nip. He was my only family. My one friend."

Elene rolls her eyes. "He was a dog. An old one. He would have died soon anyway. Hardly worth a whole week of hiding in your room. And what you did to Durand was uncalled for."

Her mask today is an exuberant, bright pink that seems to mock me and my grief. I cross my arms over my chest. Tears sting my eyes and threaten to spill. But if I am going to cry, I won't let her see it. It's bad enough that I look crumpled and unwashed in front of her, stains on my dress. "Why do you wear those stupid masks, anyway? You aren't a goddess. They're obscene, heretical."

I say it because I know it will infuriate her.

Her composure is its own type of mask, and I want to rip it off.

Elene's eyes flash, but her voice remains calm as she says, "Without the mask, people see me as too young and lowborn, unworthy of my rank. With it, I look like the queen of Bordea. You have been trained to perform your whole life. You should understand the importance of appearances."

I turn away from her and glare out the window. "Fine. Send up my new apprentice, and she will help me wash."

I can't face Lacerde right now. Not after what I did to her.

Elene doesn't move. The guards around her shift uneasily, but she just looks around the room, at Nip's preserved corpse, and takes a deep breath. "I cannot do that."

My whole body stiffens. Part of me knows what she is about to say, and still, I ask, "Why not?"

"I sent Anette away," Elene says. "I had Ren evaluate her, and he said the girl was useless . . . She was expelled last week."

I think of Anette, so small and hopeful, abandoned at the Expelled settlement. Is she in pain, still, from the procedure? How long will she last all alone, in a place where all must fight to survive?

I want to tell her that I never told Elene she was useless, that I wanted to protect her. But I will never get the chance.

Then I remember the screaming, hooded child being dragged to the performance hall, right outside my window. That could have been Anette. Could I have saved her, if only I had stood up faster, sung harder?

Wiping my eyes on my sleeve, I whisper, "Get out."

To my surprise, Elene rises and walks to the door.

# CHAPTER 14

# CADENCE

**ELENE RETURNS TWO DAYS** later with Ren in tow. For once, he doesn't look at me with contempt. No doubt he's heard what I did to Durand, and perhaps, at last, he's a little bit afraid of me.

Elene doesn't wait for me to speak before she says, "I admit that I may have been rash in my actions. I understand what you were getting at in the studio. Refusing the healing after that ordeal would have been too cruel. Even for *them*."

I say nothing. I haven't eaten again since her revelation about Anette, and my limbs feel too heavy to get out of bed. She's reaching, and I'm definitely not prepared to help her with her long overdue and insufficient apology. If she thinks words are enough, she never understood Nip's value to me.

Or how much power she's lost now that he's gone. She doesn't understand how much of myself I saw in Anette.

Elene continues, "So I've been thinking on it. It may be time to relax protocols a little regarding the nobility. Durand, Ren, and I have spoken, and we can start to . . ." She pauses for a moment and looks to Durand for support.

". . . reintegrate them," he finishes for her. He hobbles out from behind the wall of guards to stand beside the queen. Even after two days, his jaw is still clenched with pain. Perhaps none of the other singers dare to heal him for fear of being the next to face my anger. Or perhaps Elene is teaching him a lesson about the consequences of failure. Either way, I'm glad he suffers. "It's past time. Many of the older, corrupt generation are dead or dying. Their children have been raised with sufficient respect for the crown, its magic, and the law."

Ren snorts. "Respect for the law? If that were true—"

Elene silences him with a scowl.

My eyes narrow. Elene has hated the nobility—all of them, even the idea of them, past, future, and long dead—for as long as I've known her. She has never forgiven the viscount who betrayed her, or the class of people who made him reject her. She avoids them at all costs, even choosing to stay hidden in a private box at the Opera Hall. None of them are ever allowed to attend court, not even to make petitions. Why now? What does she hope to gain with this?

"I thought we could host a masquerade," Elene says. She gives me a sly smile. "To formally honor Odetta as patron of the queendom. It would be a public demonstration of a new era in my reign—"

"And a security nightmare," Ren mumbles.

"You could perform a healing song on a few people for existing ailments. Fix a broken leg, or something. It will give them a different sort of demonstration of our power."

It would be easy to let myself believe that Elene means what she says. That she really does want to begin the long process of repairing relations with the noble folk. But I know her too well.

"I have nothing else to say to you. Get out."

"A shame," Elene muses. "Ren tells me that he has a friend of yours in the dungeons. I thought we might invite her. I was planning to have a little chat with her later today to see if she might want to become a companion to you, instead of rotting away in a cage."

A friend of mine? Elene knows what the other mages say about me and the competition between us all. The closest friends I have are the nuns at Saint Izelea's, and I wouldn't go

169

so far as to call Sister Elizabeta or Mercedes my friends, despite the camaraderie I feel when I'm there.

My heart starts to race. Unless she knows about that night. Did she smell Ren's magic on me that day in the studio, or was my lie really so transparent? Did she investigate after I fought her in the studio? And if she knows about the youth, and the binding spell I undid, does she know about Remi, too?

She may need me, but Remi means no more to her than Nip did.

My fear must show on my face, because Elene smiles. "Someone spotted her horse outside the hospital," she says. Under her mask, her cheeks flush with pleasure. "When faced with losing her voice and being relocated to the settlement, the hospital's singer told Ren everything we needed to hear. I am willing to forgive you for healing a magic-bound youth. After all, it could have been a mistake."

Ren rolls his eyes. "A mistake? She knows the mark of my magic nearly as well as her own. The spell was only a few days old. Fresh. There was no *mistake*."

A phantom pain shoots up my arm, a memory from the day he broke it.

"I don't accuse Cadence," Elene says, and I wonder how badly she must need me, to allow such a thing to pass. "But it's a crime for a noble to seek aid from a singer. And what's more,

Ren and his justicars have been tracking her father's actions for years. We believe him to be part of a resistance group. Which you know quite well is treason."

"And treason carries a capital sentence," Ren says with so much relish that I shiver. He raises his eyebrows at me, grinning.

Durand grinds his teeth, then tells Ren, "Wait for us outside. You're not helping."

I expect Ren to balk. I've never seen him take orders from anyone save Elene. But he looks at me, a small smile playing at the corners of his mouth, as if he knows something about me that I don't. He sweeps Durand a low bow and says, "As you wish, my lord."

When he has gone, Elene cranes toward me. Her voice is smooth and gentle as she says, "Cadence, I think of you as my own daughter. My heir. You're much too precious to waste. *You* are not being convicted of anything, of course, but without your cooperation, we will condemn the girl."

"And the chief justicar is well prepared to take his time with her death," Durand supplies.

I know what it means for Ren to take his time. Remi will suffer over weeks, and by the time he kills her, she will be a shell of a girl, all the brightness in her eyes gone. Her screams would be an intoxicating music to him, a nectar to nourish his cruel soul.

I clench my fists, my knuckles going white. How dare Elene

arrest Remi? How dare she use our friendship—the tattered remains of it—against me? It's been a week since I went to the hospital. Have they held Remi in the dungeons this whole time?

I look at Nip's unmoving body. He's still perfectly preserved, not a white hair out of place. But no matter how hard I beg Adela or sing for him, his tail will never wag again. He will never shuffle to the door to greet me, never sit beneath my feet while I eat. We will never curl up and read together again.

This is the price of disobeying Elene. And now she seeks to offer me a substitute. A human replacement for the companion I've lost. Just so she can continue to manipulate me.

She's taken Nip and the promise of Anette. She knows that threatening to cast me out is not enough.

She just has to give me something else to lose. Well, I won't let her.

When the song tumbles from my lips, it emerges like a scream. I don't even recognize the melody, the words. It's a raw and wild composition for the storm inside me, and the effect is immediate. The guards fall to their knees. Durand doubles over, coughing stringy, half-frozen blood. I keep my back straight and lift my chin, the way Elene positioned me in the studio. The windowpanes shatter, the glass showering the floor like rain.

Elene steps toward me, humming something I can't quite

hear over the roar of my song. Whatever magic pours out of me doesn't affect her. Is this defense Odetta's gift? Or am I simply not as strong as Elene herself has made me believe?

All around, her guards lie on the floor, unmoving. Durand is crumpled beside them, a look of shock permanently frozen onto his face, blood dripping from his nose. My voice falters. I want to start a singing a healing song, but there is no life force emitting from the fallen men.

What have I done?

I am not a murderer. I'm not.

My breath comes in deep, desperate gasps.

Then it stops. All of a sudden, I can't bring any air into my lungs at all. Elene sits down at my desk chair, singing softly. Her voice is gritty, and her rhythm falters, but still, her magic overpowers mine.

No one has ever used a spell like this against me. I don't know what to do, how to protect myself. I clutch at my throat. My vision blurs and flickers. I try to think brave thoughts: If I die, she won't be able to use me anymore. No one else will be able to deliver a Performing like I did. People will be safer.

I might see Nip in the afterworld. I might see my parents.

But in the end, as the blackness starts to set in, hot tears course down my cheeks.

I don't want to die.

She releases me. I fall forward on my knees, gulping down sweet, fresh air.

"Now," Elene says, pushing her sweaty raven hair back from her forehead. She doesn't spare Durand's body a glance. "We can do this the *nice* way, and get you a new friend who will accompany you to decadent balls. Or we can do this the hard way, and keep you locked in the dungeon, given over as a play-thing to Ren, bringing you out as my broken star performer a few times a year. I leave you to make your own choices, but let there be no doubt ever again: You *will* obey my commands."

I cough violently, my chest burning. I've been foolish. Elene will always win. I've known that all along. Why had I ever dreamed it could be otherwise?

"I don't want either of those things," I whimper into my dirty sleeve. "I don't want to sing for you anymore. I don't want to be like you."

"Look at what you just did," she hisses, pushing one of the dead guards onto his back with her foot. The veins in his eyes have burst, leaving the whites the deep burgundy of wine. "You *are* like me. Stop pretending otherwise. We are what we are."

# CHAPTER 15

# REMI

MY CELL IS DARK and reeks of mold and men's sweat. As the days pass, I learn to live with the stench of my own filth. No one comes to empty the waste pail in the corner, nor to feed me or refresh the bucket of stagnant water that has started to grow a film of algae. I'm left utterly alone in the dark cell, with nothing but my nightmares of the queen's justicars for company.

Unlike the stone cells we have beneath our château, this dungeon consists of a long row of cages, fenced with bars on all four sides. The cells around me are all empty, which makes me feel even more exposed. I have no one to speak to, to ease the misery of the days.

If these are the conditions in the upper cells, I don't want to imagine what Papa has to endure.

A light flickers at the end of the dungeon hallway. I'm so

weak from hunger and dehydration that I have to use the slick bars of the cell for balance as I haul myself to my feet. I lick my dry lips, grip the bars, and wait. Maybe someone will finally bring me a proper meal. Or at least a new jug of water.

"Hello?" I croak.

A young white man wearing a trim singer's-green waistcoat saunters into the dungeon. He carries a delicate ivory candle in a silver holder that looks as if it was stolen from a formally set dining table. He leans in through the bars. His face is handsome, with high cheekbones and a well-cut jaw, but something in his eyes makes me step back.

Flashing me a wide smile, he says, "Well, my lady, what are we going to do with you?"

"Who are you?" I demand, crossing my arms over my chest. I'm too hungry to be polite. I've been told to expect the chief justicar, and I have no energy or patience for anyone else. This man must be no older than twenty-five years, likely a novice mage placed in the dungeons for training. I'll save what remains of my manners to get through the chief justicar's questioning, when he finally deigns to arrive.

The man draws out a white dinner roll from his pocket and offers it to me through the bars. I swallow hard as saliva pools in my mouth. It smells fresh and buttery. But from where I stand, I can't quite reach. I hesitate, feeling like a wild animal being lured into a snare. All of my instincts scream that this young man, with his beguiling grin, is not to be trusted.

But hunger gnaws at me. I take a step forward. The man's smile widens, and he beckons. I reach for the roll, but as my fingers brush his, he drops the bread on the dirty cell floor. I grind my teeth together. He did it to humiliate me, but I'm just too hungry. Face burning, I bend down and pick it up.

"My name is Ren," he says, as I wipe the roll on my sleeve and tear into it. It's so soft, so very sweet. "I'm sorry for the wait, my lady. We've been a little full here in our hotel as of late. Her Majesty wanted me to see to your case personally, and alas, other patrons have kept me occupied."

My blood runs cold. See to me personally?

"*You're* the chief justicar?" I demand.

He twirls around, arms outstretched, and laughs. "In the flesh."

"But—"

"I know, sweetling. You expected someone older. Maybe with a beard? Everyone does. But Her Majesty doesn't concern herself with age. I am the best at what I do." His eyes twinkle. He unlocks my cell door and sweeps me a mocking bow. "If my lady will come with me?"

I stuff the remainder of the bread into my mouth and step out of the cell. He takes my arm like a suitor, balancing my hand in the crook of his elbow. The bread sticks in the back of my throat. He seems to share Queen Elene's love of theatrics, and to be chosen so young, he must have done something truly monstrous to impress the queen. That doesn't bode well for me. Or for Papa.

"Are you a singer?" I ask.

"Of course. People without magic have no business in high positions. Unless you count that toad Durand, and thankfully, he's no longer a concern."

He winks at me, and I have to fight the urge to run. I don't know where I am in the palace, or how the layout has changed in the years since I lived here. With the palace guards lurking behind every door, I doubt I'd make it very far.

"But what kind of singer am I?" he continues in his mellifluent voice. "That's the real mystery."

Most people fear corporeal singers like Cadence above all. But I know just enough about the other magical schools to be wary. Even if Ren can't boil the blood inside me, as an elemental he could easily strike me with lightning or drown me with a flash flood. Papa says elementals are most temperamental, that their connection to the weather gives them a volatile nature. And we have all heard the tales of the queen's plant mages in battle, who summoned the grasses and trees to drag her enemies beneath the earth and bury them alive.

I follow him out of the cell block and up a flight of narrow stone stairs that winds in a tight spiral. At the top, he pushes open a door. It's been reinforced with metal, probably to render it soundproof. I wonder what kind of magic the singers work here that requires such precaution. Or perhaps it is there to protect the delicate ears of the queen's entourage from our screams.

A draft sweeps down the stone stairwell, making me shiver. Ren tugs on my arm, and I stumble into the room behind him.

I expect another, darker dungeon, lined with racks and chains and all manner of instruments for torture. Stuck in my cage over the past days, I have recalled everything I ever learned about castle dungeons in Bordea throughout the ages. But aside from its lack of windows, the space looks like the parlor Mama uses to entertain guests. Plush red and gold satin sofas line the walls. A daybed rests in the center of the room, beside a low table set with bread, a basket of fruit, and cold meats. The air smells of cinnamon and cloves, like a patisserie.

My gaze drifts to two figures standing against the rear wall: two women, naked, with their arms bound in shimmering golden rope that seems to spark with magic. One of them has long red hair, matted and dirty. Mercedes. I swallow hard. I don't recognize the other woman, but she has to be from the hospital, too.

"Do sit down," Ren says. He sings a few bars and one of the

sofas flies to the center of the room, opposite the day bed. My eyes widen. What school of magic can do that?

Recovering myself, I wrench my arm free of his hold and glare up at him. I am tired of this performance. I'm not going to act my part in yet another of the queen's absurd little plays. I am done being a polished, well-behaved puppet for her. If the chief justicar is going to hurt me, then I want it to look as ugly as it will feel.

"What's going on here?" I shout, pointing at Mercedes. I push the table out of the way, sending food and cutlery flying. "If you already have evidence against me, then why don't you tell me what it is and get whatever you're about to do over with. I'm done with these ridiculous spectacles. I still have the right to know all of the charges against me. The queen has not changed that law. Yet."

Ren's eyebrows shoot up. Mercedes turns ever so slightly in the corner, peering back at me through a curtain of matted hair.

With an exaggerated sigh, Ren sits on the edge of the day-bed. "As you wish."

The justicar clears his throat. Mercedes visibly cringes, but the other woman doesn't flinch at all. She keeps her back straight, nothing about her posture betraying fear.

I brace myself, expecting every nerve in my body to light with pain. But when he begins his baritone song, a numbness works its way up my legs like a creeping vine. The sensation flees from my toes, then my calves and knees. My chest constricts as the numbness keeps climbing higher.

My knees buckle, and I crumple to the floor. Ren stops singing, and the feeling floods back into my legs. Breathing hard, I stare up at him from the floor. He chuckles, eyes dancing. I don't know if I've ever hated anyone as intensely—not even Cadence, when I saw her onstage at the Performing. If I could move, I would grab the butter knife from the table and thrust it into his heart.

He beckons, and the two women walk over. They turn toward us, and with her face revealed, I recognize Sister Elizabeta. She looks shorter without her imposing white coronet, but her bearing is the same, strong and undiminished. Her eyes are trained on Ren's face, her chin held high. I don't know what the justicar has done to them in the time since my arrest, but the nun's stubbornness gives me courage.

"Mercedes, please repeat the testimony you gave me," the justicar says. He doesn't even look at her. Instead, his gaze bores into me, daring me to rise. "Remember, leave nothing out. The queen will grant you mercy in exchange for your assistance. We mages forgive and protect our own, when we can."

The singer lets out a choked sob. "You will not take my voice and send me to the settlement?"

"Not if you cooperate," Ren says.

"I healed her mother," Mercedes whimpers. "I shouldn't have healed her mother."

"Very good." Ren reclines on the daybed and snaps his fingers. A second later, a servant girl appears from a side door. She readjusts the table I shoved, while another servant emerges with a tray of cookies. The scents of chocolate and butter almost make me weep. He takes one of the cookies and bats his eyelashes at the girl. "Will you be a dear and bring me some milk with this?"

The girl giggles, charmed by his flirtation, and rushes out through the door.

Ren takes a bite of the cookie and closes his eyes in pleasure. "Mmm. Delicious. Now, Mercedes, tell me the evidence you have against Lady Remi. She seems very anxious to hear it. Indeed, she's spurning my invitation of tea! I want to make sure I have all the details. Her Majesty will want a complete report."

Mercedes shifts from foot to foot. She looks at me, then hastily back at the wall. "Sometimes, at night, Cadence comes to help us with the harder cases, as you know . . ." She wrings her hands behind her back.

"While I don't understand why Cadence bothers, that's not a crime. Her Majesty permits the principal to heal commoners outside the palace if she so desires." Ren lifts a cup of tea to his lips. "Carry on."

I start to extend my legs, planning to sit on the floor rather than maintain the uncomfortable kneeling position. But as soon as I shift, Ren hums a stanza, and my body numbs again from the waist down.

"That night, Cadence came to heal a young man. I could not manage it. I knew that he had been cursed, but Sister Elizabeta would not give me any other details. I knew it was wrong to try." Tears clog her voice. "But I couldn't watch him in pain, so I tried anyway."

"You have a tender heart," Ren says. "Something we will correct before you are allowed to practice healing again."

Mercedes points at me. "She came in while Cadence was working the spell. One of the other nuns let her in to pay me money, for helping her mother years ago. Cadence recognized her and asked her to stay, then she helped Cadence with some of the patients."

"Did you suspect that they had consorted before?"

"I don't know," Mercedes wails. "I don't think they had seen each other recently. They knew each other as children."

"That's everything," Sister Elizabeta interjects.

Ren scowls, then hums a few bars. The nun keels over,

moaning and clutching her stomach. She retches, and black bile bubbles from her chapped lips. He turns to Mercedes with an icy smile. "When we spoke before, you told me that Cadence worked a spell on her?"

"Yes."

I should be angrier with her—she's betraying me, my father, even Cadence, and I only went to the hospital to repay her—but when Mercedes buries her face in her hands and starts to sob, I pity her. She was kind to my mother, and now she is paying for it. I should have left the debt unpaid, forgotten in the past. We all would have been better off.

Ren snaps his fingers again, and the giggly servant appears at his side. She dips a demure curtsy, hands him a glass of milk, and then offers him a toothpick from a tray. He studies Mercedes as he cleans his teeth.

My thoughts wander back to Cadence. Will they punish her for this, too? If the boy was cursed, she must have known when she healed him. It's hard to imagine that the queen would imprison her prized singer, or kick her out to dwell among the Expelled. Now that I have met the chief justicar, I can see that Cadence is different. When she tortures for the queen, Cadence suffers, too. Ren seems to live for it. What will happen to her if the queen gets tired of a girl she must force to do her bidding?

"And did you hear the viscountess speak to any of the patients? Did she pass on any of her father's seditious messages? Remember, your pardon depends on telling the *whole* truth." He sits up, sharp eyes fixed on the singer.

Tears fall freely down Mercedes's cheeks as she whispers, "Yes. She spoke to several of them. And I thought I saw her slip a piece of paper into a man's jacket."

"That's a lie!" I interrupt, but Ren ignores me. Mercedes turns back to the wall, refusing to look at me. My pity for her evaporates. I understood, in a way, why she told Ren the truth. But to make up additional charges, ones that could end in my father's execution, is too much to forgive.

"My lady," Ren says. He lies back on his daybed and props his head up with an elbow. "You know the law. As a noblewoman, you are forbidden from visiting the city hospitals or interacting with singers. You are also forbidden from soliciting corporeal spells—"

"Soliciting?" I spit out. "Was I *soliciting* her magic when Cadence worked her other spells on me in the Opera Hall? I don't remember asking for that."

The numbness spreads up my torso. My neck goes rigid; my tongue freezes in my mouth. My eyes remain wide, but I can't blink or swallow.

"You will cease these childish interruptions," Ren chides.

Sighing, he rises from the daybed and walks over to me. Resting his hand on my hair, he says, "Soliciting, as the queen herself did not give express permission. Now, this solicitation is a serious crime in itself. But considering the other charge . . . well, aiding in a rebellion is treason. Mercedes will serve two months in the queen's prison. The nun, we will hold until she becomes more . . . malleable. But what are we going to do with you?"

Spelled to stay open, my eyes start to water. I want to paw at them, to blink, anything to fight against the forced tears. He's stripped even the smallest measure of control from me, and I feel weak and small at his feet.

A guilty part of me wonders if this is what Cadence endures. When she spoke at the hospital, she told me that I couldn't possibly understand what it was like to be around these monsters day after day.

But she is a mage. Surely she can defend herself with her own magic.

He drops to one knee and whispers in my ear, in the sensual tone of a lover, his breath hot. "Luckily for you," he says, giving a lock of my hair a tug that brings an angry flush to my cheeks, "that decision won't be made by me."

Ren straightens up and strides to the metal-lined door. "Guards," he calls down the staircase. "Take the prisoner and clean her up. The queen will see her for tea."

# CHAPTER 16

# REMI

I WAIT IN A straight-backed, satin chair, my wrists tied to the golden armrests, as a group of servants lay a long dining table for the queen. Clearly, no one intends for me to eat. The servants ignore me as they work, and no one sets my place. My mouth waters as they bring out an elaborate spread of suckling pig, stuffed dates, and delicate pastries that smell of apricot and strawberry jam. After going days with nothing to eat, the dinner roll I managed to scarf down did little to sate my appetite.

But at least I am clean. After the justicar finished with me, two guards took me from his opulent torture chamber to a small bathhouse below. They hosed me down, scrubbed my face, and stuffed me into a pale blue dress that matches the curtains here in the dining room. The humiliation should have been intolerable, but Ren's numbing spell must have worked its way into my soul as well. After everything that has happened in the last few weeks, I barely registered the indignity.

The guards were only obeying orders. They aren't the ones responsible for my treatment. I flex my wrists against the ropes that bind my hands. If the queen intends to kill me, I'm not going to die quietly.

The servants finish arranging the table and file out through the room's rear door. An elderly butler dressed in an elegant three-piece suit opens the room's curtains and stands behind the chair opposite me. I tilt my face up, basking in the ray of sunlight that filters through the window. The dining room overlooks a walled garden, filled with white and pink roses, scarlet lobelia, and cheerful winter jasmine.

Distantly, I remember this room. It was once an office for the old queen's minister of education. Lord Hureux was a jovial man, and a friend of Papa's, who always kept a jar full of sweets on his mahogany desk. I remember sitting in a chair beside the window like this, at another time, sucking on a peppermint and watching for Cadence in the garden below as Papa discussed business.

When Queen Elene took the throne, all of the old queen's top ministers were executed without trial, quietly meeting their deaths within the palace walls so the people wouldn't see. Some died in the winter garden we are overlooking. I shudder, picturing Lord Hureux's head rolling across the cobblestone path. My parents fled from Cannis to our country estate early on, keeping us away from the executions and roundups.

I hadn't understood at the time. I was angry that we were abandoning Cannis to live in seclusion at the estate. Now I know that their speedy decision probably saved us.

The doors leading into the hall fly open. A footman stands to the side and bows as Queen Elene sweeps in. I've never seen her up close before, and I'm not quite prepared for what I see.

Everyone talks about Queen Elene as if she is hideous, a monster in form as well as deeds, but the woman in front of me is stunning. She has glossy raven hair that catches the light and smooth porcelain-white skin. A gold diadem rests atop her hair. Her black lace mask does not conceal her full, red mouth, nor the striking green of her eyes. Her figure is curvy and elegant, clothed in a floor-length gown made entirely from flamingo feathers.

The butler pulls out her chair, and the queen sinks into it, her bright eyes trained on my face. "I don't think we need those bonds," she purrs. Her voice is pleasant and deep. "She knows there is nowhere for her to go. And it's not as if she can harm me without magic. Charles, set a place for our guest."

The butler's nose wrinkles, and his lips curl into a disdainful sneer, but he walks over and unties my hands. The queen begins serving herself from the silver platters on the table, heaping her plate much higher than etiquette allows.

A serving girl appears with a china plate, a fork, and a spoon for me. She doesn't offer me a knife. I hesitate, my mouth watering. For all I know, they could be planning to poison my food. The cutlery could be tainted. There are myriad poisons that have no smell and leave no taste.

But the queen has magic. Even Cadence, her principal singer, fears it. If she wants me to die, the queen needn't bother with poisons. Shakily, I reach across the table for a date and a pastry.

The queen cuts a slice of pork into small pieces as I stuff the date into my mouth. Mama would be appalled at my manners, but I don't want to go to my death hungry.

"You may wonder," Queen Elene says, and takes a sip of her wine, "why I would want to meet with you. You are a traitor, after all. What you have done is punishable by death."

I bite into the pastry. It's still warm from the oven, the jam sticky. I take another bite, swallow, and savor the weight of it moving down my throat to my stomach. "It shouldn't be a crime to heal someone else's pain."

The queen's eyebrows shoot up. I help myself to a second date. I'm walking close to disaster, and I know it, but I'm not going to die a coward, either. The queen has already made up her mind about my guilt. Whatever I say won't change her verdict.

"You are too young to remember how things were before, when the greedy nobles of this land stripped our country to its bones and hoarded all its resources for themselves." She picks up her wine glass and studies me over the rim as she drinks. "You are a child. You cannot possibly understand the complexities at work in keeping a queendom in balance."

"Try me," I say. "Your Majesty."

The queen sets down her glass, her lips pursing. "Your crimes are not in question, and I have not brought you here as an advisor in matters of state. We are here to talk about Cadence."

"Cadence?" I scoff. "Your justicar already knows that she healed that boy. He said you weren't charging her. I don't have any other information to offer you."

"Oh, it's not about her crime," the queen laughs. The butler dabs the corner of her mouth with a napkin. "Ren's justicars will hunt the rebel youth down and put that right, never fear. But she's been difficult as of late. I think having a companion of her own age, someone outside the mages' school, might improve her . . . disposition."

"A companion?" I can hardly believe what she's saying. I have been imprisoned for a week, starved, and left in darkness. My father is rotting below ground, accused of treason without evidence. Now the queen tells me she knows of Cadence's crime, does not doubt her guilt, and the singer's punishment is to be . . . a friend?

"You knew each other as children, didn't you? I spoke with Madam Guillard, who heads the mages' academy. She said that back then, you and Cadence were inseparable."

The injustice of all this makes the pastry stick in the back of my throat, but slowly, I nod. "Yes, but that was many years ago. A lot has changed."

"According to the singer at the hospital, you two were getting along quite well," the queen says. "We could ask any number of girls to join Cadence at the palace, and I am sure they would jump at the chance. But Cadence is not an easy girl to befriend. She never has been. She isolates herself. If she has taken to you already, then it may be easier for you to calm her tantrums."

Tantrums? I don't remember Cadence ever throwing a fit when we were young. *I* was the outspoken, precocious, boisterous child, whereas she'd always been reserved, even shy. From what I observed of her onstage and at the hospital, that hasn't changed. Lord Durand menaced her at the Performing, and she was hesitant even when she summoned her courage to ask me to stay at the hospital.

"You will persuade her to behave reasonably," the queen

continues. "You will act as an intermediary between her and me. You will relay information to her as I provide it."

I start to piece together what the queen doesn't say. I stuff the rest of my pastry into my mouth and chew as my mind races. Cadence was terrified to act against the queen. She told me it was pointless. What happened in the time since I saw her? Whatever it was, if I can somehow encourage Cadence to keep working against the queen, Papa and I might get home alive.

"As an incentive," the queen says, and raises a finger, "I will move you and your father into better accommodations. You will have every luxury and comfort. I will hold your father as a prisoner, with excellent food and care, because I cannot allow the supposed leader of a rebellion to converse with the public."

"What if I say no?"

She shrugs. "You and your father will die. Your suffering will be prolonged over months, even years. Ren is very adept at torturing a person to the brink, then putting them back together so he can start again."

"But your information is wrong! My father isn't leading some secret rebellion. I'd know if he was. He is innocent."

"He is not innocent." The queen presses her lips into a thin smile. "And even if we can't prove, yet, exactly who his contacts are in the movement, he *did* bring your mother to

Saint Izelea's. We could prosecute him for that, and arrest your mother, too."

I grip the edge of the table. The queen is as good as admitting she has no real evidence of Papa's treason. He is to be a hostage, then, kept in exchange for my good behavior. He was so careful with Mama all those years ago. No one would ever have found out if I hadn't been so foolish. All of this is my fault. And no matter what it costs me, I have to fix it.

I want to bury my face in my hands, but the justicar has already forced enough tears out of me today. I can't fathom a life in this queen's service. But the alternative is unthinkable.

"What of my mother? My father is required at home to help manage the château." I can picture Mama, sitting in her parlor alone, staring out the window and watching for any sign of our return. Who knows if Rook even made it back to give her the message of our arrest, or if he, too, has been detained? My parents' relationship has been strained these past years, but I know there is still love between them. Worse yet is the thought of Mama traveling to Cannis to speak on our behalf. I can imagine how the queen will twist her defense of us into further proof of Mama's own guilt.

"I can send an attendant to help your mother manage. Do well, and I may even send a healer."

"Her condition can't be healed."

"Perhaps," the queen muses. "But she hasn't seen a palace healer. Mercedes is second rate at best. In the absence of a cure, there may still be things a more skilled singer could do for her. Treatments to ease her pain."

"How long will I have to do this?"

"However long I require it. However long it takes for Cadence to cooperate again."

She needs Cadence. I've met Ren, and while I know corporeal mages are rare, the queen has to have others like him. Whatever unique power Cadence holds, the queen must need it badly, or she wouldn't bother with me at all.

A magic like that might be stronger than even Cadence herself knows. If I can convince her to stop being afraid—to use magic even the queen fears—I might be able to help more than just my family. When I think of all the people we could help, it doesn't seem like a choice at all. It's a duty.

I take a deep breath, then give the queen the smallest of nods. The queen lifts her glass to toast me, her lips curving into a smile.

# CHAPTER 17

# CADENCE

I DREAM OF MY first lessons at the palace, after Elene snatched me from the academy's embrace. I sit in the corner of my studio, memorizing lines I don't understand from a volume of theory. The door to the room is locked, barred from the outside.

For hours, I try to study, until exhaustion takes me, and the words on the page start to blur together.

Then the dream shifts away from memory. Elene appears at the door, fury etched across her features. She sings, and I am thrown backward into my bookshelf. Her magic fills the air with perfumed smoke. A high, childish cry escapes my lips.

Durand leads Remi into my studio by the hand. She's a child again, too, and she smiles up at him, expression guileless and carefree. As I sob in the corner, clutching the theory volume to my chest, Elene makes a fist. Flame erupts from her hand, and she hurls it at Remi, engulfing her. Weakly, I try to sing a freezing song to counteract the fire, but it's no good. Remi screams and screams, until her charred form disintegrates into a pile of ash on the floor.

Lacerde shakes me awake. She pulls my duvet back, exposing my legs to the cold air. "The queen has a guest with her. They're waiting to see you." She doesn't meet my eyes as she speaks, and her lips are pressed into an angry, thin line. She hasn't forgiven me yet. I don't know if she ever will.

I want to apologize, but I don't know what to say that can make up for how I treated her.

"I'm not going," I mutter instead. I pull the covers back over my legs, hoping she will leave. My voice sounds hoarse again. Since Elene's spell stopped my breath, my chest has ached. The dream left my throat clogged with tears.

Lacerde squats down, then tips my mattress so I tumble onto the floor, knocking my wrist on the bed's metal frame. "Enough," she snaps.

I glare up at her and cradle my arm against my chest.

She takes a deep breath and glances toward the door as if to assess the distance to escape, and says, "This isn't like you. I've always known what you are capable of, but I was never afraid of you. I know losing Nip was painful." She lifts the mattress back into place. "But you killed innocent men, men with families."

I climb slowly to my feet. Durand deserved his fate. He orchestrated the spectacle of pain that became the Performing. I knew what he was from the first day we met, when he procured that poor urchin boy for me to torture.

But Elene's guards? I can't even recall their faces. I know nothing about them, where they came from. I don't know what circumstances led them to serve her.

Lacerde goes to my wardrobe and selects a lilac gown. It's a fine thing, made from sheer muslin and embroidered with pale pink roses and mint vines. It's one of Elene's favorites for me. Lacerde lays it out on my bed alongside a pair of silk gloves. I stand like a doll while she dresses me, lifting my legs when instructed and stretching out my arms. After so long in my room alone clothed in only a shift, even the loose-fitting dress feels restrictive. I need a long, hot bath.

"Who is it?" I ask, holding up a foot so Lacerde can adjust my stocking. "The queen's guest?"

When Elene invites me to meals, she usually means for me to provide a demonstration. She and her guests will laugh and applaud as I heal an old scar or regrow a patch of missing hair. Foreign dignitaries, from countries unblessed by the goddesses and therefore untouched by magic, are filled with wonder at such displays. It's beneath my skills as principal, but important guests demand an important performer, and Elene likes to show me off.

Lacerde shrugs. She plucks a horsehair brush from my dressing table and dusts my cheeks with rouge. Her strokes are brisk, all business. "She didn't say."

She stands back to admire her work. With a nod, she takes my arm and steers me toward the door.

I can't let what I did hover between us any longer.

Before she can open the door, I blurt out, "I should never have used magic on you like that. I'm so sorry."

Her expression softens into a smile that is almost tender, but she takes me by both shoulders and looks in my eyes. "No, you should not have."

She doesn't say that she forgives me. Instead, she opens both doors and steps aside for me to pass through.

The two servant girls wait in the hall, arms full of clean linen for my bed. When they see me, the color drains from their cheeks. One of them drops the linen on the floor as she stumbles into a curtsy. The other mumbles something in greeting, but her voice is so shaky I can't make out the words.

Shame burns my face. They're afraid of me. Talk spreads

like wildfire in the servants' hall. By now, everyone will know what happened to Lacerde and to Elene's guards because I lost my temper.

"Thank you," I force myself to say, and dip my head to them. "My bed was starting to smell."

Lacerde wrinkles her nose in disgust, but I think I see one of the servants' lips twitch with a smile before she disappears into my room.

I'm used to the palace being busy with servants, guards, cooks, and novices scrambling from room to room. But today, the halls are quiet. It's as if everyone is hiding, waiting behind doors for me to pass by, so they can resume their lives away from my shadow.

Even the portraits of our former queens stare disapprovingly down at me from their positions on the wall. Queen Celeste's was removed, so there is a bare patch of wall where her likeness once hung, but I imagine her scowl nonetheless as I clutch my prayer stone, whisper a plea to Adela for the old queen's soul, and scurry down the hall.

I want to appear brave when I face Elene again, but fear creeps up my spine with every step we take. The silence makes me anxious. Elene choked the air from my lungs with barely a blink. She could kill me, if she wanted, and no one would step in to stop her.

Lacerde's grip on my arm tightens. "It'll be all right," she says. "Her Majesty was in a good mood when I saw her earlier."

I nod and give myself a little shake. As long as I keep doing what she demands of me, Elene may never mention our confrontation again. She tells me often that she thinks of me as a daughter, though what mother would leave her child with Ren as a governess, I do not know.

Elene has a private dining chamber on the other side of the palace. Once, the room served as an office for one of the country's ministers. Their dismissal left many empty rooms, which have largely been repurposed into lounges or bedrooms for Elene's darlings—people of many genders who catch the queen's eye when she ventures into Cannis. Some are mages, others are commoners brought to the palace to live here surrounded by fine things.

Her darlings all seem happy enough, and I've never heard of any of them being cast out, even after Elene's favor turns to others.

While the practice of taking multiple lovers fell out of fashion among the nobles of the court several centuries ago, it is still common among us mages. Many in the palace share chambers among three or four lovers, living and raising families together. We have never bound ourselves to the restrictive marriage rules of the nobility.

Of late, I've mostly seen a plump silver-haired elemental mage with youthful, mischievous eyes accompanying Elene. Most likely, Raquelle will be with the queen at the meal today. It's hard to imagine Elene as a lover. With me, she's always been distant and cold. But I've seen her laugh with Raquelle, their heads buried together in conspiracy when they think no one is looking.

Two guards watch the entrance to the dining hall. When we approach them, they stiffen. One reaches behind his back as if to grab a musket before realizing it's not there. A look of panic flashes across his handsome features. I stifle a sigh. He must have come from the army, patrolling the borders, or from the city guard. Companies outside the palace still carry mechanical weapons.

"Oh come now, chickens," Lacerde snaps. She elbows them aside and drags me behind her. "She's just a wee girl."

"A wee girl," the older of the two scoffs. He runs a hand over his bald crown. "Didn't you hear what she did to the queen's last escort? Those were all trained men."

"Of course I did. I was there," Lacerde says.

Their eyes widen in amazement.

I wrap my arms around my chest, wishing I could sink into the walls. In the moment, working my spellsong against the queen made me feel strong. Even respected. But it has also made me feared, which is not the same thing at all.

I can feel their hatred burning behind their eyes as acutely as I can sense a tumor. I only wanted everyone to leave me alone, to realize that what Elene had done was unforgivable. Instead, I've done something unforgivable myself.

Without waiting to be announced, Lacerde pushes the door to the dining room open. I step inside after her reluctantly. As much as I dread seeing Elene, I can't stay in the hall making the guards uneasy.

Elene sits at the head of the table, surrounded by enough food to feed a city block. She smiles demurely at me and raises her wineglass. In front of her is a carved pig. Its aura smells like strangulation. I press my handkerchief to my nose and look away. Her pretty silver-haired lover is nowhere to be seen, but when my eyes rest on the room's other occupant, I freeze in the doorway.

Dressed in a blue cotton gown, her copper hair still wet from bathing, Remi sits opposite the queen. At first glance, she doesn't look as though she's been taken from the dungeons. I've seen prisoners emerge plenty of times before, all of them dirty, with torn clothes. But her cheeks are gaunt, and her eyes are slightly glazed. Her jaw is locked tight. Her hands, tucked carefully beneath the table, are balled into fists.

I focus my magic and cough the softest note into my hand. Her heart beats wildly against her ribs, as fast as a rabbit's.

"Do sit down, Cadence," Elene instructs in her smoky voice. "We'll get a plate for you. I believe you already know the viscountess."

"Yes," I say cautiously, and ease myself into a chair. I reach for a glass of wine and take a hasty gulp. With the remains of the pig sitting so near, the wine is all I can manage without gagging.

"I thought . . . ," Elene says, stabbing an olive with her fork. She adjusts her mask, then pops the olive into her mouth. "That Remi might move into the palace to be closer to you, as we discussed?"

Remi's brown eyes shift to me, her stare so intense I feel my cheeks warm.

"If you don't like her, we can send her back to the dungeons and execute her father. It's really up to you, Cadence." Elene lifts a morsel of pork to her lips as Remi sucks in a sharp breath and my stomach churns. "I would be perfectly happy with either outcome. But I'm worried that you are lonely. You need someone around you can talk to. Someone your own age."

I glare at her, wishing I could sing a heat song to fry her where she sits. She's trapped me. If I refuse Remi as my companion, I'll be responsible for her father's death. I have enough innocent blood on my hands already. If I agree, I'll place her in constant danger.

Still, it feels wrong to decide the outcome of Remi's life for her. It's been years since our days at the palace together. Even if we were once close, how can I possibly know what she wants now? I can't consign her to the existence of a hostage without her consent, even to save her life.

"What do you want?" I ask Remi, my voice barely above a whisper.

She blinks twice, as if my question surprises her. The shock in her expression stings. She lifts her chin and says, "I will stay in the palace with you. The queen has already promised to bring my father out of the dungeon if I cooperate."

The way she says *cooperate* sets my jaw on edge. I want to trust Remi, but she owes me nothing. If she believes I betrayed her—betrayed her *family*—it makes sense for her to agree to work with Elene against me. What has she already promised in exchange for her father's life? If I could make a deal to get my own parents back, what would I be willing to give?

Elene beams and claps her hands. "It's settled! I'll have the servants arrange a room for our guest."

# CHAPTER 18

# REMI

**WE FINISH THE REST** of our dinner in silence. I eat like a wild creature, ripping pork off the bone with my fingers and dripping sauce down the front of my new dress. It's the most delicious meat I've ever eaten: juicy, tender, and full of flavor. If Mama saw me now, her scolding would last for days. My stomach cramps with the richness of the meal, and sweat breaks out on my brow, but I don't stop eating until every morsel on the table has been devoured.

Whatever the queen may say, I don't trust her. She may yet decide to return me to my prison cell and leave me to starve again. I need to be prepared.

Cadence barely touches the feast. She glares at the queen over the rim of her wineglass, occasionally lifting her fork to push food around her plate. The queen either does not notice or does not care, and eats with almost as much gusto as I do. They say nothing to one another, and I wonder if things have always been this strained between them, or whether I am the cause of this new enmity. As we finish the pork, Cadence's alabaster skin takes on a greenish hue. She covers her nose with her napkin and stares pointedly out the window, away from the table.

The servants seem on edge, their hands trembling as they pour more wine into Cadence's glass. I don't miss how closely the butler stands behind Cadence's chair, as if waiting to reach out and restrain her. The muscle in his jaw twitches, and though he stands his ground, his knees shake.

When we have finished eating, the queen rises. Cadence jumps to her feet, the movement automatic and practiced. I have been away from court so long that it takes me until the butler clears his throat to realize that I should stand, too. Snatching the last crust of pastry, I push my plate away and stand. The queen's eyes narrow behind her mask.

The doors bang open, and the chief justicar strides in. He nods to the queen, and to Cadence, in turn. "Good afternoon, Your Majesty, Principal. I'm here to collect my prisoner."

He doesn't bow as he ought, but the queen smiles at him anyway. As he crosses the room, he walks close enough to Cadence that the sleeve of his robe brushes against her. She visibly cringes before rearranging her features back into a vacant smile.

"Remi and I have come to an arrangement," the queen says. "You may escort her to the east wing. And please have her father moved to more suitable rooms."

A devious grin twists Ren's lips. "More suitable? For a rebel?" he asks, the eagerness in his voice unmistakable.

"Nicer, if you please," the queen laughs. "I *did* promise."

The grin slips from Ren's face, replaced by a scowl so petulant it's as if he were a small child, rather than one of the most dangerous singers in the country. I half expect him to stomp his feet. "I thought I might—"

The queen raises her hand and cuts him off. "For now, you thought incorrectly. Just make a note of whatever plans you may have devised. Should Remi prove unsuitable as a companion for Cadence . . ."

I swallow hard. Her threat is clear enough. Whatever anger I feel toward the queen, I have to bury it for my father's sake.

"I'm sure we will get along fine," Cadence whispers.

Ren takes hold of my elbow. "Well, my little sweetling, come along. I'll show you to your new accommodations."

I curtsy as low as I can to the queen, my knees dipping almost to the floor. She holds my whole family's fate in her hands, and I can be the picture of a dutiful courtier if I must. But I keep my eyes trained on the plush, floral rug at the queen's feet, scared that if I meet her gaze, she will see the anger simmering inside me.

As Ren leads me from the dining room, Cadence gives me a hesitant wave.

Instead of taking me through the gardens on the direct path to the east wing, Ren marches us along the long hallway that leads west. We walk past statues and rooms I half remember, in foggy fragments like the remnants of a dream. I played in these halls as a child, running their lengths countless times. I remember sitting pressed up against these walls, my eyes covered with my hands, counting and waiting for Papa to hide.

This hall was once full of courtiers and servants, ministers and mages. All with their part to play in palace life. I imagine the doors that line the hall flying open, and all the people I remember bursting out to greet me, to reclaim this silent wing with their energy and joy.

But of course, they will not.

Most of the people I remember have been gone for years. Either dead on a battlefield, or their bodies rotting in the gardens, their faded joy feeding the roses. My hands curl into fists.

A group of students linger in the hall, none of them older than nine or ten. They all stare openly at me. They wear emerald-green robes like the justicar's and pins that mark their school. Most clutch stacks of books in their skinny arms. Two have dark purple shadows under their eyes that could be from lack of sleep, or something more vicious.

"Our most promising young students," Ren says. "They come to live here in the palace, so I can personally supervise their education on behalf of Her Majesty."

I'm sure that it's considered an honor to leave the academy and dwell within Cavalia's hallowed walls, but these children don't look like they're benefiting from the queen's patronage.

A slight blond girl stands a step behind the rest of the pack. She bears an angry, red cut across her cheek. She looks so much like Cadence that I feel a lump rise in my throat.

Papa's words ring in my ears. *Don't look away.*

"Who did that to you?" I demand, and jerk my head at Ren. "Was it him?"

The girl shakes her head so furiously her hair comes free of its pins. She moves behind her friends, clutching her books to her thin chest.

"She's a *noble.*" One of the boys says the word like a curse and makes to spit on the carpet, before Ren's severe glance forces him to swallow.

"Run along, Jeffrey," the justicar hisses.

The child shrinks back, as if bracing himself for pain, then races down the hall.

The other children scatter like minnows. Ren's hard gaze

follows them until they turn the corner. He looks like a heron in the water, waiting for his prey to regroup, so he can devour them all in a single gulp.

We continue walking until we are nearly at the end of the hall, and Ren stops me in front of a door. I bite my tongue to keep my emotion from flowing out. I would recognize that oak frame anywhere, the knots and whorls in the wood almost as familiar as the planes of Mama's face.

"Open it," he urges, and pushes me forward.

My hand curls around the doorknob, and I have to swallow an angry refusal. Slowly I open the door, half expecting Mama's laugh to spill out and embrace me.

But inside the room is bare, and my mother nowhere to be seen. A simple, small bed sits in the corner of what was once our parlor. In place of the thick, woven rug I remember beneath my toes, books and papers litter the floor. The beautiful stained-glass windows, which Papa had commissioned specially for Mama, have been replaced with yellowing paper. All of my family's things are gone, and dust has taken the place of our memories.

"Go on," Ren says, shoving me farther into the room.

Seeing my old home like this, I can't contain my anger any longer. There is no reason for him to bring me here, other than to upset me. I whirl around, planting my hands on my hips.

"I've seen enough, thank you," I snap.

His eyes widen and his mouth opens, as if to sing. Part of me wants to cringe, like the little boy in the hall, or Cadence in the dining room. But Ren is nothing but a bully who thrives on fear, and I will not give him what he seeks. He can control my body, but mage or not, he will not bend my will.

"I don't think the queen wants you to hurt me. She wants my cooperation, and if you hurt me, I will tell her."

"I'd like to see you try it without your tongue," he growls. "I know that your kind still think you're due our obedience, but let me correct you."

All the arrogant, theatrical charm from his studio falls away, replaced by raw, ugly anger.

My heart is pounding, but I roll my eyes. "You could try being a little subtler. It's hard to take you seriously when you say something so ridiculous. You don't think the queen would notice my *tongue* is missing?"

He stares at me, expression bewildered.

"Take me to the east wing," I say, walking out of the room and away from my past. "Do as your queen commands."

His lips close without a sound.

# CHAPTER 19

# CADENCE

I WAIT UNTIL EVENING before seeking Remi out. I take the candle from my bookshelf and venture into the hall. Lacerde might know where to find Remi, but after what happened, I don't dare ask her. Elene may intend for Remi's role as my companion to be for appearances only, and Lacerde may no longer keep my secrets.

I head for the laundry instead, intent on seeking out the maid who rescued the white kitten. If I can get her to talk to me, I know she'll have the answer. The servants have their own webs of communication. By now, the whole staff will know where Remi sleeps.

One of the servants has left a frayed brown traveling cloak on a hook outside the kitchen. I pull it on and arrange the hood to cover my hair. Keeping my head low, I sprint through the kitchens and hum to dull the senses of the other servants. The cooks, intent on preparing separate meals to the specifications of all the court mages, don't notice me as I slip into the washing rooms.

I find the maid standing on a wooden stool, churning a boiling vat of water and linen with what looks like a boat oar. Sweat has broken out on her brow, and I wonder why we don't just station a mage in the kitchens to do this with magic. I am sure that we used magical flames in Queen Celeste's days. An elemental could easily have managed all the vats at once while sitting in a chair, casually reading a book.

The maid jumps as I come up behind her and drops the stirring rod into the vat.

"Damn," she hisses under her breath. Then she takes in my face and stammers. "Principal. I'm sorry—I didn't expect— what are you doing here?"

"I need some information," I whisper. "And I'm afraid to ask my attendant for it."

It's not fair to ask for her help again, but I have nowhere else to turn.

She glances around the laundry. Two other servants sweat over vats like hers, lulled into daydreaming by the monotony and my song. I hum to block their hearing, just in case.

The maid shudders as she listens to the song. "The kitten is well," she says. "She has made a place for herself in my brother's barn. But I can't be seen speaking with you. The queen wouldn't like it."

I take a deep breath. The last thing I want is for her to get in trouble. Not when she already took a risk by bringing the kitten home. "If anyone asks, I will say that my bleeding started, and I required fresh linen. I just need to know which rooms the queen has given my new companion."

The maid flushes at my openness and stammers, "If—the queen—has appointed her to serve you, why not just ask Her Majesty?"

"She might not want me to see Remi unsupervised. Things are always complicated when it comes to the queen," I say.

Her lips quirk in a wry smile. "How well I know."

"My friend?"

She sighs. "She is being housed in the east wing, in the suite at the end of the hall. I prepared her bed myself."

"Thank you," I whisper, praying that no one will find out she helped me. "What is your name?"

"Etienne." She peers over the rim into the vat. "I'll never get that stirrer out. They'll be very angry with me. The wood will soften and ruin the linen by the time I can cool the water and fish it out."

The room's other servants have continued stirring, senses

dulled by my song. From behind, all they can see of me is my servant's cloak. "Reach into the vat," I say.

Etienne's gray eyes jerk up. "It will boil the flesh from my bones."

"Do it," I urge, gesturing toward the waist-high vat. "Trust me. If I can bring an opera hall full of people to their knees, I think I can protect your arms from a little bit of hot water."

Etienne gives an uneasy laugh. Then, slowly, she extends her hands. I begin to sing, my voice soft. I use the magic to cool the surface of her skin, layering a protective barrier of ice between her flesh and the boiling liquid. She brushes the surface of the water with outstretched fingertips.

Grinning at me, she says, "It feels like bathwater."

She pulls her sleeves back, then leans forward into the vat. The water continues to boil. Steam rises from the vat and spills over onto the laundry's floor. When she straightens, she holds the wooden stirrer, a wide, triumphant smile on her face.

I stop singing, and she claps my shoulder in farewell. A strange happiness bubbles in my chest. If only all magic could be as sweet and uncomplicated as helping a new friend.

I creep out of the laundry room. Behind me, one of the other maids exclaims, "Marena's teeth! I think I fell asleep on my feet!"

The east wing is across the courtyard from the main palace. It's connected by a garden walkway: a cobbled bridge, framed by planters of lobelia and an evergreen hedge. I shiver as I step outside. The night is cool, and a gust of freezing wind nips my cheeks. The moonlight casts a path through the garden. On either side of it, white roses glimmer like stars against the black earth. I pick my way carefully around the plants, lifting my skirt to keep it clean.

I need Remi to know that I didn't betray her, and there are a thousand questions I want to ask.

Two guards stand at the entrance to the east wing. Both of them hold muskets, and the sight of the guns' metallic gleam is almost enough to send me scurrying back to my room. Ren has never allowed the commoner guards who complement his retinue of justicars to carry weapons within the palace walls.

I wonder if the weapons are to prevent Remi's escape or protect the guards from me. In years past, Ren would have stationed justicars to contain high-profile prisoners, but fewer corporeal mages have graduated from the academy recently. There are no longer enough of us that we can be wasted standing at doors. The role of justicar is a dangerous position. Without replacements, Ren's force is dwindling.

Adela has not chosen as many children, which some believe is a sign of the goddess's displeasure. Of those who have been destined, many have defied the queen and been sent to the settlement.

The guards stare straight into the garden. Since I can't doctor memories, I don't dare send them straight to sleep. Untrained folk often rationalize magic away, preferring to believe that they fainted or dozed off, but trained men such as these will wake with the knowledge that someone compelled them. I have no choice but to speak to them and convince them to let me pass.

"Lovely evening," I say.

When the moon catches my face, the guards step closer together. "Principal. What are you doing here? This isn't your wing."

"I'm just out for a walk," I lie. "It's such a clear and perfect night. I needed to stretch my legs. I wanted to see if Lady Remi might accompany me."

"I'm not sure that is allowed. We were told to monitor her closely," the older of the two says. He wears a silver captain's armband. This, too, is unusual. Ren does not like to promote common folk. He must be growing more and more desperate to fill his squads.

For a moment, I consider pulling rank on them. I am still the queen's principal singer, even if I am at odds with her.

"Why don't you escort us?" I offer my arm and a smile. "I'm sure no one would object if a captain were to escort me on my walk."

The guards exchange looks.

"No, Chantrix," the captain says shakily. "We will keep to our posts here, but when you leave the wing, please keep to the gardens, in our sight."

"Of course," I say.

"Please, allow me." He opens the door and steps aside, bowing so low his hair brushes his knees.

I beam at him and step into the warmth of the hall.

The east wing is the oldest part of Cavalia, built centuries before the luxurious west and southern wings, when Bordea first declared its independence from Solidad under Queen Maude IV. Unlike the rest of the palace, the wing is made from gray slate—built for war, for defense. It has narrow, crooked hallways, spiraling staircases, and slit windows, designed for archers rather than light.

I follow the dark hall until I reach the end, where a grandfather clock stands. It's an old piece, made of glassy mahogany and nearly as tall as the ceiling. Ancient numerals decorate its face. The smell of jasmine blossoms and aging paper emanates from it, the magic that compels its mechanical heart to beat. The spell is old, and the mage who cast it long in the grave.

When I reach Remi's door, I'm surprised not to find more guards posted outside. But then, I suppose Elene's real security comes from keeping Remi's father imprisoned. As long as the viscount remains under Ren's guard, Remi will never run.

I knock. Inside, I hear rustling and the wet sniff of a nose being blown.

"Come in," Remi calls.

I push open the door with my shoulder. Remi is sitting rigidly on the edge of her bed. It's obvious from the room's condition that no one has stayed here in a long time. The curtains that hang over the stained-glass windows are dusty and faded. The furniture looks antique, inherited from another age. No one has lit the fire in the brazier, and the room's only source of light is a stubby tallow candle on the bedside table that emits black smoke into the air.

So much for treating her like a guest. At least I know that the linen is fresh.

I close the door quickly and, before I can lose my nerve, blurt out, "I didn't tell Elene anything. I would never betray your family like that."

Remi shrugs. Her long lashes are wet, and her voice has a nasal resonance, but now that I'm here, she doesn't let a single tear fall. "I did wonder, but the chief justicar had already interrogated Mercedes when he brought me for questioning. The queen promised to lessen her sentence if she gave him information." She curses under her breath. "She even made up a few charges."

I sigh. Mercedes never was a strong mage. She left the academy at fourteen with a lesser classification because she failed the higher-level examination. She has no experience with court politics, either. Ren must have terrified her.

"I'm sure she was scared," I finally say. "Did they arrest any of the nuns?"

"They brought in Sister Elizabeta for questioning, too." Her lips curve in a wry smile. "But she didn't tell them a thing."

I sit beside Remi on the bed. My tongue refuses to move. I can feel the heat emanating from her shoulder. Sitting with her like this is both familiar and strange. Though she is physically close, somehow the gap between us feels unbridgeable.

"The queen told me she was having trouble managing you," Remi says, her brown eyes intent. "What did she mean?"

"We fought," I say, and look down at my lap. "So she murdered my dog."

It sounds like such a trivial thing to say now. The queen took Remi and her father as prisoners, threatened to execute them. Her life is in danger, and here I am grieving for my lost pet. I don't know what to tell her about Anette. The loss I feel is disproportionate. I only met the girl once, and though I felt connected to her by our shared past, we hadn't been given enough time to form a real bond.

"Oh, I remember him," she says, her voice so gentle that it squeezes my heart. "He was always with you."

I nod. Nip was with me since my first week at the mages' academy, when I was five. One of the old queen's hounds had escaped and mated with an unknown sire, and no one at court had wanted the puppies, so Madam Guillard took them. She sent most of the puppies to her brother's farm in the countryside, but she kept the smallest for me. Even as a child, I had an anxious disposition, and Madam thought that Nip would help calm me, so she allowed him to live in the dormitories.

Nip was mine from the moment I laid eyes on him. Though small, he was the boldest of the litter. When I scooped him up, he licked my chin, and his whole body trembled with joy. Those first nights he slept curled under my arm, his snores as constant and reassuring as the ticking of a clock.

A few days later, I met Remi for the first time. Her father was taking a break from his meetings with the queen's ministers. They were playing a game together. He chased her through the halls as she shrieked with laughter, auburn curls tumbling everywhere. I hid behind the curtains and watched them, wishing and praying that I could bring my own family back as I held Nip in my arms.

When Remi's father went back to work, Nip struggled free. He ran straight to Remi, and I followed.

"Why would the queen kill him?" Remi asks. "Was it because of the boy you healed?"

Tears brim in my eyes. "She came to my studio the day after I met you at the hospital. Between the Performing and treating so many patients this week at the hospital, my voice was almost gone. Elene said we should have skipped the healing at the Opera Hall after the heat song."

"I wouldn't be walking now if you had." Remi shudders. "Why do you let her push you around? I've felt your magic. You could stand up to her if you wanted to." Her voice is soft, but her jaw clenches and her hands twist in the bed linens.

"My magic doesn't work on her," I explain, then take a deep breath. "That's the reason she brought you here. After she killed Nip, I *tried* to hurt her. Six guards and Durand are dead because I lost my temper, but Elene wasn't affected at all. She brushed off my spell like it was nothing."

"How is that possible?"

"I don't know." I bury my face in my hands. "Everyone else in the room died. The guards. Durand. But Elene just stood there, humming, and when I stopped singing, she choked me with her spell. It could be some new magic, a gift from Odetta. Or maybe she really is just that powerful."

I trace a circle around my neck with my fingers, where Elene's song cut off my wind.

Remi's brow furrows. "Are there blocking spells? There must be. When mages used to fight in the wars, they must have had some way to defend themselves. Maybe the problem isn't your strength or what goddess you worship, but that you never learned how to defend yourself."

"I've spent years studying corporeal spells. I'm one of the best taught in the palace. There are things I haven't studied, but I know what they are. Elene made sure I had the best—" I stop and bite my lip. Elene has always chosen my tutors. She has directed my curriculum from the day I arrived at the palace. I always thought her interest was in making sure I was as well trained as I could be, as strong as possible.

But what if Elene tailored my education to make me into the perfect tool? One that could do her bidding, and perform with devastating effect, but never turn against her.

No one ever taught me a song to defend myself. Madam Guillard didn't once mention that there were spells I could learn, even when I ran to her sobbing after Ren had hexed me. She always told me it was impossible to block.

Has my tutor, my mentor, left me vulnerable by choice?

"Even if such things exist," I say as my broken heart hammers in my chest, "Elene has known the spells for years. I don't even know where to look for volumes on self-magic like that. It's forbidden. And I'd need to practice."

"Isn't that a risk worth taking?"

I get up and pace the length of her small room. Elene almost killed me at our last encounter. To challenge her again, unprepared, will certainly mean my death.

"I hate Elene," I say. "I hate the Performings. I hate what she does to folk like you, to Nip. But I don't want to die."

And if Elene doesn't kill me, she'll take everything from me: my magic, my position, my home. I have no family, no wealth. I will end up like Anette, alone and on the streets with nothing.

"Since I was a child, everyone I know has lived in fear of her," Remi says, closing her eyes as a shudder rips through her. "Every time we go to the Performing, we wonder if it will be the last time. We wonder if she'll execute us in the Opera Hall. My father is trying to marry me off to a boy I don't love, just so I can be safe. If I had any chance of deposing her, without magic, I would risk *everything*."

I look away from her, ashamed. If our positions were reversed, and she were the chantrix instead of me, I don't doubt that she would risk her life to save her family. To save everyone she knows. But I am too afraid.

"Don't you think you owe it to the people you hurt in Elene's name?" Remi says, getting up from the bed and coming to stand beside me. "Just talk to someone. See what spells the queen has withheld from you!"

A tendril of her hair comes loose from its pins. She moves to the desk to fix it and lights an extra candle to illuminate the mirror. In the flickering candlelight, her face looks rounder, younger.

Nostalgia makes my stomach clench. I remember the pitch of her laugh, the warmth of her fingers. Spending time with her made me happy. I don't have many good memories of the years since her family left Cavalia.

I could go to Madam Guillard and demand to know what was left out of my education. I know that my old tutor shares my religious beliefs. She knows song magic is a gift, to be given and taken at Adela's pleasure, to be used to help others. She told me that on the day I entered the academy, clutching my mother's necklace. And she repeated it over and over again in my early lessons, before Elene took power and the reminders abruptly stopped.

"I'll ask about the blocking spells," I say. "But my magic may just be weaker. Or maybe some gifts allow you to use shields and others don't. Magic isn't a science. It's not exact. I don't know what my powers will allow until I try."

Remi's eyes meet mine, shining almost as brightly as her smile.

"Do you have everything you need here? Did the servants bring you food?"

She nods and gestures to the bed. "They did, and this is a little better than a dungeon floor."

"I'll send for you tomorrow," I say, hating the way it sounds. "Since the guards let me pass tonight, I don't think anyone will object to me seeing you in my studio. There will be witnesses there, but I can try to tell you what I find out."

I go to the door and wrench it open. I half expect to find one of the guards listening on the other side, but the hallway is deserted.

"Cadence," Remi says as I step out.

I hesitate in the doorway.

"Thank you."

Her gratitude brings a blush to my cheeks and makes my chest flutter. But I've done nothing worthy of her thanks, and I'm not sure I can be the person she wants me to be.

CHAPTER 20

# CADENCE

**THE GUARDS NOD TO** me as I leave the east wing, relief evident on their faces. I'm shaky from my talk with Remi, but now is as good a time as any to speak to my old tutor. If I wait, I might lose my nerve.

I try to look at ease as I cross the palace green. I stuff my hands into my cloak pockets and keep my pace slow. The clouds have started to roll in, but I can make out the barest twinkle of stars, muted by gray muslin fog. I've always liked the palace best at night, when everything is still.

Remi really seems to believe that everything could be different. I wish I could share her optimism, but I have too much experience with Elene.

The mages' academy sits atop a hill on the far side of the palace gardens. The servants often call it a wing, but the academy has its own building, a spherical tower built from seastone surrounded by a black slate wall.

I wrap my cloak tighter around me as I begin the climb up the hill. The path is slick with ice from our first autumn freeze, and the wind is starting to pick up. A lone guard paces the length of the low wall, carrying a clipboard instead of a weapon. He's not here for our protection but to report our comings and goings to Ren. I suppose everyone in the queendom expects a group of mages to protect ourselves, though any of us could have told them that singers sleep just as soundly as anyone else.

The emerald-green paint on the front door has started to chip, and the bronze knocker is covered in blue-gray tarnish. The door creaks when I push it open. The academy needs money for repairs, but now that all the best singers reside in the palace with the queen, they no longer pay rent toward the academy's upkeep.

Most of the young mages in Bordea used to live here. We all worked, ate, and sang together, regardless of school and classification. Now most students are sorted on arrival. The best immediately go to the palace, to train where Ren can watch them, their instructors brought in each day. Those with lesser magic, or who take more time to develop their skills, train here. The only part of the academy that maintains its former splendor is the library, as mages from all over the country flock to study its volumes.

The marble hallway is dark. The torches on the walls have been snuffed out, to be rekindled by an elemental when morning comes. Madam Guillard still enforces a strict curfew and bedtime with her students. I creep forward, leaving the heavy door open a crack so the moon can light my way.

Something warm brushes against my leg.

I jump and brace myself to bolt for the door. If there is a new ward spell guarding the hall, it might not recognize me. If I take another step, I could find myself caged in air, trapped and floating until morning.

But it's only Madam's old silver tabby, rubbing his cheek against my calves. I scoop him up, and he purrs into my ear.

Madam Guillard's rooms are on the ground floor, away from the dormitories. When I was a child, some of the older students told me it was to keep them from sneaking out at night. Madam's sharp ears miss nothing, and she was rumored—though no one has ever confirmed it—to sweep unruly students up in a cyclone of wind, transport them via tornado, and deposit them into their own beds.

The cat perches on my shoulders as I make my way down the dark hallway until I find the entrance to her suite. The door is slightly ajar, and candlelight makes snake tracks across the floor. I knock twice and wait.

"Who is it?" Madam calls.

I push the door open and step into the pool of light. Madam sits in her bed, wearing an emerald dressing gown. Her silver-blond hair hangs loose about her shoulders, and spectacles balance on the end of her nose. She rests a book on her knees. The cat jumps down and bounds up onto the bed beside her.

"Cadence?" she asks. Her smile is warm and comfortable. "What brings you here? I'd have put the kettle on if I'd known to expect you."

The lightness of her tone brings tears to my eyes. How many times have I visited her like this over the years? As a child, I used to climb straight into bed with her, and she would read me a story before donning her cloak and walking me back to my bedroom in the palace. When loneliness overwhelmed me, I came here. When Ren hurt me and I needed a kind word, I went to Madam. She held me and soothed my aches with peppermint tea.

And yet. She never taught me how to stop him. Did she know that she was sending me back for more of the same every time she patched me up and comforted me?

"I need to speak to you," I say, swallowing hard, "about songs that block other magic."

She stiffens. I hover in the doorway, waiting, as she strokes her cat's fur. A war of emotions plays out on her face. Like me, she's complicit, and I know how it feels to come face-to-face with that truth.

Finally, she whispers, "Close the door and lock it."

After I fasten the lock, Madam takes a deep breath. "You have to understand that the queen set your curriculum. From the time she took you to the palace, your education has been out of my hands."

"I know that." The air in the room is too close, too warm.

"Her Majesty wanted you to learn a certain set of songs, ones that would be useful to her in the work she wants you to do. She wanted you to learn them perfectly. That is why we have neglected much of your training with plants."

"But this isn't about plants," I force out, before I lose my nerve. "I came to you, again and again, when I was in pain. You never once mentioned that there might be a way for me to stop Ren. I'd never even seen a blocking spell until I saw Elene perform one. There is nothing about them in the library."

"I *wanted* to show you!" Madam's voice cracks. "But if you had used one against Ren, the queen would have found out. When you were young, she could still have chosen another. It would have been worse for both of us."

I've used that excuse myself. Elene always makes things worse. I told Remi that. But thinking of myself as I was—so small, scared, and helpless in the face of Ren's hexes—makes it harder to swallow.

Madam sighs and points to a bookcase beside her window. "Bring me the red leather volume. You're old enough now to use discretion."

Madam's bookcase is as tall as the ceiling and stretches across the entire back wall of her room. I walk over to it and run my fingers over the books' soft spines. Most are fiction: small, tightly packed volumes with paper covers. That makes me smile a little, despite my sadness. I've never imagined Madam Guillard reading romances beneath her covers like I do.

The volume she wants is easy to spot. It's a huge tome, with gold embossed lettering, sitting alone on her top shelf. Too late, I see that a knife rests in the cradle of its pages, and the blade falls at my feet when I pull the book down.

The knife's hilt is encrusted with pearls and glimmers gold in the candlelight. The smell of countless magics coats its blade, mingling together into an overpowering stench. I stoop down to pick it up, but Madam's warning shout makes me jerk my hand away.

"Don't touch that!" she cries. "Just the book, if you please."

My gaze lingers on the knife for a second longer. It's a fine blade: well crafted and expensive. And illegal on this side of the palace walls. I want to believe that Madam enchanted it with a heat or binding spell, as I did with the shears at the hospital.

But it doesn't smell of her magic—like a whisper of magnolia—and I have the same sense of unease around it that I feel from meat that has been cruelly slaughtered.

But I came here for information. If I pry too far into something else, Madam Guillard may tell me to leave.

I carry the spell-tome over to Madam. She lifts it from my arms with a grunt and begins leafing through it.

Clearing her throat, Madam taps the book's open pages. "I always keep this book in my room, out of the palace libraries. As you know, we do not encourage self-magic of any kind. Too many things can go wrong, and yet, in order to protect ourselves, it is a road we must sometimes travel." Her eyes linger on my face, soft and intent. "I wanted to show you these. So many times, when you came to me, I ached to teach you. When most of our corporeal students reach ten years of age, we begin teaching them these songs of protection. But Her Majesty did not want you to know them, and I couldn't risk the chief justicar's ire."

I swallow, my throat dry. So instead of facing Ren's wrath herself, she let it fall on me. A child.

I peer down at the pages. The notes are foreign, the melody entirely new. Self-magic. Since I was a little girl, I have been warned against it by all of my instructors.

Remi was right. It *does* exist. It's not something only Elene, with Odetta's blessing, can do. I simply wasn't taught.

Many singers have joined the queen's army over the centuries. We learn about their valiant history in the academy. The mages were instrumental in securing Bordea's independence from our northern neighbor, Solidad. They squashed the noble forces who resisted Elene. Of course those mage-warriors needed a method of defense as well as attack. Just as Remi said.

I drag the chair beside Madam's dressing table over to the bed and sink into it. Madam pats my arm, but I flinch away.

She hastily pulls her arm back. "I heard what happened in the palace between you and the queen. I'm sorry, Cadence. Truly. I know I should have taught you these spells earlier, to protect you from her. From both of them."

I let the tears fall down my cheeks. I wish her words could comfort me, but they don't. Ever since the stern matron at the children's home brought me to the palace, Madam has been the closest thing I've had to a parent. But our interactions have been scripted by Elene, and it hurts to know how much. Madam has never been free to stay with me in the palace, or take a meal with me in my rooms. I assumed that she didn't want to. After all, she didn't protest when Elene took me, or when she insisted that I become her principal.

And yet, I can't hate her for it. I know what we all must do to survive.

"Although this volume contains many spells, you should only use self-magic for defense," she says. "I don't want you getting the idea that the spells in this book are safe. Even for defense, working magic on yourself is as dangerous as I've always told you. You must promise me that you will only ever use these defensive songs in an emergency."

"I promise," I say. "I'll be careful."

She flips a few more pages, then passes the book to me. I cradle it in my lap to study the music. The page shows a simple, two-stanza refrain. The musical notes are inked in dark red above spell words printed in black.

When I work a spell, the melody is the most important, followed by the pitch. I can work magic without speaking the words as long as I hum the refrain. The goddess who grants our powers hears our thoughts. It's the music itself, the tone, the chromatic scale, the rhythm, the cadence, and the uniqueness of each human interpretation that enthrall her, not the words.

"Take the book with you," Madam says. She reaches down and bends the corner of the page, which makes me wince. "This page and the two after it contain defensive spells. This one will turn your skin to metal, so you can deflect most corporeal surface spells. The others will change your body temperature or relax your muscles so that impact or choking won't affect you. Elene's magic is strong, but she has favorite spells like we all do. These will be enough so long as she is not expecting it. Practice them in your studio. Keep the book hidden. I don't have to tell you that she will be furious if she finds out."

"Did you ever teach her? Elene?" It's a question I've always longed to ask but never dared. With her graying hair and the faint lines etched around her mouth and eyes, Madam Guillard has to be nearing sixty. Elene is not yet forty—still a young woman.

"I was a young instructor when the queen was brought to the palace, but I taught some of her lessons, yes."

"Is she as strong as people say?"

My tutor sighs. "Stronger. Madam Olivette ran the academy in those days. She thought Elene would take over from her and run things here when she retired."

It's strange to think of Elene as a student, and even stranger to consider the course her life might have taken. She might now be sitting in Madam Guillard's bed, with a romance novel balanced on her knees. With power like that, her future must have seemed so assured back then, a destiny built. And yet, she had longed for more. If she had never met the young viscount, could she have been content with life as a teacher, a headmistress? I can't imagine it.

"Was she always as she is now? Ambitious?" I ask carefully.

Madam Guillard barks a laugh. "Yes. She was always competitive, always had to be the best at everything she did. The academy was not as ruthless then as it is now when it comes to positions, but still, the best patronages were competitive. Only the brightest students secured them. Most of her instructors encouraged her."

"Did you?"

My tutor looks down. "I suppose I did not discourage it. She came from a poor family, and they struggled to pay her yearly tuition. I think she felt she had something to prove to some of the other students here, and I saw her potential. But when the viscount started to call on her, sending her messages and jewelry, I should have said something then."

I nod, then open my cloak and slide the book inside, under my arm. Even at night, someone is bound to notice if I hold it uncovered. I'll need to bring it straight to my studio.

"Thank you for this," I whisper. If the spells are as powerful as Madam Guillard seems to think, I might have a chance. I don't forgive her, but I can understand her. "Do they always work? Are there ways around them?"

"There are always ways around. These spells do not guard against every possibility, and once Elene realizes that you have used one, she may try a less common attack." She shakes her head. "Unfortunately, we have devised more spells for violence than protection. And now that Elene prays to Odetta, she may have been blessed with special knowledge. Odetta is famed for her bloodlust, after all."

"So how can I fight her?"

Madam glances out her window, and when she speaks again, her voice wavers. "If you use one of these spells against the queen, or her justicars, you must be prepared. You must be ready to strike as soon as her guard is down, because I guarantee that once she feels your magic protect you against her, Elene will not wait for you to do it a second time."

"You *want* me to attack her?"

"Of course not. Not unless there is no alternative." She presses her cold palm to my cheek and looks me in the eyes. "I taught both of you. I do not look forward to burying my students."

# CHAPTER 21

# CADENCE

**WHEN I REACH MY** studio, I quickly close the door behind me. I don't want anyone to walk in unannounced, though the hour is much too early for Elene to bother me.

I smooth my fingers over the book's red leather cover. Its creamy pages are made from vellum, soft calfskin, a material we barely use anymore in Bordea. The thickness of each page and the bright, gold-leaf ink make the book feel infinitely more powerful and ancient. I sit down on my pianoforte bench and flip through the tome until I find the songs Madam showed me.

The melodies are simple, to be sung presto. I hum the spell-song as my eyes scan the music bars. The lyrics are harder. The tight, black script under each musical bar is a language I've never seen.

Most spellsongs are written in a kind of alliterative poetry, easy to memorize. Almost all of them are in Bordean, though the library has a few volumes left over from Solidad's occupation that are written in Soli. I sound out each syllable of the words in front of me. My tongue slips clumsily over the phrases, and even though there is no one watching me, my face colors.

Reading didn't come easily to me as a child. I remember the humiliation of standing in front of my class, tripping over letters that rearranged themselves on the page. The other students laughed as my teacher sighed with frustration.

When the academy learned the strength of my magic, Madam Guillard took over my literary instruction. She showed me a new, phonetic method of sounding out each word. Learning still wasn't easy, but with her help, it became possible. Then the books that had seemed so inaccessible opened like metal gates, revealing hidden worlds beyond.

"Shall I bring your breakfast here, Principal?" a deep voice shouts through the closed door.

I rest the volume on my knees. Although I haven't slept, I have a rare appetite. "Yes," I say, then hesitate. Even though the palace servants are afraid of me, I'm not sure they will obey any direct orders concerning Remi. Whatever her title here, they know she is Elene's prisoner. "Will you bring my new companion? I want to sing for her."

A pause. I rise from my bench and go to the door. Opening

it a fraction, I peer out at the servant. He's young, with a fading tan and a crop of freckles that covers his nose, suggesting he's very recently worked outdoors. His unruly ginger hair sticks up at the back, an offence the head butler will not allow for long. He may not yet know the way of things here.

"Well?" I bark, trying to replicate Elene's queenly scowl.

The boy's eyes widen, and he nods. "Yes, Principal. Right away."

He bows twice and scurries down the hall. As I close the door, I hear him shout to the maids about my breakfast. Perfect.

I carry the book to my music stand and prop it up. Difficult lyrics or not, if I'm going to practice these songs, I need to do it before the mages in the castle wake up. To common folk, these songs will sound no different from anything else I practice. But I can't let Elene and Ren, or any of their spies, overhear me. Madam Guillard is right. If I'm ever going to challenge Elene, I need the element of surprise.

Inhaling deeply, I relax my diaphragm and straighten my shoulders. I read over the lyrics a final time and internalize them. Then I project my voice and begin to sing. When I learn new songs, I like to sing as loudly and strongly as I can. Later, once the magic and music are more familiar, I can refine them. My studio's thick walls contain most of the volume.

I expect self-magic to be grand, blazing. It's a forbidden,

dangerous power, and it seems as though it should come as fire or a devastating cold. A power to shake my very bones. But when I sing, the magic whispers. It wraps around my skin, as gentle and soft as new fleece.

Something is wrong. This can't be how a powerful protection spell should feel. Self-magic is a treacherous art, but this feels mundane, like the healing spell for a paper cut. I stop singing as frustrated tears sting my eyes. My spell is weak. I scan the words on the page again and try to pronounce them differently, with exaggerated breaks and hard consonants. But this time, when I sing, the magic doesn't come at all.

I kick the music stand, and it crumples, the book falling to the floor and landing in a splay of pages. I should have known better than to place any hope in Remi's plan. Elene probably excluded these songs from my education because they are useless.

Maybe there are other volumes like this book with more powerful, resilient protective spells. But if they exist, Elene has likely sealed them away in her private library. Or Madam Guillard simply doesn't trust me with their secrets. Perhaps Ren has consigned them all to a bonfire. The thought of beautiful, hand-scripted ancient pages curling into ash causes a sob to rise in my throat.

"Cadence?" Remi's voice cuts through my sorrow. She pushes the door open. I sniffle, wiping at my nose.

The red-haired manservant lingers in the hall behind her.

"Your breakfast will be along soon, Principal," he says.

I usher Remi inside and shut the door in his surprised face.

Remi wears a light gold taffeta gown that rustles when she moves. It has a white lace collar, with small, perfectly round pearl buttons. She's swept her auburn curls into a bun, held in place by a multitude of tiny pins. I cross my arms over my chest in a feeble effort to hide my wrinkled tunic. Even the perfume of my magic can't conceal how bad I smell.

Her eyes travel to the book on the floor, then to the tears on my cheeks. She kneels and picks up the book, then places the book reverently back on the music stand.

"You look nice," I blurt. When we were children, I was always jealous of Remi's looks: her plump, round cheeks, the way she always had a new, beautiful dress every day. I'm still envious, but it's a different kind of envy, one sharpened by longing.

A smile quivers on her lips. She's highlighted them in pink, and they are bright and tempting. "The queen had some dresses sent to my room last night. A mage must have taken my measurements somehow, because everything fits perfectly. Her note said she hoped it might rub off on you."

I give an awkward, high-pitched snort of laughter. When Remi's eyebrows shoot up, I mutter, "Typical."

Elene would furnish me with a hundred dresses if I allowed

it, each a hundred times finer than the one Remi wears now. When I first came to live at the palace, I delighted in all the fine new clothes she provided. I finally had the wardrobe I'd long envied Remi for having.

But no matter what I wear, Elene is never satisfied with my appearance. Even when I make an effort, she will comment on the sallowness of my skin, my protruding collar bones. After a while, dressing to please her lost its allure. It's easier to bear her commentary on my clothes, rather than on an unchangeable part of me.

Remi jerks her shoulder toward Madam Guillard's book. "New magic?"

"A new book," I groan, and sink onto my bench. I drop my voice to a whisper, just in case the new servant stands outside listening. "My old tutor gave me this. It's supposed to teach me how to do self-magic and protect myself, but I tried the spells and they don't work. Not for me, anyway."

She steps over to the music stand and pages through the ancient book. "Not at all?"

I shrug. "I can feel the spell a little. But it's not as it should be."

Remi adjusts her skirt and sinks gracefully to the floor like a dancer, leaning her back against the wall. "Have you ever used magic on yourself before?"

"No. It's forbidden. We can go too far."

"Then how do you know what your magic is supposed to feel like? If you used the spell, and you felt something, then maybe it's right."

"You've felt my magic. You know how strong I am."

She doesn't get it. Non-magical folk never do when I try to explain my abilities, how I know if a spell is working. My protection spell was feeble, the work of an unskilled child.

"I pushed the spell as hard as I could, and all I felt was a trickle. If I sang one of the spells I know for you, and tried to force as much magic as I could into it, you'd die. Even from a healing spell."

She glances up at me. Under the flutter of her long lashes, her eyes brim with hope. "So this is gentler? Maybe that doesn't mean it isn't working."

I exhale slowly. I still think she's wrong, but self-magic is new to me. For her, I could practice a little more and see where it goes. "I'll practice. No promises, but I'll try."

Her grin widens; then she arches her back and twists from side to side. "My mattress is as hard as a rock." She works her fingers into her neck, massaging. "I don't think anyone has replaced the beds in the east wing since the reign of Marianne V. If I dared to look under the bed, I'd probably find all manner of dead things."

It's the kind of joke she would have made when we were

children. But now, I stare down at the nape of her neck, at the soft sweep of a loose curl brushing her skin. My fingers twitch in my lap.

"I could fix it for you," I say. My face reddens as soon as the words escape.

She glances up at me out of the corner of one eye, then folds forward so that she rests on her elbows. The movement is fluid and elegant. She smells of frost and lavender perfume. As the early-morning sun catches her hair, it lights with amethyst and bronze.

My breath quickens. One of the buttons on her gown has come open, revealing a sliver of the smooth, perfect skin of her back. I wonder what it would be like to undo them one by one, to trace my fingers down the hollow of her spine, to follow the touch with my lips. What would her skin taste like? Would her back, so supple and firm, quiver when I kissed it? Would she arch up into my touch?

Or would she recoil?

I *am* a monster, and everything about this daydream is perfect, except for me.

I bite my lip. Remi has never given any sign of . . . an *inclination,* as Madam would call it. I have always been free to love any gender I choose, but I am a mage. I know how the rest of the queendom views relationships between two women. Things are slowly changing among the non-magical folk, but Remi was raised in the old beliefs of Queen Celeste's court.

We are only beginning to be friends again. More than anything, I want her to think well of me, as she did when we were children.

I can't hope for anything else.

She closes her eyes as I begin to sing and lets out a little sigh. I don't need to look at her to loosen the knots that have formed under her shoulder blades, but I can't tear my eyes away. Her head tilts ever so slightly to the side. Her long lashes flutter down.

I've never considered healing to be intimate before, but as I heal Remi, I am aware of every breath, every subtle change my magic works inside her. Despite what I did to her in the Opera Hall, she is trusting me to do this.

Some of the other mages use their corporeal magic for another type of restoration. I heard two young men speak about it once. I was sitting in the garden out of view, reading a book behind a cherry tree, as they fed each other from a platter of fresh fruit. They spoke of songs used to bring explosive pleasure, songs that set every nerve of the body alight with a gentle kind of fire. I'm not exactly sure how it works—Marie and I only kissed—but I wonder what would it be like to bring Remi to bed. To watch her hands grip the white headboard of my four-poster, her feet scrambling for purchase on the white linen sheets as her body battles a crescendo of bliss.

My song starts to shake, and I clear my throat.

Remi sits up slowly. All of her hair has escaped from its pins. She pushes the strands back off her face. Her eyes meet mine, sleepy and warm, and I feel indestructible.

# CHAPTER 22

# REMI

IN THE MORNING, CADENCE comes to my room before dawn. She pulls open the drapes, and I wake as starlight bathes my face. At home I often sleep until noon, and it's clear to me that Cadence needs to learn a thing or two about the pleasures of sleeping in. This is the second day in a row that she's been up and wanting to see me before the sun even lights the sky.

While I pretend to dose, she tosses herself onto the bed beside me. Her eyes glitter with excitement. Groaning, I pull my blanket back over my head.

"What time is it?" I moan. "Why are you here? The guards can bring me by your studio in a few hours."

"I have a surprise for you," she says. "Get dressed. You can just wear yesterday's clothes. It won't matter for this."

She seizes the duvet and pulls it off me. Though I am wearing a lace nightgown, my calves are bare. I yelp when the cold air touches them. The servants keep forgetting to light my brazier in the evening. Cadence's gaze lingers on my exposed skin for a blink too long.

"It better be good," I mumble. "I was hoping to sleep until sunrise, at least."

I heave myself up and reach for yesterday's dress, casually strewn over the foot of my bed. My hair is a mass of tangles. The dress smells faintly of honey, a scent I'm coming to associate with Cadence's magic.

Once I'm dressed, Cadence seizes my hand and leads me from the room. A shock seems to pulse from her fingers to mine, making all the hairs on my arms stand on end.

The two guards stationed outside the east wing regard us with suspicion as we approach. The older of the two extends his arm, blocking our path. Cadence's brows furrow and her lips part, as if to sing, but then she seems to think better of it. The barest hint of that honey smell hovers in the air around us, a sweet threat that dissipates on the breeze.

She fixes the guard with a smile instead. "Don't worry—we won't go far. We'll just stay on the palace grounds."

"It's early. Shouldn't both of you still be abed?"

"And miss the best part of the day?" I say with a grimace.

The guard cocks his head and narrows his eyes, but he lowers his arm. His gaze sweeps Cadence's simple breeches and my wrinkled dress. "Have her check back in with us before the tenth bell."

"I'll be here," I say, and tighten my grip on Cadence's hand. The queen made herself clear: If I try to run, she will execute my father. I won't risk it. "Come on, I want to see this surprise."

The corners of Cadence's lips twitch. They are a delicate, pale shade of pink, slightly chapped from the winter weather.

Outside, a fresh dusting of snow covers the walkways. In the time I've been imprisoned, I've missed the end of autumn. Back at the château, our tenants and stewards will already have brought in the harvest. In any other year, Mama would be directing the preparations for the Bone Festival to honor Marena.

I follow Cadence through the gardens and around the back of the palace. Here, the servants are already awake. Maids scurry across the grounds, bearing chamber pots and jugs full of boiling water. Stewards carrying leather folios trot toward their offices. The smell of baking bread and roasting meat emanates from the kitchen block. Wagons laden with goods from the city are parked beside it. Servants unload their cargo while a minister, wearing a gold rose pin to mark him as a mage, counts coins into merchants' hands.

As we pass the dungeon, my eyes linger on the iron gate leading into the stone keep. A company of common guards and mages is posted outside the prison. They rub their hands in the cold and pass a long pipe between them. Red smoke snakes up into the air. One of the guards, a slight girl with a white-blond ponytail, wears the same heart badge as Cadence.

I want desperately to see Papa, but there is no way we can sneak past so many guards. I look down at the snow, afraid that even looking at the gate will compel my body to do something rash. I would give anything for a minute with him, just to see that he is okay.

We enter a stone building at the edge of the palace grounds. The gentle sound of horses nickering reminds me so much of home. Even here, where I am a prisoner, horses have the power to calm me. The stable is a single, long corridor, lined on either side with airy horse boxes, similar to our barn at home, but on a grand scale. Each stall is made from burnished mahogany wood, with brass fittings and lacquer bolts. The horses smell of sweet hay and leather, and they press forward, ears pricked, to inspect us. Some call out, thinking we bring their breakfast.

A stallion inquisitively bumps his muzzle against my shoulder and leans over the low door of his stall. He has a magnificent, muscular crest and a coat whiter than the new snow outside. A long, silver forelock falls elegantly over one of his bright blue eyes. Only horses from Solidad have eyes like this. Papa always wanted a Soli stallion, but since Queen Elene took the throne, none can be brought across the border. I stroke the horse's nose and allow him to lip my palm.

"I don't have any sugar," I chuckle.

"He's Elene's favorite," Cadence says. She stands a few steps back from the horses, hands in her pockets. "She rides him to processions and hunts with him."

"You beauty," I murmur, lifting my hand to scratch behind his ears. "She doesn't deserve you."

"His name is Monsurat." Cadence scuffs her foot along the stable floor. "He was taken from their château, after."

I swallow hard. She doesn't need to tell me the story. Everyone in Bordea knows what happened at Monsurat.

A few months after Queen Elene took the throne, Duke François of Monsurat, the old queen's beloved nephew, assembled his army and prepared to march on Cannis. But when Queen Elene heard of his plan, she traveled to Monsurat with a small company of mages.

With fewer than fifty singers, she completely slaughtered the duke's forces. The duke sought shelter in his château with most of his household. But a handful of the queen's mages were skilled with plants. At Queen Elene's command, the singers encouraged the trees around the château to creep closer.

Roots and branches grew through the walls and sought out the family hiding inside. They impaled the duke and his family.

As though that death wouldn't have been horrific enough, the queen appointed two singers to remain at Monsurat to heal the duke a little at a time, to keep him alive and suffering for weeks.

This stallion is far more than a beautiful horse. He is a symbol of the queen's victory, a spoil of war.

"My tutor told me the duke rode him out into the field to meet Elene," Cadence says. "And that Elene told him that first day that the horse would be hers."

Shuddering, I give the stallion a final pat and move down the block. If the queen were to find concrete evidence of Papa's rebellion against her, would our household share Monsurat's terrible fate? All noble families keep the stories of Monsurat and Foutain alive. We all know how dangerous resistance is, and yet, when I imagine Papa as a revolutionary, I can't help the pride that swells in my chest.

A familiar, demanding whinny pierces my thoughts. Gathering my skirt, I race down the row of stalls.

Chance stands in the last box. He's fiddling with the bolt on his stall door, trying to grip it with his teeth, but when he sees me, he stops, and his ears prick forward. In the chaos of our arrest, there wasn't time to make provisions for Chance.

I'd hoped that Rook would be allowed to return home with the horses, but I'd still worried that he would be detained in the capital and Chance would be returned to his dark, cell-like stable at the hotel.

I unlock the stall door and throw my arms around his neck. He snorts affectionately, then lips my ear. A laugh catches in my throat, and happy tears brim in my eyes.

"I've missed you," I gush into his neck. "Where have you been? Has Rook been good to you?"

Chance's piebald coat is shiny, and his mane has been meticulously brushed. I've never seen it this free of tangles. I was worried that no one would feed him, but if anything, my pony has grown chubbier in the time we've been apart.

Cadence leans over the stall door. A silly, lopsided grin on her face. "Surprise," she says, with a roll of her eyes. "I remembered how worried you were about him that night at the hospital, so I asked around."

"This is a wonderful surprise." I smile at her, and a blush creeps up her neck.

She gestures toward the saddle rack next to the stall, where a new, suede sidesaddle rests. "Your stable hand was detained a few days ago, then allowed to go home. They took most of your things into custody, so I had this made. I hope it fits him. It's singer-made."

"He hasn't really been trained to go sidesaddle yet. He's still very green."

"Oh." Her face falls slightly, but she recovers with a quick shake of her head. "Well, there are plenty of other saddles you can borrow here. I thought we might go for a ride. We'll have to stick to the palace grounds, of course—"

"That's perfect," I say. After so many days cooped up inside, I can't wait to feel the wind in my hair as we fly across the grounds.

Cadence rubs the back of her neck. "Only, I'm not very good. Sometimes I even have to sing to the horses so they don't buck me off. I don't leave Cannis very often, and I usually just walk, or take a carriage if Elene makes me. When I had Nip . . ."

She trails off and bites her lip, grief clouding her blue eyes.

"Why don't we ride Chance together?" I ask. "You can hold on to my waist while I steer us."

Cadence raises an eyebrow. "Won't that be too much weight for him?"

"Look at the size of him."

She presses her lips together, shoulders shaking with laughter. "He does look sturdy."

She opens the stable door and sidles in with me, so close I can feel the fabric of her tunic brush my hand and the heat of her breath on my back. The past few days have proven that she has not entirely become the queen's creature. Despite what she's done, she is still the girl I knew. I turn to look at her, and the intensity in her blue eyes makes my heart jump into a gallop.

But maybe I'm reading something in her expression, in the inviting part of her lips, that isn't there. When she healed my back in her studio, it felt different than it had in the hospital, like there was a connection between us, something deeper than magic. I want to believe she felt it, too. Cadence has healed so many patients that perhaps for her, it was all just routine.

"I'll just go and find a saddle," I say, and slip past her out of the stall.

"There's a tack room at the end of the row. Hand me the bridle."

I lift the bridle from the peg outside Chance's new stall. It matches the new sidesaddle, with red fastenings and a diamond headband. The reins are made from the softest suede I've ever held. I'm no stranger to expensive things, but the bridle is a treasure. I pass it over to Cadence.

Our fingers brush, and she jerks her hand away. I race down the hall.

Once Chance is ready, we mount up and set out across the palace grounds. Cadence sits well behind the saddle, putting careful distance between our bodies, her arm only loosely curled around my waist for balance. Neither of us speaks much, but occasionally, Cadence points out a statue or a pavilion, and I rack my memory, trying to picture what it had looked like in my childhood.

Chance is eager. He dances sideways, and it's all I can do to hold him to a trot. He fights my grip, and his muscles bunch beneath us. I'm grateful for the curb bit on the new bridle. I can feel his longing. He wants to gallop through the gardens, jump benches and hedges, as we would have done at home.

I decide to take the path that winds up the steepest hill, to tire him out. After assuring Cadence that I am an adept rider and can keep us safe, the last thing I want is for my over exuberant cob to make a liar of me.

At the same time, I wouldn't complain if she slid a *little* closer.

Chance gives a playful buck at the base of the hill. I nudge him hard with both heels. But when Cadence's grip tightens around me, I scratch his withers in thanks.

We thunder up the hill in a burst of speed. The winter wind stings my eyes and cheeks, but it feels so good to be on a horse again. Though her grip is like iron, Cadence is laughing. Up here, the palace is hidden from view by tall trees. I am free to think of nothing but the horse beneath me and Cadence's arms around me. It almost feels like being at home again.

We turn a bend in the path and nearly trample the servant who scurries forward from the bushes to meet us. He gives me a haughty sneer, but nods to Cadence and bows.

"Principal," he says. "I come straight from the queen. Her Majesty has requested that you take your breakfast with her."

Cadence sighs. "I guess we'll head back, then." To me, she says, "You can drop me off by the entrance to the west wing. I'll get one of the stewards to see you back to your rooms."

The messenger shakes his head. "The invitation was extended to both of you. Her Majesty requested that you come immediately, as you are." His lip curls as he considers me. "I'm sure your friend agrees that dining with Her Majesty is an honor?"

Chance shifts beneath us, nickering. Unease brings cold sweat to my face. Does the queen think we were trying to run away? If she takes it out on my father . . .

"Surely, the queen does not wish to dine with us dressed like this and smelling of the stables," Cadence insists. "What is the reason for your haste?"

The messenger fishes in his satchel and holds out an envelope to Cadence, bowing again as she takes it. The envelope is scarlet and bears the queen's seal. The wax shimmers in the low winter sun. "My apologies, Principal. I forgot to present this to you. I believe Her Majesty wishes to start discussing the particulars with you."

Cadence breaks the seal to draw out a black card. It's shaped like one of the queen's masks, and the paper is cut to look like lace trim. It reminds me of the invitations the palace sends out before the Performing. As she studies it, all the color drains from her cheeks.

"I didn't think she was serious. I didn't think she would actually host this," she whispers, closing her eyes as if in pain. She holds out the card for me to read. "It's an invitation to a ball."

# CHAPTER 23

# CADENCE

**STILL DRESSED IN OUR** wrinkled clothes, we find Elene in her conservatory.

She had the room commissioned years ago—the only room she has added to Cavalia since she took the throne—and it's her favorite place in the palace. The vaulted ceilings are made entirely from pink mageglass. Little sparks of elemental magic still glimmer along the ceiling's ribs. The glass is transparent enough to allow daylight to filter in, but everything in the room takes on a rose tint. The room's furniture is concentrated on a stone platform at the center, and Elene's gardeners have planted a living floor of white roses. Under the tint, they are the color of sweet wine. Obsidian stepping-stones dot through them, creating a path that leads to the platform.

Remi gazes up at the ceiling in wonder, then cautiously toes the nearest stone. It's strange to see her nervous, but it makes sense. Everything in this space has been touched by magic. If I had ever suffered a Performing, I might be afraid of the stones, too.

Elene sips tea from a glass cup. She reclines on a pink-quartz throne, eyes closed. A plate of macarons rests on a cushion beside her, and a young white man I don't recognize sits at her feet, massaging her ankles. His brunette curls are bound back with a singer's-green tie, and he is wearing a simple white mask. Raquelle sits to Elene's right on a bed of cushions, silver hair styled in neat braids, sipping wine and gazing at the new young man with a mixture of hunger and affection.

"Sit," Elene says, gesturing toward the quartz bench opposite her. "We have much to discuss."

We sit as directed. Remi perches on the edge of the bench, every muscle in her body tense. I study Elene's face, trying to gauge her mood. Her tone is light and her posture relaxed, her lips curled slightly in an almost playful smirk. When Elene opens her eyes, they dance with mischief; I see no malice in their depths. She leans forward to stroke the man's hair as Raquelle offers him a macaron. Whoever he is, I thank him silently.

If Elene would spend more time with her lovers and less with Ren, the whole queendom would be better off.

"I brought you here to discuss my ball!" she exclaims, and

claps her hands. "Cadence, I know you and I have spoken about it before, but I wanted your new friend's input as well." She flashes Remi a conspiratorial wink. "Seeing as she is the only living person at the palace today who has ever been to one. Besides her father, of course, but I won't consort with rebels."

She emphasizes the word *living* as she gazes at Remi. Beside me, Remi is as still as a statue, her breathing shallow, face blank.

"I was a child," Remi says. "I never actually attended the balls. I was eight when the old queen—died."

Elene scowls. "Well, I suppose you might not be very useful after all."

Remi's eyes flash with anger, but she bows her head. "I am sure that anything Your Majesty can plan, with the aid of so many skilled mages, will make any other ball seem dull in comparison."

"Oh, it will be magical. An evening to be remembered, to be sure," Elene says. All traces of honey leave her voice, leaving only the familiar, cold rasp. "My tailors will come to your rooms tonight to fit you with something appropriate for the occasion."

"My—my thanks," Remi stammers.

"I'm trusting you to encourage Cadence to dress up." Elene pats me on the leg. "Leave us now. I would speak to my singer alone."

Remi's shoulders sag with relief, while I tense. I don't want to be left alone with Elene. Although I've been practicing the songs in Madam Guillard's book, I'm not ready to defend myself if I need to. The young man rises and takes Raquelle's hand. They accompany Remi out of the conservatory.

Elene's gaze follows them, her expression wistful.

"You like her, don't you?" she asks, when they've gone.

"What?" I croak. It's bad enough that Elene sees us as old friends, but if she suspects that I feel anything else, Remi will be in even more danger.

Elene's green eyes narrow. "I'm not a fool. I can see the way you look at her. My servant says he found you riding together. On one horse. Your arms around her stomach."

"We did that as children, too. Because she was my friend."

"And now she's something else." Elene offers the tray of macarons to me. When I shake my head, she shrugs and pinches a teal cookie between two lacquered nails. She bites into it, swallows, and shudders with pleasure. "We may have had our differences recently, but you know I am fond of you."

I am a weapon to her, nothing more. She has made that painfully clear.

"I am," Elene insists, noticing my skeptical expression. "I have no children. As my protégé, you are as close to a child as I have. And I care about your safety. I need you to understand that the nobles are dangerous. They are all thirsty for power, being born with none of their own. If you give her the chance, Remi will use you and throw you away."

She comes to sit on the bench beside me, cups my chin with her hand, and forces me to meet her eyes. There's a sincerity in their emerald depths that I've never seen before. And for a moment, I catch a glimpse of the girl she was years ago, in love with a boy who cast her aside when their purposes no longer aligned.

"Remi isn't like that."

Her fingers ghost over her mask. "Do not be naive. She doesn't feel anything for you. All these nobles—their only ambition is to regain what they lost. They think of themselves and their families' positions, and nothing else matters. Your friendship is a task Remi must perform to save herself and her father. That is all."

I pull away from her. "I thought you wanted to hold this ball as the beginning of reconciliation. I thought Bordea was moving on."

"Yes, after a fashion." She takes a deep breath and goes to sit on her quartz throne again. "We are moving forward because we must, but we will never forget. This ball will be a reunion, but no less a demonstration of our power."

"I won't hurt any more people," I say.

In my head, I think the words to a brutal freezing song, but no sound emerges from my lips. Panic makes my breath catch in my chest, as surely as if Elene held it back with her song. I miss Nip's calming, steady presence at my side.

I want to be brave, to stand up to her, for my sake as well as Remi's, but a small pulsing doubt creeps into my thoughts. Elene's nobleman betrayed her. He thought nothing of abandoning her, of trying to kill her, once he had gotten what he wanted.

Elene sighs and looks out across the sea of roses. Her lips press together, and for long moment she says nothing. I toy with the hem of my sweaty tunic, bracing myself.

When she finally speaks again, her tone is much harsher than before. "I thought we had already put this argument to bed. You will do as I ask. If the ball goes as planned and all the attendees behave, there will be no need for you to inflict pain. We will do a healing demonstration. But should anyone step out of line, I will make you perform the most terrifying song of your career. People will talk about it in reverent whispers for a hundred years. If you refuse, your friend will die, and you will spend the rest of your life in the dungeons. Do you understand?"

Heart pounding furiously against my ribs, I nod.

CHAPTER 24

# REMI

I WAIT IN MY room for hours, but the guards do not come
to take me to Cadence's studio. Outside, the sun blazes high in
the sky. Servants and gardeners bustle past my window, pushing
wheelbarrows and dragging carts. Everyone is busy preparing
the palace grounds for the queen's ball. I am an afterthought.

Cadence's absence troubles me. Did I do something wrong
on our ride together? Did she somehow know what I was thinking? Was I too forward? I don't want to believe that I have mis-
read all the signs again, that I have made the same mistake I
did with Elspeth.

Worse yet is the thought of Cadence practicing some new
and vicious magic on the queen's orders. As much as her indif-
ference would sting, I can put aside my feelings if only my family can stay safe.

My new dress for the ball is draped over the open door of my wardrobe. The bodice is dark mauve silk, the skirt a burnt orange with hints of gold along the hem, the color of rising dawn. A note pinned to the lapel stated that the dawn colors were to signify new beginnings. Like the rest of the clothes the queen has sent me, the dress has been made by a singer. In this gown, I will look round and decadent and strong.

In any other circumstance, I would have loved it.

A gold mask lies on the dressing table, chosen to perfectly complement the dress. I try it on, fastening it into place with the ivory silk ribbons.

I wonder if Cadence will remember the promise I made to her all those years ago as children: that I'd take her to a ball and ask her to dance. Neither of us are children anymore. For all I know, Cadence might have a sweetheart in the mages' academy. Yet I've visited her studio almost every day for a week and have never seen anyone else come or go.

Footsteps drum down the hallway outside my room. A moment later, the captain of the guard unlocks my door and steps inside, not even bothering to knock.

"Let's go," he grunts.

"Go?" I stand and plant my hands on my hips. "Go where? I've been waiting here all morning."

"You're a prisoner, not a princess. We don't owe you a time.

Everyone is busy," he says. "The queen wishes to see you. You have a visitor."

My brow wrinkles with confusion. All of our friends and their families moved out of Cannis years ago. I close my eyes and grip the brass bed frame for support. The only person I can think of who might try to come is Mama. What if the queen has summoned her to the ball early? Maybe this is why Cadence hasn't come. She's unable to face me because she knows something has happened to my mother.

"Who is it?" I ask, fighting to keep my tone cool.

The guard shrugs. "Don't know. Some craftsman's boy. He says you and he had an arrangement. He says the queen can't hold you here because you're promised to be married, so your rank is forfeit. That there is no crime."

My jaw drops. I hastily shield my mouth with my hand. Nolan? What game is he playing? I can imagine him kneeling in the queen's throne room, holding his cap in his hands, his beautiful eyes beseeching the beast sitting on the gilded chair. The image makes me feel sick.

We've only met once. Why would he risk this for me?

I wring my hands as I follow the captain out the door. If the queen finds out Nolan is lying, that we don't have a precontract, he'll end up in the dungeons or worse.

I expect to find the captain's usual entourage waiting for

us at the door, but he leads me from the east wing alone, a sweaty hand clamped on my wrist. The gardeners avert their eyes as we pass them, as if they know that the queen waits to condemn me. My stomach sinks. Nolan is probably in chains already.

The captain marches me across the palace green, half dragging me in his haste.

The door to the audience chamber is made entirely from emeralds and diamonds and framed by pink marble pillars. The stones seem to glow from within, lit with magic.

Placing a hand on my back, the captain yanks the door open and ushers me inside. The chamber is dark and windowless, with only a few sparsely placed torches for light. I scuff my toe along the black marble floor. It glitters with tiny inlaid gemstones, an extravagance the queen probably bought by selling off properties from broken noble families.

I've been in this chamber before. I remember playing at the foot of the throne as Mama spoke to Queen Celeste. The old queen loved children and clapped her hands joyfully when I recited a poem from my lessons to her. Somehow, I can't imagine children playing while this queen laughs.

Queen Elene sits on her throne, legs crossed at the ankles. Her nostrils flaring, she is glaring down at a boy who sits on a wobbly, three-legged stool at her feet.

Sunlight strikes and illuminates Nolan's face as he pivots to face me.

"What are you doing here?" I demand, my voice trembling. My hands curl into fists, but I can't decide if I am more scared for him or furious at his presumption.

Still, our fathers have been friends for years. Jon is a well-connected craftsman, with an exalted position in his guild. It's possible that Nolan's presence here could have nothing to do with me. His father could have sent him to rescue me and free Papa. Hope springs inside me, and my heart beats faster. But Jon might not understand the true danger Nolan faces. The commoners have never been forced to sit in the Opera Hall during a Performing. Many of them love the queen.

But even if Nolan's only trying to save me, to go through with his plan would mean marrying him after all. If I agree, we will both be unhappy. But I can't contradict his story now. Lying to the queen is a crime in itself, tantamount to treason.

The queen claps her hands. "So you do know each other. I was worried this was all a trick."

Nolan rises from his stool and strides over to me. His steps are confident, but his hazel eyes are unsure. His gaze travels rapidly across my face. He takes my hand, places it in the crook of his arm, and leads me toward the queen. "As I said, she is my betrothed."

"We had only discussed it," I murmur.

Nolan frowns and looks down at his shoes. He is wearing craftsman's boots of worn black leather, covered in a thin layer of dust, as out of place in the queen's hall as he is. Elene lifts her skirt and steps daintily from the dais. She stands only as high as Nolan's chin, and yet, he cowers before her. I have a sudden protective urge to step between them.

"It sounds as if everything is not so settled after all, but I will grant you a reprieve to speak alone." The queen leans up to Nolan's ear, shielding her ruby lips with her hand, and hisses, "Do not enter my presence again until you are certain."

If Nolan were a nobleman, I am sure we would both be in Ren's custody now, bound for the dungeons. But his station gives us some freedom. Even with her army of mages, the queen relies on the commoners for support. A guild master like Nolan's father, with his numerous friends, could make things difficult for her.

She snaps her fingers, and two guards scurry to her side. They have young faces, with patchy, barely grown beards. Mere children. My stomach tightens.

"Escort these two to my clerk's chambers," the queen barks.

Heads bowed, the two guards escort us through a plain wooden door at the rear of the chamber. We follow them down the candlelit hall to a small, empty room littered with papers and scrolls. A scuffed wooden desk and a leather chair dominate the space. There are no windows. We enter, and the guards shut the door behind us.

When we are alone, I wrench my arm away from Nolan. "What are you thinking, coming here like this?" I demand. "How could you have been so foolish as to try to deceive her? Please tell me your father has a plan."

He chews his lower lip, eyes glued to the door. "It's not a deception," he stammers, keeping his voice low so the guards will not overhear. "Your father wrote to mine after we met. He invited us to your château. We thought—"

"You thought it was decided."

He nods and gives me a shy smile. "I thought we were getting along well at the pub. You seemed to enjoy my company, and . . . I think you are beautiful."

"And you think that is enough to build a marriage?" I exhale sharply and shake my head. "I do enjoy your company, but not in that way. I told my father I would like to see you again because I thought it would make him happy. After this year's Performing, he needed to have hope that I would escape it next year."

Nolan crosses his arms. "What's so wrong with me?"

I scan his rich umber skin, his chiseled jaw with its trace of black stubble, his hurt, gentle eyes. I think back to our meeting at the pub. He made me laugh, then helped me devour a steak pie. But I compare his square, broad shoulders to Cadence's slight, delicate frame, and there is no question of what I prefer.

He's perfect, but he isn't *right.*

"Nothing," I say honestly.

"Is it because I am a commoner, then?"

"We barely know each other, and—"

"*Is it because I am a commoner?*" he repeats. His voice deepens into a growl. "You want to keep your title? Afraid that your noble lady friends will laugh at you if you lower your station? The country has changed, in case you haven't noticed. None of those things matter anymore."

"No," I hiss, my own anger flaring. "It's because you're a *man.*"

"What?" Nolan asks. His nose wrinkles in confusion. Then, slowly, his jaw slackens, his eyes widening as he plays over what I said. "Oh."

"You see? What you're telling the queen is impossible," I whisper.

"Does your father know?"

I shake my head. "No. I'm afraid of how he'll react. He's only trying to marry me off to protect me. If I lose my title, I'll never have to go through the Performing again."

Nolan stands frozen for a moment, then sits on the edge of

the desk. He pushes the clerk's papers aside and pats the space beside him. Sighing, I sit.

He takes my hand and squeezes. "What if we just tell the queen we're betrothed?" he asks. "We can keep up the game long enough to get you out of here. We carry on for a while, play the giddy lovers, and then quietly call it off once the queen has found other prisoners to occupy her dungeons." He grins and gives me a roguish wink. "Then you'll be free to marry the second most beautiful girl in the world."

I roll my eyes at him, then lean my head against his shoulder. "As if it could ever be so simple."

He shrugs. "Why not? We know lots of folk in the city with spouses of the same gender, and some who are living in polyamorous households, like the mages."

Even if I can't love him the way he wants, I feel a rush of affection for him. He's only the second person I've ever told how I feel about women. And the first not to condemn me for it.

"I still don't think that will work. The queen has appointed me as a companion to her principal singer. If she lets me walk out of here, she will watch us for the rest of our lives."

"Principal singer? That creature who tortured you at the Opera Hall?"

I wince. "She doesn't truly want to do it. She's almost as

much a prisoner as I am. They all are. You should see what they do to the children."

"So you're both just going to stay here as prisoners?" Nolan lifts a brass seal from the clerk's collection and points to the queen's crest on its face. "She'll kill you. Maybe not now. But eventually."

"It may happen soon. She's hosting a ball. Maybe I'm to be the main attraction."

He cups my cheek and exhales. "I know."

"You know? I thought the invitations were only going out to nobles."

"Things are in motion," he says seriously. "My father is in communication with the leader-elect in the Expelled settlement. They are giving us key information on the queen, the palace, even magic. Many of the Expelled have worked in the palace. They're mages. They still have friends in the academy."

I nod. So many mages have been exiled since the queen took power. It makes sense that at least a few of them still have connections to old friends at the palace. "Aren't you afraid to send letters there? In case one of the queen's spies intercepts them? They watch the settlement closely to make sure no one sends aid."

Nolan makes a series of gestures, fingers moving too fast for me to follow. "They have their own language in the settlement, complex hand signals, that neither the queen nor her spies understand. I'm learning. So is my father. We have an apprentice who is Expelled, kept hidden, of course. He's been helping us and arranging meetings."

"Dangerous for him. He must be very brave."

"He was a corporeal mage. He failed his examinations on purpose. He knew he'd be expelled and sent to the settlement, but he didn't want to pass the exam only to be forced to join the justicars."

I let out a low whistle.

After a quick glance at the closed door, Nolan reaches inside his jacket to pull out a letter. "We received this."

I recognize the broken seal immediately: copper wax, a rearing horse with a mane of flames. It's our house crest. The handwriting is Mama's, tight and practical. I snatch it from him and tear it open, desperate for news of her. As I scan the letter, my eyes widen. It's addressed to Nolan's father.

The letter details the circumstances of Papa's imprisonment, and mine. It urges Jon to carry on, to continue building forces for the rebellion in secret. The queen's allegations about Papa are true, and my mother has been involved the whole time.

My eyes well with tears. I don't understand why my parents kept this a secret from me. Nolan's father trusted him. My own mother trusted Nolan more than me.

I brandish the letter at him. "So it's true. My parents are traitors."

His eyes flash. "They are heroes. My father is proud to be involved in the work they're doing."

"They've never told me anything about it." Deep down, I know that they probably believed they were keeping me safe, but it feels like betrayal all the same. I had been so sure of Papa's innocence, and my own responsibility for our situation.

"How long have you known?" I ask.

"A year. It's one of the reasons I agreed to meet with you, when my father proposed that we might be married. And why I was so shocked that my class might matter to you. I never wanted to marry a spoiled aristocrat, but I would be happy to wed a daughter of revolution."

A smile pulls at my lips. "And? Am I a spoiled aristocrat?"

He takes my hands solemnly. "Not even a little bit." Extracting the letter from my hands, he tucks it back into his coat pocket. "If the queen tries to execute anyone at the ball, we'll be ready to act in the city. The queen proclaims that she's done so much for the common people, but most of it is lies. In theory, we commoners have more legal rights than we did under the old queen, but in reality, justicars roam the streets attacking anyone who gets in their way. The city coffers are empty, and business is dry. No one is thinking about her new universities when so many can't afford to eat. Her spies are everywhere, and people just disappear, like you and your father, shepherded away to the palace dungeons without a trial. The old system may have been broken, but this is no better. As far as most of us are concerned, the queen's mages are the same as the courtiers before. She just traded one set of nobles for another."

I let out a low whistle. "Whatever you're planning, I hope you know what you're doing."

Nolan smooths a hand over his hair and grins. "I hope we do, too. But no risks, no gains, right? Do you think you can get your singer friend to help us?"

"I believe in Cadence," I say. "I think she's ready to stand up to the queen. She just needs a push."

Nolan shakes his head. "Her life at Cavalia is good. Probably better than whatever she had before coming to the queen's service. What would motivate her to risk this?"

"She knows what this life costs. She goes to the hospital of Saint Izelea to heal people. I think if the queen weren't making her Perform, it's all she would want to do."

"Saint Izelea's?" Nolan frowns. "How often does she go there? Was she there the night before you got arrested?"

"Yes. She was healing a boy—"

Nolan cradles his head in his hands.

"What?" I ask.

"That boy is the eldest son of a craftsman in my father's guild. He works for a tailor with wealthy clients, so we can pass messages without suspicion."

I nod, pleased that I know something. "Master Dupois."

"He was delivering a package outside a tavern on the outskirts of the city when one of the queen's police squads apprehended him. It was led by the chief justicar."

The memory of Ren's spell, numbing my legs so I couldn't move, freezing my eyes so I was forced to cry, floods back. I wince. "I've met him."

Nolan nods grimly. "Then you know what he's like. He saw Clarence and thought he looked suspicious. The tavern is in Breclin—it's not the nicest neighborhood, and Clarence was wearing his best suit, on account of the person he was sent to meet."

"Who was he meeting?"

"I'd rather not say."

When I give an offended grunt and cross my arms, Nolan rushes to say, "It's not that I don't trust you. Even in the resistance, we get told information on a need-to-know basis. That way, if we're caught, we can't give everything away, even under the worst torture." He rubs the back of his neck ruefully. "Though your father knows an awful lot. Dad is desperate to get him out."

Despite our situation, a glow of pride settles inside me. These people trust Papa. They know my father would never betray them. He's strong, and if Mama is caught up in this, too, he'll die before he gives her away.

"What happened to the boy?" I ask.

"Ren put a binding spell on him. At first no one thought anything was really wrong. He went home and ate his dinner with no problem. But when he woke up in the morning, he said he felt like a snake was constricting his chest. A day later, the first of his ribs cracked."

"And he went to Saint Izelea's? Did the nuns know who he was?"

"Only the Superior knows for sure," Nolan says. "She can be trusted."

I remember Sister Elizabeta's stalwart defiance of Ren in his torture parlor, her unyielding posture. The way she silenced Mercedes. "Yes, I'm sure she can."

"It's Cadence I'm worried about," Nolan says. "The usual singer at Saint Izelea's isn't very good. When we arrived, Sister Elizabeta told my father she would send a courier for someone who might be able to help Clarence. We didn't stay, but I never imagined she would write to the queen's principal."

"Cadence isn't going to tell anyone."

Nolan takes my shoulders and turns me to face him. His eyes

bore into mine. "Do you know that for sure? Would you stake your father's life on it?"

"I—"

Would Cadence risk everything for me? I've grown comfortable with her again. I like her. I want to believe in her. If Nolan were asking me only about my own life, I might have said yes. But would I trust Cadence with Papa's life?

"If we are to act on the night of the ball, we need someone on the inside to distract the queen and her mages," Nolan says. "If Cadence decides to help us, that's fine. But we have someone else inside already. My father and a small militia will be standing by."

"If she won't act, *I* will," I say through clenched teeth.

"It's too dangerous for you. If she won't do anything, you need to go somewhere you'll be safe. There will be carnage when the militia storms the palace, and if it all goes wrong, you will be among the queen's first suspects."

If fighting breaks out in the palace, I have no intention of hiding in a dark corner somewhere. I need to find my father and get us both out alive.

"I wish you were coming with me today," he says softly.

I rise and take his hands, tugging him to his feet. "You know why I can't. You'd better leave before the queen comes back."

Nolan hugs me. His navy wool coat still smells of pine smoke from his father's workshop, and for a moment, I wonder if I'm making the worst mistake of my life. I can't fall in love with him, but I could love him in a different way. He's right: Believing in Cadence might come to haunt me. She may never stand up to the queen. The city rebels, armed with guns and swords and not magic, might not be enough. At the ball, the queen might finally kill us. Or I may remain a prisoner forever.

"If you change your mind, send word. My family will go along with the marriage. I know they will. And even if you don't love me, I can do this for you. You'd be free to have an affair with any girl you like. I wouldn't take that from you," Nolan says.

Slowly he curls his right hand into a tight fist and taps it on his outstretched left palm. "This is the sign for help in the language of the settlement. A few of the new guards are part of the cause. If you are in trouble—if you need me to come early— light a candle and make this sign at your window."

I mimic his action twice, and he nods with satisfaction.

"Aren't you worried that someone else might notice? Someone who is not a friend?" I ask.

Nolan's lips curve in a wry smile. "These mages put too much stock in their songs. They never notice how much you can say in silence."

He walks to the door and opens it. The guards still linger

in the hallway, leaning against the opposite wall and sharing a smoking pipe between them.

"I need a minute," I say when the guards beckon. "Alone."

Nolan waves to me over his shoulder as one of the guards escorts him down the hall. The other nods to me, then shuts the door again. My eyes stay locked on the closed door long after Nolan's footsteps have faded.

# CHAPTER 25

# REMI

AT MY REQUEST, THE guard agrees to escort me to Cadence's studio. I find her inside, singing lines from an ancient, yellowing sheet of music, her fingers lightly clutching the edge of the wooden music stand.

At first, I hesitate in the doorway. I still don't know why she didn't send for me today. Nor what passed between her and the queen. But then I see that the sleeves of her lilac tunic are pushed up past her elbows, and a faint, pink glow emanates from her skin.

"How does it feel?" I ask, after closing the door.

Cadence jumps at my sudden question. Her skin dims, and her eyes flutter drowsily. "Still weak." She lies down on the floor with a sigh and spreads her arms wide. "And I'm exhausted."

"I was worried when you didn't send for me today."

She grimaces and flicks her wrist toward the music stand. "I went to the library. Some of the other mages use enhancement songs to help their magic along. I wanted to see if I could find one that might work with the defensive spells. I've never needed to use one, so I didn't think of it before." Her cheeks redden. "I didn't want you to see me practice again until I had something to show you."

I flop down beside her, my skirt in a jumble. "A boy came to see me today. He told the queen we were engaged."

Cadence's eyes fly open. Framed by long blond lashes, they are as wide as a doll's. She turns sideways to face me, propping her chin up on her hand. "Are you?"

She offers a smile, but it doesn't reach her eyes.

"No. We were going to be. Our fathers introduced us the day before I met you at the hospital." I clear my throat. "He's the commoner my father wants me to marry. So I won't have to go to the Performing again."

Cadence looks away.

I sigh and adjust my hair self-consciously. The more time Cadence and I spend together, the more anxious I become when we talk about that day. I shouldn't have to feel guilty for mentioning it. *I* didn't cause her pain. And yet I hate the way she closes off as soon as I mention what happened in the Opera Hall. The memory of that day haunts us both, only in different ways.

"Mages are commoners," she murmurs under her breath. Then louder, she asks, "What did you say to him?"

"I said that I couldn't."

"Why not?"

I shrug. "He wasn't right for me."

"But he is right about the Performing." Cadence sits up and tucks her hair behind her ears. I notice for the first time how endearingly large they are for her face. "If you marry him, you'll be free. Elene is even changing some of the old laws. You could still inherit land."

"I don't think I could keep up the charade," I say. "The queen wants me to spy on you. She wants to use me. If I ruin that for her, she'll watch me for the rest of my life. Nolan and I would have to stay married."

"To the end of your life and beyond," Cadence agrees. "Elene can hold a grudge. This whole queendom is in disarray because of it."

"I wish I could talk to my father about it."

Cadence toys with the hem of her tunic. When she looks back up at me, her eyes glimmer with a mischief I haven't seen in her since we were children. "We could go and see him."

"How?" I ask, unable to keep the suspicion from my voice.

I glance toward the door. On the other side, two guards await to return me to my chambers once Cadence is finished with me. All of my comings and goings are monitored, and at night, the captain personally locks the gate to my wing. My father will be under even tighter supervision.

"Elene is holding a briefing in her audience chamber before dinner. She wanted me to come, but I told her I needed to practice, and that satisfied her. She wants the guards to hear their orders from her directly in advance of the ball. She won't leave anything to chance, since so many of them are new." Cadence says.

I point to the studio's door, where I know the captain waits. "What about him? He'll be staring right at us."

Cadence stands and goes to the studio window. She fumbles with the latch, then pushes it open. A gust of cold wind blows into the room, carrying the scents of winter roses and lobelia with it. "We'll have to climb down."

"What?" I join her at the window and peer over the ledge. The palace walls are made of smooth, slick stone, but a delicate vine of browning ivy creeps up to the window. Cadence's studio is on the second level. The ground looks a long, long way down. Maybe Cadence's magic gives her bones some extra resilience, but mine will surely break if I fall.

"I used to do this all the time when I was trying to avoid Ren," Cadence says. She crouches on the windowsill and points to the vine. "Just walk along it. It won't break."

"Only for you," I grumble as she swings her leg over the edge and begins to descend.

She smirks. "I've never known you to be afraid."

"Heights are my weakness," I mutter. There are so many ridiculous things I've imagined myself doing to rescue Papa: charging in aboard Chance with a raised pistol, defending him in a courtroom, sneaking through the dungeons in the dead of night . . . Scaling a wall has never featured in my daydreams.

"Are you sure about this? What if we get caught?"

She doesn't answer me. I lean out the window as far as I can and watch her. She moves nimbly, shuffling along the vine's main branch until she reaches the frost-blanketed grass below us. She waves up at me, beaming.

This is the price if I want to see Papa. I've told myself I would do anything. Now is the time to prove it.

I gather my skirt and step out onto the ledge. Trying not to look down, I lower my left foot until I feel the vine beneath it. My head swims with vertigo, but I slowly ease my full weight onto the vine. The wind makes the leaves billow around my ankles, but the vine does not give way. I exhale a cloud of frosty white steam. I scoot along the vine, growing more confident with each movement.

As I shuffle closer to the ground, I speed up. I will see Papa.

I *will.* I'm going to tell him I'm sorry. That Nolan told me everything. I'm going to tell him how proud I am of him and Mama.

Without warning, my shoe catches on the hem of my long dress, and my right foot slips from the stalk of the vine. I bite my tongue to hold back a scream.

"One step at a time," Cadence whispers from below. "Just one step."

I grit my teeth. "I'm doing it."

By the time I reach the ground, I'm dizzy from the blood pounding in my ears. I flex my numb fingers. My grip on the vine was so tight that the texture of the plant's gnarled stem has imprinted on my palm. I button my wool coat up to my neck, the cold wind in the garden nips at my cheeks.

Cadence laughs. She slings her arm over my shoulder and whispers the eerily familiar words of the heat song. At first, I tense in recognition. The words of the song are burned into my memory after what I suffered in the Opera Hall. But as a quiet, gentle warmth spreads up from my toes, I slowly relax. Despite the snowflakes sticking to my hair, I feel summer sun kiss my skin. I strip off my coat and fold it over my arm.

Cadence is dressed in only her tunic. The hairs on her arms are standing on end. Snowflakes cling to her eyelashes, melting into winter tears that make trails down her flushed cheeks.

To warm herself must be another type of forbidden self-magic. Something inside me stirs, and I imagine what it would be like to kiss her tears away. I shake out my coat and drape it over her shoulders.

She bites her lip, cheeks glowing. "Thank you. I can't use the same spell on myself."

"I know."

"Come on," she says, and reaches for my hand. I stare at our entwined hands. I think that I should pull away, but I don't want to. Even if this is another sign I'm misreading, I want it to last. Her fingers are so small, her nails short and jagged.

Cadence leads us through the gardens, around the back of the west wing. She's right about the guards. A few stand at their posts along the outer wall, but none pace the walkways. The palace's central courtyard is nearly deserted. A trio of novice mages gossip beneath a barren tree. They wear bright red hoods and emerald mittens. None of them look older than twelve. When they see Cadence, two of them curtsy to her before dispersing.

The third walks over to us, her eyes on the ground and her hands pushed deep in her pockets. When she reaches us, she looks up at Cadence, eyes shining with tears.

Then she spits at Cadence's feet.

The action has so much venom in it that Cadence does a

double take; then she snaps, "Novice, what is the meaning of this?"

The child's chin trembles, but she lifts it defiantly. "That was for Anette."

She darts away, leaving Cadence to stare after her. I marvel at the girl's courage. After seeing how the mage children are raised in the palace, she must know the consequences that could befall her for such a display. The brightness that lit Cadence's features dims. She stares at the snow, her lips pressed together.

"Who is Anette?" I ask, as I try to reach for her hand again.

She crosses her arms and doesn't meet my eyes. "She was to be my apprentice. It didn't work out."

"What happened?" I ask, resting my hand on her shoulder.

She closes her eyes as tears leak from under her lashes. "She wasn't strong. I was giving her private lessons. We have exams every year, but it is the ones after fourth year that really matter. If you fail, you have to leave. It used to be that mages who failed just went home, became apprentices, and the like. But now . . . well, Elene doesn't want trained mages out there who don't work for her, so they're all sent to the Expelled settlement. Vocal cords cut. It's a miserable, hopeless place."

My tongue itches with the knowledge Nolan gave me, that in the Expelled settlement, the mages are organizing, fighting back. But even though I know it would comfort her, I can't tell Cadence. Not until I'm sure where her allegiance lies.

"When I stood up to Elene, I asked for Anette to be made my apprentice. I thought it would give me time to work with her, and that no one would question her abilities if the principal picked her," she continues, her tone bitter.

She sits beneath the tree, in the space the novices vacated. I sit beside her, our shoulders so close I can feel the moment when she breaks. Her body tenses and begins to shake as a wave of sobs crashes through her.

"She was so young," Cadence whispers. "She looked like a doll when we practiced together, just a tiny girl stuffed into an expensive velvet dress. She must have spent hours curling her hair. She really wanted to impress Elene. Impress me."

Watching her cry, when I know there is something I could say to make it a little better, is one of the hardest things I've ever done. But all I can do is sit here and watch her suffer. I run my hand over her hair. Her sobs grow deeper and more desperate, until I'm sure that she's not just crying for Anette, but for herself and her dog, and everyone she must have lost over the years to the queen's viciousness.

"I didn't ask about her," she says. "When she was taken, I heard her outside my window. I tried to help, but afterward I made myself believe it wasn't her. I was so consumed with my grief over Nip, I didn't want to believe it. I didn't ask Elene about her until days later. Far too late."

Cadence leans against the tree's trunk and stares up at the patches of sky visible through the sparse leaves. She sniffs and wipes her face on her sleeve. Then she pushes herself to her feet. "Let's go. We don't have much time before the briefing is over."

# CHAPTER 26

# REMI

AS WE DRAW NEAR, the sight of the dungeon makes all the memories of my time in the cells and Ren's parlor rush back. I feel sick with rage that my father is still in there. The queen promised me Papa would have rooms of his own, servants, and ample food befitting his station. She lied.

"Don't worry. He's not in the cells anymore," Cadence says, when she notices I have stopped following her.

"He shouldn't be here at all," I hiss.

We edge closer to the door. Cadence begins to sing, her voice so soft I can only catch the barest hint of melody. The guards on the palace walls do not turn to face us. I reach for the door handle, my hand shaking, then slowly ease it open, just wide enough to squeeze through.

We slip inside. A staircase sits behind the door, with steps leading down to the common dungeon and up to the cells where I had been held. Ren's torture parlor is near the top. I reach for Cadence's hand again, and this time, she does not pull away.

"The prison has five levels," she explains as we begin to climb the steps. "Political prisoners like your father are housed at the top. There are actual rooms up there. It's fairly comfortable. We'll have to sneak past Ren's rooms, though, and I expect him to be in. He and Elene have already met to plan for the ball. His studio is on the fourth level."

Papa might still be so angry he'll refuse to speak to me. From what Nolan said, my parents have been involved in the resistance for years, evading arrest. My visit to the hospital jeopardized everything.

On the fourth landing, the door behind us flies open. Ren bursts out of his parlor, clothed in a simple dressing gown, his feet bare. "Stop," he commands, almost sleepily. He rubs his eyes and *giggles*. "In the name of the queen. You do not belong up here."

I brace myself to run. Even if Ren chases me, even if Papa won't speak to me, I've come too far not to see him. Ren has a strangely dazed expression on his face, as if we've just woken him up from a luxurious nap. I believe I can outrun him and snatch a few precious seconds with my father. It will be enough to see what promises the queen has kept, to make sure he's alive.

But Cadence lets go of my hand and steps around me. Ren towers over her by a foot. "You reek of wine," she mutters.

"You should not speak to me in such a way, little Quarter Note," he slurs. He takes a wobbly step toward her. "Her Majesty's instructions are explicit. No visitors for the viscount. Now be a good girl and run back to your room, and I won't have to punish you."

Cadence is trembling, her fingers shaking at her sides. But she speaks anyway, her voice slightly higher than usual. "Really? Her Majesty didn't make that clear to me . . ."

"Oh no," Ren cackles. "You don't fool me with your little act. Her Majesty may have chosen to believe you didn't know about that boy at Saint Izelea's, but I know you did. You knowingly aided a criminal—"

He takes another step toward us, and, unconsciously, I move to shield Cadence with my body.

Ren reaches for me, and a hint of awareness flickers in his eyes. He opens his mouth.

Cadence begins to sing. Ren staggers backward and falls. He

knocks his head against the wooden doorframe, and a trail of blood seeps down from his hairline. He moans, already asleep, and a soft snore escapes.

"Goddess's bones," Cadence whispers. All the color has drained from her cheeks. She seems as surprised as I am by her own actions. "What have I done?"

I stare down at Ren's limp form, then give his side a little kick. "That was amazing."

"He's going to be so angry."

"Shh." I take her shoulders and turn her to face me. "He's not going to do anything. He's drunk. He might not even remember this."

Cadence stares at the justicar, then stoops and grabs one of his arms. "You're right. Quick, take his other arm. If we can get him onto his couch, he may think the whole thing a dream. And even if he doesn't, Elene won't believe his story. She hates it when he drinks. She thinks it ruins him for his job."

Wrinkling my nose in distaste, I snatch the justicar's forearm. Ren's skin is clammy, cold to the touch. His breathing is shallow but even. His state doesn't quite seem like sleep, but I don't dare ask for more details of the spell Cadence used.

Cadence pushes open the door to the parlor with her hip. We drag Ren between us, through the center of the room, not caring if we knock him against the furniture. For a slight man, his weight is impressive. My shoulders scream with the effort of dragging him.

When Ren brought me into his parlor before, everything was orderly, sickeningly reminiscent of my home but for the trembling prisoners in the corner. But the justicar clearly has a different way of living when he is alone. The couches are pushed together. A plate of half-eaten doughnuts rests on the cushions, and empty wine bottles litter the floor. The acrid scent of vomit lingers.

We hoist Ren onto the couch beside his food. Cadence picks up a jam doughnut and smears it down his front. Then she takes a bottle of wine from the table and wedges it under his arm. Some of the red liquid sloshes onto his breeches. I grimace, but Ren's eyelashes don't even flutter.

Cadence points to the wine rack across the room. "Pull another bottle down and pour it over him."

"What?"

"We want him to think this was a drunken dream," Cadence says. "But if he wakes up and the first thing he smells is my magic on his skin, he'll know he didn't imagine it. Worse, if he goes straight to Elene, she'll smell it, too. Dump the wine on him."

I retrieve the bottle and uncork it with my teeth. I give

Cadence another questioning look, but when she nods, I upend the bottle over Ren's hair, face, and clothes.

"Won't he question why he's soaking wet?"

Cadence shrugs. "Maybe, but Elene will just think he got in a brawl or did this to himself. He does this a lot. Drinks too much. They fight about it."

She presses another doughnut into his free hand, then straightens. "We should get going. Ren won't wake up for a while, but the guards will be finishing up."

I nod. Ren's color has started to return, but his snores are growing louder. We pick our way across the room, taking care not to step on any of the discarded bottles. Cadence eases the door shut behind us. I wait until the latch clicks, then race up the remaining stairs.

At the top of the staircase is a lone door. It's made from black glass and reflects our likenesses. There is no handle that I can see, only an empty keyhole and small slot along the bottom that I assume allows the guards to pass Papa his meals.

I walk up to the door and push. It doesn't budge. I kneel and squint through the slot. I can just make out the leg of a plain wooden chair and a carpeted floor, bathed in candlelight.

"Papa?" I hiss.

I hear the sound of a book snapping shut, followed by footsteps. Then Papa's nose and lips press up against the slot. "Remi?"

My shoulders slump with relief. He's alive. "Are you all right?"

Papa extends his hand through the slot. I grasp it. His fingers are almost as cold as Cadence's were outside, in the garden.

"It's certainly better than where they kept me before," he says. "Tell me, are *you* all right?"

"I am," I choke out. "I'm housed in the palace's east wing."

"Good. It means everything to me that you are safe."

"I can't see inside your cell. Does Ren have the key?" I don't relish the idea of trying to steal the keys off Ren's spelled body, but I want to hug Papa so badly it makes my whole chest ache.

I need to talk to him about the resistance. And if I'm going to tell him about Nolan, and about me, then I need to see his face. I want to know his true reaction, see the look in his eyes, not just hear whatever he will say.

"The door is specially made," Papa says. "From what I can tell, it requires two separate keys to open. They fit together, like a puzzle. The captain of the guard has one, the chief justicar the other. They always come together."

"Damn it," I curse.

Papa laughs, but it ends in a string of coughing. "Don't worry about me."

"Do you have a fire in there? Have they been feeding you?"

He doesn't respond, and his silence tells me everything I need to know.

"We have to get him out of here." I rise and take Cadence's hands again. "We have to."

She glances out the tower's slit window and bites her lip. "We have to leave. I just saw one of the guards outside take his post. The briefing is over. They'll be taking their evening-shift stations soon."

I gesture to the glass door. "Can't you do anything about this? Blast it apart or something?"

Cadence scowls. "The door is made from mageglass. Even a mage who is skilled with the elements wouldn't be able to break it alone. I can't do it."

On the other side of the door, Papa sighs. "Don't worry about me. I'll be fine as long as I know you're safe. Have you heard from your mother?"

But I ignore him. The queen has broken our agreement. While Papa might not be in the lower dungeons anymore, she promised me he would have every comfort. And yet he is here, freezing and alone.

"The queen, then. You can do something about the queen at the ball! You could demand his release in front of the court," I plead.

"She wouldn't listen to me. It may make her order me to torture all of you, just to prove she could."

"You just bested Ren! Surely that's proof that you're strong enough to stand up to her?"

"He was drunk! And I didn't mean to. I just sang before he could hurt you. Elene will be expecting me to fight her. She'll be prepared," Cadence growls. She pulls on my arm and moves toward the stairs. "I'm not sure of any of my shield spells yet. I might not be able to ward against her. I can't take the risk. Not yet. I have to wait until I'm ready."

She offers me a conciliatory half smile, but anger swells inside me. Nolan was right. She's willing to leave my father behind, in this cell, without food or a fire. He doesn't matter to her.

As much as Cadence might hate what the queen makes her do in the Opera Hall, she's safe in the palace, protected by her status. She is the queen's principal singer. If the queen loses her throne, Cadence's position, maybe even her life, are forfeit. Why would she choose to help us?

"You said that when you let Anette be taken, you were only thinking about yourself and your grief," I snap, knowing how cruel my words are. "You're only thinking about yourself again, and how scared you are. You haven't changed at all."

I know as soon as the words are out that I pushed too far. She bites the inside of her cheek, and her eyes swim with grief.

I open my mouth to apologize, but she storms down the stairs without another word to me. With a parting tap on the mageglass door, I follow.

# CHAPTER 27

# REMI

I KNOW THAT MY words hurt Cadence, but I don't have time to dwell on how to fix things between us. Almost as soon as we scramble up the vine and back into her studio, the captain of the guard knocks on the door. He takes in our sweaty and slightly disheveled appearances, clucks his tongue, and insists on returning me to the east wing.

In my room, an entourage of royal tailors waits to fit my dress for the ball, accompanied by Cadence's maid, Lacerde. The head tailor steers me over to the mirror, and her assistants strip off my clothes. They prod and pinch me, spinning me around until I feel sick.

But when they finish and turn me to face the mirror, I stare at myself. I thought that the gown was perfect before, but now it melts onto my body. I gawk and swish my skirt, twirling and twirling. Mama has always made sure that I dressed well, but I've never owned something that fits like this. The tailors trim the gown's hem until it floats just above my feet to skim the carpet.

They seat me in the room's lone chair so Lacerde can style my hair. The maid piles my copper curls atop my head and secures them with diamond pins. Then she dabs rouge powder that tastes of sawdust on my lips.

I glance out the window as carriages file through the palace's open gates. It reminds me of my childhood, of happier times in Cannis. Despite the dangers, everyone will come to this ball, as they always do to the Performings, so grateful to still be alive that they will demonstrate every obedience to the queen.

Everyone will want to believe that this is the year things finally get better.

And this year, they will. Outside the palace gates, in the heart of the city, the resistance stirs.

As the tailors put their kit away, I snatch a pair of scissors and hastily hide them in the folds of my skirt. I'm to provide a distraction, but once the resistance forces break in, I need to be able to defend myself. If the queen sets her guards on me, I don't want the only blood spilled to be my own. I need a weapon.

When the mages have finished with me, they leave the room without a word. Lacerde lingers behind. She presses her fingers to her lips, and we wait as the sound of the mages' footsteps grows fainter down the hall.

"I saw you take those scissors," she says.

Cold sweat collects on my forehead, and I curse myself for being so foolish, so brash. I think about denying it, but that will only make me look guiltier.

I draw the scissors out from under my skirt and lay them on the dressing table. It is a crime in Bordea to bring weapons into the palace. If Lacerde turns me in now, Queen Elene may suspect that I am working with the resistance. I must convince her that I had another use in mind for the scissors.

"I thought I might need them later. My hair never stays put, and I might need to trim the edges . . . ," I say.

It sounds completely implausible, even to my own ears.

Lacerde raises an eyebrow. "I would be more than happy to trim it for you."

"What a relief." I smooth my skirt and give her a wide smile.

Lacerde does not smile back. If anything, her stern frown grows deeper. She holds out her hand. Swallowing, I place the scissors on her palm.

She tucks them into her bag and draws out a white suede pouch. "If you're going to do what I think you are," she says. "Then you should be better prepared."

She passes the pouch to me and heat radiates through the

leather. When I untie the laces that hold the pouch closed, a pungent vinegar scent assaults my nostrils. Bracing myself, I reach inside and draw out a pearl hairpin inlaid with diamonds and rubies.

The metal of the hairpin's back is so hot, I drop it on the floor. Lacerde stoops to pick it up, using her skirt to protect her fingers, then deposits it in my lap. "Lay your hand on it," she instructs. "It will only burn for a moment. Then it will get used to you."

I don't argue, even though the idea of a hair accessory becoming familiar with me, as if it had thoughts of its own, is unsettling. I rest my palm atop the pearl face. A tickling sensation ripples up my arm. The heat drains out of the pin, leaving it temperate. I pick it up again and turn it over in my hands. It has a strange clasp; the beautiful facade conceals a clear glass box filled with orange liquid. It fastens with a long, flat pin, the edge serrated like a steak knife.

"What is this?" I ask.

"What does it look like?"

I scowl at her. "You know what I meant."

Lacerde smiles then, and wrinkles crease around her eyes. "Young Nolan thought you might try to take things into your own hands. If he was right, I think you should have this."

I stare at her. Cadence's own maid, part of the rebellion?

"It's magical," I accuse, running my finger along the pin. Now the edge is dull like a butter knife, but somehow I know that it would pierce whatever I drove it into.

She nods.

"But how?" I demand. "Is one of the mages in the palace working with you, too?"

For a breath, I dare to hope that Cadence might have made this. That she has changed her mind and is ready to confront the queen at last. "Did Cadence—"

"No. This was made by a mage in the Expelled settlement."

I shake my head. She must be mistaken. Those who live in the settlement have long since been stripped of their magic. "But Adela only gifts singers with magic."

Lacerde gives a sharp bark of laughter and rolls her eyes. "As you know, the goddess of song ordains her disciples by choosing the time of their conception. She alone controls who will be born a mage. The queen might believe that she can strip away Adela's gifts by mutilating her chosen, but only the goddess can remove that divine power.

"Last I checked," Lacerde continues. "Her Majesty is still mortal, no matter how she fashions herself. The Expelled can no longer sing, but their magic endures. Adela, in her fury, chooses to hear the song inside them."

My heart pounds in my chest, so strong my ears ring. If there are mages in the settlement, mages who have every reason to work against the queen, it changes everything.

"How do you know all of this?" I demand.

"I was an administrator in the palace many years ago, in the old queen's days." Lacerde gives me a sad smile and looks down at her hands. Like Mama, she has a thick callus on her index finger from years of writing correspondence. "I met Francine then, and for many years, I was one of her partners. Even after I chose to leave the palace, met someone else, and had my daughter, we remained very close friends. It was a risk for me to come back here, even as a lowly maid, but Francine needed someone who knew the palace, and who could get close to Cadence. It was so many years ago when I'd last worked at Cavalia—I was a young woman then—that no one remembered me."

"Francine Trevale made this? And the queen has no suspicions?" I ask breathlessly.

Francine Trevale is the most famous mage ever to be cast out of the palace. She was so powerful that the queen didn't dare arrest her publicly, only managing it through deception. Francine's downfall had been a turning point in the war, the time at which many lost hope. I run my fingers over the suede pouch in my lap, my confidence surging.

I have to tell Cadence. She has to know that there are other mages working against the queen.

"The queen does not," Lacerde says. She takes the hairpin from me and gently tucks it into my hair. "Nor can she. Her mages outnumber those in the settlement, and they have had years of training with their voices. In the settlement, they are still figuring out how to access their powers again."

I start to rise from my chair. "I have to talk to Cadence."

Lacerde puts her hands on my shoulders and pushes me back into my seat. She takes a deep breath, and her eyes shine with tears. "You cannot. If Cadence is to help us, she must make her own choice. After everything she's done, it's the only way the resistance will accept her. I have been hoping for it, encouraging it, for years, but Cadence herself must take the leap."

# CHAPTER 28

# CADENCE

**I SIT ON MY** pianoforte bench and rest my head on the keyboard. Tears flow freely down my nose, and I bang my fists on the keys. The discord of notes gives voice to my pain. I opened up to Remi, confided in her, and she threw it all in my face.

I am still wearing Remi's thick, wool coat around my shoulders. It smells of her hair oil, buttery with a touch of vanilla. I strip it off and toss it into the corner of the room.

She's angry with me for leaving her father behind in the prison, but there was nothing else I could have done. He's sealed behind mageglass. He isn't getting out unless Elene orders it.

I chew on my fingernails, now bitten so low my nail beds are red and weeping underneath. In her own way, Elene has helped me. She saw my potential and took me from the academy. She gave me a role at her court. I could have ended up like Mercedes, scraping a living in the city hospital. My song is powerful, but I've always known that without a patron to support me, I will have nothing.

Elene is the reason that so many now live in poverty and disgrace, but she is also the impetus behind my ascension.

I open my hollowed-out volume of music theory and take out the romance novel concealed inside. I've read the book three times, but it's one of the first books Sister Elizabeta ever procured for me, and just holding it makes me feel closer to her. Saint Izelea's has been given over to a new Superior and I am forbidden from visiting.

The book tells the tale of two women, both mages, who met during the Brogan Wars as rival generals. I flip through it to a section in the middle. Here, the pages are creased and stained, the edges torn. In the chapter, the two women make love for the first time.

The author of the volume is a man. And he isn't a mage. One of the generals uses single-word spells to bring pleasure to her lover, and I'm not sure if the author understands magic or anatomy.

Still, I find comfort in the pages. I don't have friends at the academy I can discuss this with: passion, love, sex. Resting the book on my knees, I lean back against the wall. Would Remi like this sort of magic? Under my breath, I whisper the single-word spell, my face aflame.

The door bangs open suddenly, and Elene enters, a petite red-haired girl trailing in her shadow. I hastily shove the book aside, but Elene doesn't spare it a glance. She wraps her arm around the shaking girl's shoulder and steers her forward.

"This is Margaret," Elene says. She smiles at the girl, who offers her a trembling grimace in return. I vaguely recognize her as one of the older students who was in the library when I worked with Anette. "She is a sixth-year novice, and a corporeal singer. Madam Guillard tells me she's very promising. I thought you might like to work with her. She's too advanced to be an apprentice, but she can be an understudy, of sorts."

"An understudy?" I echo. After what Elene did to Anette, I will never allow myself to become attached to another student again.

"Yes." Elene smiles. "I've given her rooms in the palace just down the hall from yours. I think it's best if we have you two training for the Performing together, don't you? I know your nerves have been a bit fragile of late, and Dame Ava has been so ill."

Though her smile is friendly, her meaning is clear: *If you can't do your job, I will replace you with someone who can.*

I swallow and climb to my feet. Margaret curtsies to me, her eyes glued to the studio floor. "Principal."

I remember her laughing in the library. In the past few

weeks, she's transformed into a fearful shadow. I wonder if Ren has already taken over her training.

Elene wants to rattle me, to make me say something she can use against me. So I keep my face blank and passively friendly. "What a wonderful idea," I say. "You'll need someone else to take over my duties if I were to fall ill."

Elene's eyes narrow.

"Hello," I say softly to Margaret, like I might to a frightened kitten, and give her what I hope is a warm smile. "Why don't you show me your scales?"

When I return to my suite, my dress for the ball is arranged on my bed. It's a pale beige, the same color as my skin, with ornate embroidered flowers in pink, purple, and pastel green. The bodice is fitted, made from sheer material. The skirt is full, made of taffeta and structured with bone hoops.

Running my fingers over the fabric makes me smile. I will look beautiful in this dress, but will Remi even notice? She said she couldn't marry Nolan, that he wasn't right for her. But she did not say why. Her *why* threatens to eat me alive.

A mask sits on my bed beside the dress. It's made from bright pink lace, the same shade as the flowers on my gown. I press it to my face, then tie the ribbon behind my head. The eyeholes are not quite wide enough to allow full vision. I see the world as if from behind a sheer veil, all of it tinted pink.

I walk to the dressing table to study my reflection. I'm afraid I will resemble Elene, but I'm shocked to realize I look almost exactly like a painting of the goddess Odetta that hangs in the throne room. Our hair is the same shade of cornflower gold, and the pink of the mask makes my blue eyes look lilac.

So I am to be the centerpiece of Elene's occasion. But in this mask, all I see is a little girl, a frail and delicate thing, playing at divinity. Remi wants me to stand with her, to demand her father's freedom, but pretending that I'm fit to lead a rebellion is fanciful thinking, *playing*, too.

The dress taunts me from my bed. I pick it up and rip the sleeves from the bodice. Flinging it across the room, I ring the bell for Lacerde.

I will wear something else. A dress that makes me feel powerful.

When Lacerde doesn't appear immediately, I press my ear to the oak door that separates my rooms from her small bed-chamber. I can't hear her inside, and a soft song confirms that there is no live matter in the room. For a heartbeat, my stomach seizes with panic, thinking that she is dead behind the door, sliced open on Elene's cruel order because I did not show enough enthusiasm about Margaret.

I sniff the air. I can smell my own songs, and faint layers of other magics from older spells. But there is no fresh hint of cinnamon or iron in the air. I breathe deeply. Ren has not been here in the past few days, and Elene would not send anyone else.

I ring the bell again.

Lacerde rushes into the room out of breath. She carries a leather-bound music folio under her arm, its front cover stamped with Elene's wax seal.

"The queen asked me to bring this to you," she gasps, still panting, though Elene's rooms are in the same wing as mine. "It's what she wants you to sing tonight."

I accept the folio, biting the inside of my cheek to disguise a grimace. I flip open the cover. Inside, Elene has enclosed just two sheets of music. On the top sheet, in her curvy, flamboyant handwriting, she has written *Folio A*. The song is simple, for setting broken bones. I've performed it hundreds of times at Saint Izelea's. Even in front of a crowd, it will be a short performance and not terribly flashy. But the song is rarely rejected by the body, and I am unlikely to embarrass Elene with failure.

Sighing, I pull out the second sheet, which Elene has labeled

*Folio B.* I suck in a breath, and my knees start to shake. The words and notes are unfamiliar, but embossed in gold lettering beneath Elene's handwriting, the title of *Constrictor* appears. It's the same terrible song Ren used to bind the young man from the hospital. This music is the harbinger of a slow, painful death.

Elene told me that if things go well, she will show mercy. If not, she promised a demonstration that would be remembered for a hundred years. The folio is not accompanied by any performance notes. It's not clear who Elene's intended victim is. If there is to be one or many. The melody is not complex, and even without practice, I could sing it to ten or more people. But for a spell like this, even one victim is far too many.

If I do this, there will be no coming back from it.

"What is it?" Lacerde asks gently. "You're shaking."

"I'm going to be sick," I whisper, and then lunge for my chamber pot.

I kneel, then sit back on my heels with the pot in my lap, my shoulders hunched over it as I vomit.

Lacerde crouches on the floor beside me. She pushes my hair off my face and rubs my back in circles as I heave again.

I start to cry as vomit dribbles down my chin, but inside, my resolve hardens. I've never been both so afraid and so sure in my life. I have rationalized doing nothing a hundred times, because it was easier and safer to believe I wasn't capable of doing anything else. But even if I can't defeat Elene, I've always been capable of making the choice to disobey her.

I am not going to sing this song.

I will pray to Adela that nothing will go wrong tonight, that Elene will be happy and refrain from calling for such a terrible demonstration. But if she does, I will refuse. I will get Remi and her father out of Cavalia no matter what. Even if it means being imprisoned, or expelled. Even if it means never seeing her again. Because if I can't stand up to Elene, I don't deserve Remi anyway.

I push the chamber pot away and reach for the music sheet again. I exhale deeply through my nose, then rip it into shreds.

Lacerde's mouth hangs open for a minute, but then she rises and fetches me a glass of water from the table by my bed.

I take a sip and, trying not to look at the pile of shredded paper on the floor, say, "I would like to wear something else."

Lacerde gives an approving nod. She stoops down with a grunt and picks up the gown. "Good. This is hideous. What do you have in mind?"

A smile tugs at my lips. I've missed her brusque manner. Our late-night conversations, the click of her knitting needles, and her barbed comments. I've missed *her*, and at least for an hour, things between us will be as they should be.

# CHAPTER 29

# REMI

I CAST A FINAL glance at myself in the mirror, making sure the hairpin remains in place. It glimmers and sparkles as the diamonds catch the candlelight. A pretty, deadly bauble that no one will suspect of being anything more.

Someone knocks on my door. I gather my skirt and rise to greet them. The ornery captain waits in the hallway, eyes on his brass timepiece.

He wears a new uniform with a burnished velvet coat and cream breeches. He offers a stiff arm to me. At his belt, a set of keys jingle. They are all simple, made of brass and iron, and any one of them could fit in the mageglass lock of Papa's cell.

"The queen will be satisfied. You look nice," he mumbles.

"Shouldn't I? Does the queen plan to ruin all of our clothes?"

I think of the Performing, of all the blood spreading over the floor, and the splashes of vomit on my satin shoes.

The guard rolls his eyes. "As far as I know, the only display of magic tonight will be to set a duke's riding injury—nothing flashy. So long as no one steps out of line."

Beckoning me to follow him, he turns his back and marches down the hall. My hand instinctively goes to my bun. The hairpin pulses warmly against my fingers.

He leads me out into the gardens, and I can't help but gasp. Everything has been transformed for the occasion. Candles lit with blue flame line the cobbled paths. The rosebushes have been dressed in silver garland, their petals teased into full bloom. Paper lanterns hang from the trees. Elegant ladies walk arm in arm, clad in white mink furs and gowns of vibrant silk.

Under the old queen, this is what the court was always like. Opulent and beautiful. But back then, there was a carefree ease to the court that is long gone. Now, the ladies who stroll the garden are gaunt with fear under the rouge dusting their cheeks, their smiles more like grimaces.

The guard tugs me along the widest path toward the west wing and the ballroom. Despite what I know I must do, my mouth waters thinking about all the delicacies the kitchen has prepared for the occasion. There will be pies stuffed with venison and figs, pastries filled with almonds and lemons. My stomach rumbles.

A dozen more guards stand by the entrance to the ballroom. Like their captain, they wear new uniforms of pressed velvet. They all look uncomfortable, not only from the stiff fabric, but at the sight of passing nobles.

As the queen's guards, they are no doubt schooled in tales of our corruption and greed. They probably believe that we ruined the queendom, and that it was Queen Elene who rescued Bordea from chaos. Most of them look far too young to have worked at the court under the old queen.

The captain takes hold of the door handle. He glances down at me. "Ready?"

I smooth the front of my dress. "Of course."

The ballroom is a vision of winter paradise. Real snow carpets the floors, and the immaculate walkways are covered in red rose petals that smell impossibly, magically sweet. Icicles dangle from the ceilings like chandeliers, lit with cold, blue elemental fire. An ice table laden with food stands beside the door. At its center, a living rosebush grows, and tiny, translucent ice hummingbirds flutter beside it. Though they are not technically alive, they glitter in the winter light, their movements joyful. One of the queen's mages stands in the corner beside the table, wearing a white gown and mask, so she nearly blends in with the decor. She sings softly as the birds alight on the shoulders of passing guests, chirping merrily before disintegrating into snow.

Beyond the dance floor, an ice floe stage floats on a shallow, artificial lake. Lightning dances across the water's surface. Fish made from ice swim around the stepping-stones that lead onto the stage.

The dances have already begun. Lords and ladies in masks twirl and cavort in front of the queen's dais. Two mages, also clad in white, sing a duet together. The queen sits on a throne entirely made of ice, wearing a snow leopard's fur fastened into a shawl around her shoulders. Her dress is as red as amaryllis, covered in pearls that form a snowstorm across her skirt. Her mask is simple and white, without adornment. Her silver-haired lover sits to her left, clad in evergreen and looking bored with the proceedings, slouching as she holds an empty wine glass.

On the queen's other side, Cadence sits in a carved, straight-back stone chair. Her long blond hair has been curled into ringlets, and she is wearing gold lip paint that sparkles under the icicles' light. Her gown is made from rich, royal purple velvet, with one long sleeve that ends in a gold cuff. Her other shoulder is bare, dusted with a faint gold shimmer. The skirt is short at the front, cut just below her knees, with an elegant train at the back.

Unlike everyone else at the party, she holds her mask in her hands. It is made from pink muslin and doesn't match her dress at all. It's a small act of resistance that makes me wonder what she would have said if I'd trusted her enough to tell her everything.

I disentangle myself from the captain and step toward her. But before I can make my way over to the dais, I feel a tap on my shoulder.

I turn to find Baron Gregor Foutain, my friend from the Performing, smiling at me. He's dressed in his finest, no holes in his waistcoat or smudges on his lapel this time. His black suit has a long black cape that brushes the floor behind him, and his eyebrows are curled upward in the latest style. He walks toward me with a mahogany cane and a slight limp.

"Baron!" I dip a curtsy to him. "You look in better spirits than the last time I saw you."

His eyes dart anxiously around the ballroom, and he dabs his sweaty face with a handkerchief. "Don't take this the wrong way, my lady, but I had hoped never to see you at a function such as this again."

One of the little hummingbirds lands on my shoulder, chattering. "I don't know," I say as I stroke its cold breast. "Tonight may be full of surprises."

The baron gives a sharp laugh. "You don't believe that."

He taps the pin on his lapel, depicting his house crest. "My brother was wearing this the night he died. I had it recovered and shined up a bit. If I'm to die, I'll go out a Foutain."

The hummingbird disintegrates into a puff of snow. The cold is just a whisper against my cheek, but I feel it course through my whole body. "I'm sure it won't come to that."

Shaking his head, the baron rises on his toes, looking over my head. "Where is your father? I had hoped to catch him here."

"He was detained," I say carefully. If news of Papa's arrest hasn't leaked out beyond his close friends, I don't want to trust the wrong person with the information. Especially not tonight.

"Smart man," the baron mumbles. "I should have detained myself better. When he does arrive, please give him my regards."

He spins me around in a dance circle, so that my back faces the dais, then fumbles inside his coat to draw out a letter. He presses it into my hands. "From a mutual friend. I was asked to give this to your father if I saw him, and to you if I did not. I didn't ask questions, and I don't want to know. I knew Claude well enough back in the day to suspect that not all of his activities are entirely legal."

The letter bears a plain wax seal, and through the thin paper, I can make out boxy, practical handwriting. I stare at it for just a moment before tucking it into my bodice.

The queen stands and claps her hands. We all turn to face her. Two guards lead a child forward, and Baron Foutain's cheeks drain of color. She has copper hair just like mine and is dressed in a perfect replica of my gown. A knot of dread forms in my stomach.

One look at Cadence's stricken expression tells me this was not part of the plan the queen relayed to her.

Queen Elene extends her hand to the child, and, trembling, the girl walks to her. The queen situates the child on her lap, and the room goes silent. Even the dancers still, their gasps of frosty breath and the hummingbirds' flutter the only movements in the ballroom. The mages who stand guard behind the queen's throne take a step closer to their sovereign.

"I'm bringing back a Sapphire Age tradition!" the queen proclaims. "And this child shall be my princess of the ball. Isn't that delightful?"

Everyone around me laughs, but Cadence's jaw hangs slack.

In the Sapphire Age, it was customary for the queen to bring a peasant girl into the court, dress her up, and nominate her as princess of the ball for one evening. If the child, with no instruction, could mimic the manners of the court, then she was said to be an orphan of noble parentage, and the queen would have her brought up in the palace. If not, she would be cast back out onto the streets, saddled with the memory of wealth she could never have.

It was a test, just as this is now. Only this test is not for the child, but for Cadence. The queen is playing with her, making her believe that her behavior will influence the night's events. Perhaps the queen will allow the healing of an old duke, perhaps not. But whatever outcome she chooses, she will make sure Cadence believes it's her fault.

The queen bounces the girl on her knee. She smiles at Cadence. "Why don't you find someone nice to dance with? We will have our demonstration later."

There is a threat behind her words. Cadence wrings her hands as the queen offers the child a chocolate strawberry from the tray beside her.

Through the crowd of people, Cadence's eyes find mine, pleading for a reprieve. I take a deep breath and walk toward the throne's dais.

The guests of the ball are my parents' friends, the highest of our society. If I show them what I am, a noble marriage will never be an option for me. I will be deemed tainted by magic, too prone to strange and liberal beliefs to ever make a proper noble bride.

I don't care. Long ago, I made a promise to Cadence, and here, in front of everyone, before I risk everything, I am going to keep it. If the baron is right, and we're all going to die tonight, then I don't want to have any regrets.

I walk to the dais and curtsy so low my knees brush the snow. When I straighten, I look Cadence in the eye and offer her my hand. The queen sucks in a breath, but there is no disapproval in her gaze, only curiosity.

Cadence blushes as my hand hovers, outstretched. Then she takes it and slowly rises.

The other dancers clear the floor. Whether from disapproval at my actions or fear of Cadence, I'm not sure. Our dresses rustle together as we move. I stand opposite her and give a gentlemanly bow. She dips her head, laughing now. Still holding her hand in mine, I wrap my free hand around her slender waist. Her body presses against mine, warm and supple. I look at the two singers by the queen's throne, expecting them to begin the song anew.

"They expect me to sing it." Cadence's lips are so near my ear that her breath makes me shiver. "I outrank them, and they must show deference."

I tighten my arm around her. She begins to sing, and my feet start to move as if by instinct, driven by the spell. I could listen to her forever. Her voice is hauntingly lovely. I watch her full golden lips form many words, but I can only hear *dance, dance*, echoing in my very soul. We move in a whirl of colors, velvet, and taffeta. Cadence's eyes are radiant, alight with careless joy. My body knows only her song. I spin and twirl, letting myself laugh until I cry, forgetting everyone, caught in the thrall of her magic.

When she stops singing, we stand facing each other on the dance floor once more. Still alone. But it's perfect, and I don't care who watches us.

"Beautiful!" the queen exclaims. She gives the court an impervious glare. "Don't you think that was beautiful?"

Everyone begins to clap mechanically.

"Come, come!" The queen motions us toward her.

Cadence squeezes my hand and leads me forward, but the noise and the queen's intrusion break the dance's spell. I can't focus on Cadence anymore. I just stare at the little girl with copper hair in the queen's lap. She's even younger than I was the last time my parents took me court.

We climb the steps to the queen's throne, my feet as heavy as wood.

"I didn't expect that from you." The queen looks up at me and smiles. "It gives me hope that your generation has learned well from the mistakes of your parents. Perhaps it is time to move forward, after all."

There is no way to move forward with a monster who would use a child like this and who believes that the only way to rule is through fear. We have all been puppets in her spectacles long enough.

Nolan said his forces would be ready if I was prepared to provide a distraction. I have to trust that this is true.

I think about Papa, hungry and cold behind a mageglass door. I might never see him or Mama again.

I pull the hairpin out of my bun and plunge it into the queen's heart.

# CHAPTER 30

# CADENCE

**I'VE FORGOTTEN WHAT IT'S** like to sing for the sheer pleasure of it, for the glory of the goddess, for myself. For so long, my songs have been dictated by other people. When I open my mouth to sing for our dance, for only the second time in my life, the words that come are my own composition. They flow as easily as water and guide us as surely as Remi's practiced steps. The music reverberates through my whole body. I'm drunk with magic, brought to life by the hunger in Remi's eyes.

I want to sing away the whole night, held firmly about the waist in the solid arms of a beautiful girl. But slowly, I become aware of the silence in the rest of the ballroom, and of Elene's eyes on us. I stop singing, breathless.

"Beautiful," Elene announces. She raises her hands above

her head and claps. Then she leans forward, glaring at the trembling nobles before her. "Don't you think that was beautiful?"

The mages and common folk around us clap enthusiastically. There is scattered applause among the nobles—a few look delighted, while others bite back barely constrained fury.

Elene beckons us. "Come, come!"

I take Remi's hand, squeezing it. Elene is smiling. She holds Raquelle's hand. For the first time, I wonder if she might actually *approve* of Remi, of me.

When we sat together in the gallery above, overlooking balls like this, I never believed I would be part of one, the center of it.

Elene still holds the child in her lap, but I no longer feel afraid. Tonight at least, she is happy. Everything will be all right. She will present the duke, and I will heal him. The child will be released to her parents. Someday I know I will have to stand up to her, but tonight, everyone will be safe.

Smiling back at the queen, I lead Remi up the dais to the sound of relieved applause.

"I didn't expect that from you," Elene says. "It gives me hope that your generation has learned well from the mistakes of your parents. Perhaps it is time to move forward, after all."

Remi's hand has started to sweat. I want to whisper that it

will all be all right, but Elene's bright eyes are trained on us as she waits for us to answer. So I let go of Remi's hand and curtsy to Elene.

Remi yanks her diamond hairpin free. Its pin is sharp, serrated, and at least as long as my handspan, coated with bright orange fluid. Before I can react, she steps forward and embeds it in Elene's chest.

No one moves. Remi hovers over Elene, her breath still ragged from our dance. Elene's eyelashes flutter in shock. Her hand goes to the pin protruding from her chest, and in that moment, I don't know what to hope. For Elene's death? Her forgiveness? That dancing with me hadn't been Remi's ploy to get close to the queen?

I can still feel Remi's warm, steady hand on my back. I don't want to believe that was a lie.

Cheeks wet with tears, Raquelle slowly pulls the pin from Elene's chest. Around the wound, Elene's flesh has turned purple. Green pus along with blood flows from the injury. Mages flock to Elene from all over the ballroom, already murmuring the words to healing songs. I hum softly with them, not to heal but to form a picture of the wound. Another inch to the left and Remi would have stabbed her clean in the heart. Elene would be beyond the aid of any singer then.

Elene's dress is torn, and blood stains what remains of her bodice, but her expression shows more shock than pain. She touches the wound and stares down at her bloody fingers.

And then her mask slips from her face.

It's the first time I've ever seen her whole face exposed. And for a moment, all I can think is how young and bewildered she looks, nothing like the cold, powerful ruler I know. Her skin is smooth and porcelain white, poreless. Her wide eyes are wet, framed by long black lashes. Her chin trembles as she bites back whimpers of pain. Her hand flies to her cheek in disbelief, feeling for the mask.

Remi stumbles backward, tripping over the steps that lead to the dais. Her eyes are wild with surprise, as if she can't quite believe what she has done. The queen's guards descend on her like a pack of wolves, and the captain hauls her to her feet. The other guards form a phalanx around her. Some of the mages create a wall around the guests at the ball, blocking them from helping Remi. The guards tighten their formation, then march her out of the ballroom. Ren emerges from the shadow of the curtains to follow his guards out.

I want to scream at them not to hurt her, but my voice, which flowed so naturally only a few minutes ago, is stuck in my throat.

As the mages sing, Elene's wound knits together. It closes, but purple lines stretch from the pink scar. Whatever poison coated the hairpin remains in her veins. Elene's eyes lock on my lips. She can see that I am not singing.

"Traitors," she hisses through gritted teeth. "Traitors, all of you."

Elene stands and Raquelle lets the pin fall to the floor. I'm too stunned to move, and everything I rehearsed to say if I had to confront her flies out of my head. Elene seizes me by the hair. I yelp and squirm, but she keeps her hold, her grip steady despite the poison in her veins. She nods to the few remaining guards, and they seal the doors of the ballroom, trapping everyone inside.

"My queen, we have done nothing!" protests a lord near the throne.

Elene's fingers tighten in my hair. My scalp sears with pain. "You planted one of your resistance spies in my court. You have all conspired to assassinate me. You will remain here while we question the traitor."

"That isn't true!" I wail, flailing to get away from her. "You brought Remi here. *You* were the one to arrest her! No one conspired against you. I didn't know a thing!"

"Silence," Elene shrieks. She shakes me so hard I wonder if she will tear the hair straight from my head. "You've had more than enough time to plan this. I'm only surprised you chose such an ineffective method. What was the matter? Afraid to do it yourself?"

She drags me down the dais. The crowd parts like a curtain, too terrified to stand in Elene's way as she marches me out. "I can only imagine how such ideas of treachery got into that girl's head. *You* will be the one to question her, and maybe, once she is dead, I will consider allowing you to remain here."

Trailed by the guards, we march across the courtyard. Cold wind flays my bare shoulder. I fall and scrape my knees on the frosted cobblestones. But Elene doesn't release her hold on my hair until we enter the dungeon. By then, my scalp is numb and my neck screams with pain. I descend the stairs into the lower dungeon, dragged behind her.

The walls of the lower dungeon are damp and covered in hanging moss. Fear seems to drip down them. The air smells cloyingly of mildew and cinnamon. The hairs on the back of my neck rise. How many people have died down here at Ren's hand? Or been left to rot, entombed beneath the earth, held prisoner in the dark at Elene's will?

I will not let that happen to Remi.

A cluster of guards and mages stands in front of a cell at the end of the corridor. Elene marches toward it. Water pools on the dungeon floor, soaking through my shoes. The smell intensifies, so strong that I can taste blood and cinnamon in my mouth.

When we reach the cell, my stomach drops. Unlike the other stone cells in the dungeon, this one is made entirely of transparent mageglass. Remi stands inside, up to her waist in dirty water. Her gown is sodden, weighing her down.

As I watch, Ren flicks his hand at two elemental mages. Sometimes he, like Elene, enjoys the theater of choreographed magic. The elementals sing in unison, their pitches perfectly harmonized. The water in the tank rises at the command of their song. Remi screams as the water pools up to her neck, then covers her entirely. The glass cell fills to the brim. She thrashes wildly in the water.

"Stop!" I shout to the mages. They don't even look at me. They may know what I can do, but they fear Ren and Elene more.

"Yes, stop," Elene says. The water in the glass cell recedes. A small pocket of air appears above Remi's head, and she gasps for breath. Elene grabs me by the bicep, digging her nails into my flesh hard enough to pierce the skin. "You will finish this. It is the only way I will believe you are not a traitor as well."

Remi wraps her arms around her chest and shivers violently. She glares through the glass at Elene with angry, defiant eyes. But when her gaze shifts to me, there's nothing but sadness there.

She no longer believes in me, and that is the worst thing of all.

"I won't do it," I say, and turn to face Elene. "I won't."

Elene just smiles. She studies me for a moment, and then bursts into song.

I feel her magic claw at my throat, but this time I am ready. I belt the words to the defensive song I practiced, praying to Adela to help me. A gentle warmth envelops my skin, and the pressure at my throat becomes as soft as a kiss.

The smile slips from Elene's face, but before she can reconsider her attack, I change my tune. I sing the words to a binding spell, raising my voice and forcing magic into my song.

But my spell doesn't so much as ruffle her hair. She laughs, and frantically I try a heat spell instead, but Elene's lilting cackle just grows louder.

She hums a tune I don't recognize, and the force of it throws me back into the dungeon wall. I crack my head on the stone, and wet blood congeals in my hair. My ears ring. I fall forward onto my knees, coughing. The scents of a winter garden, hellebore and witch hazel, thicken the air like meringue.

I cannot rely on my education. Elene knows what songs to expect from me, because she dictated every part of my curriculum. I was a fool to think that she would not prepare defenses against what I know. Madam Guillard probably told her when she gave me the volume on self-magic to study.

Ren steps forward—too finish what Elene has started, no doubt—but Elene holds up her hand.

He winks at me, then spreads his arms like a conductor. "And one, two, three," he says, nodding to the elementals.

Remi screams, but the water filling the tank soon drowns her cries.

Twenty seconds. Thirty. The blood from my scalp trickles down the back of my neck. The dungeon spins.

Ren looks to Elene again. She nods curtly in response. I notice that her cheeks have taken on a greenish hue, and she has to brace herself on the dungeon wall. The lines of poison have extended above the neckline of her dress.

Ren bows and then grabs me by my hair. The pain is so searing that my stomach heaves. He hits me across the face with enough force to make my vision swim, and I am reminded so vividly of all the times he did this when I was a child, that I whimper.

Forty seconds, then a minute. Remi's fists beat frantically on the glass.

"And release," Ren instructs.

The water lowers, draining to Remi's waist. She gasps and splutters, her skin tinged with blue.

"How many times do you think we can do it and keep her alive?" Ren asks the elementals. "Twenty?"

The respite is not a mercy. Ren means to make her suffer, to relive the horror of drowning again and again, with no hope of survival. The look in her eyes—she's given up. If I don't act, she will die. And after Elene makes me witness it, she will kill me as well.

I clutch the lapis prayer stone around my neck. I have perverted Adela's gift and knowingly served a heretical queen. I don't deserve the goddess's help, but I beg for it anyway. I visualize the prayer candles in my bedroom and recall the reedy voices of my music boxes. My breathing slows, and some of the panic ebbs.

A tune comes to me, the melody of a song I barely know. A well of magic opens inside me, power that isn't mine. I begin to mumble the words of the sleeping death. It's a delicate piece, sung above my natural range. I have never been able to master it, to hit each note with the precision the magic requires, because Elene never allowed me to dedicate the time. It's effective, but painless, and therefore of no use to her.

An unfamiliar scent fills the air around me, a warm summer perfume of sunflower and meadow grass cutting through the damp. It's not the lavender aroma of my own magic, but the signature of another, working through me. Adela, making her will known at last. Elene doesn't expect the force of the spell. She isn't ready to defend herself. When it hits her, her knees buckle, and she crumbles to the floor, unmoving.

The mages and guards standing around me fall to their knees in supplication. Even Ren kneels, his eyes wide with astonishment. In her cell, Remi laughs, and her breathless rasp is the sweetest music in the world.

"You will unlock the prison," I say, clenching my hands at my sides.

My voice is steady, though I still feel an unfamiliar power roiling inside me. The sight of Elene, motionless on the floor, both terrifies and thrills me.

I swallow hard. In attacking Elene, have I started another war? Maybe I should kill her and end the power struggle before it can begin. But I'm not fit to judge Elene, and I can't bring myself to end her life.

I focus my attention on Ren, who cowers behind two of his mages. He has hurt me more than Elene ever has. I'm glad he's afraid, so he will finally understand some of what I have felt for so many years. I want to hurt him, but whatever I do to him now isn't going to chase away all my memories.

I turn to the elementals instead. "Drain the cell."

The rest of the water in the cell slowly vanishes. The guards step forward and unlock it. As soon as the door opens, Remi rushes from the cell to throw her wet arms around me. Her eyes glisten with hope. Her skin is freezing, but when her cold lips crash against mine, heat flares inside me.

We break apart, conscious of our audience, but the shock of the kiss leaves my stomach fluttering.

Remi looks down at Elene and kicks her in the side. None of the guards move to stop her.

"We have to get back to the ballroom," I say. "The mages there will be arresting the guests, trying to get information."

A wry smile twists Remi's lips. "I think those who remain are about to get a shock."

One of the elementals steps forward, wringing her hands. Without meeting my eyes, she asks, "Shall I dry her clothes?"

I nod, and the mage summons the water from the fabric of Remi's dress, from her hair and skin. She lifts the dirt particles and lets them fall to the floor in a pile of sand. When the girl has finished, Remi looks almost as good as she did on the dance floor.

Elene stirs and rolls onto her back, groaning. The guards immediately leap into a protective circle around her, their loyalty swinging like a pendulum. My eyes widen. The spell should have lasted for hours. Somehow, Elene must have managed a few bars of a defensive spell before my magic hit her, or else Odetta is making her protection known.

The idea of a war within the quartet, of two goddesses using us as proxies for their fight fills me terror, but I push the guards aside. I have to act quickly, before she is able to get her bearings again, so I decide to stick to a song I know well, something I have practiced again and again to perfection.

The heat ballad tumbles from my lips.

Elene shrieks as I focus my power on her forehead. I want to conjure a fever, which will keep her on the floor.

Both of Elene's hands fly to her head. She shakes it from side to side, as if she can expel the magic like water from her ears. Then she curls into a fetal position, banging her forehead on the dungeon's stones. Sweat drips from her brow, and tears leak from her eyes.

"Please," she begs. "Please."

"You have to kill her," Remi says.

My throat is so dry I can't speak, but I shake my head.

I beckon the captain of the guard forward. "Take her and the chief justicar into custody. Take the prisoner out of the mageglass cell on the fifth level and release him. Put these two inside, instead."

"Don't be so naive!" Remi hisses. "He'll free them as soon as you walk away! You know he will!"

The captain ignores her. "It will be done," he says with a curt nod to me.

One of his men grabs Ren by the arm and hauls him over to Elene. The queen eases herself to her feet, trembling. The guards form a cluster around them and herd them up the stairs.

"I can't believe you. How can you be so foolish?" Remi snaps. "You know what she's done. She's murdered hundreds of innocent people—slaughtered entire families! If she's dead, then there is no chance for another war to begin. It will all be over."

"This is my choice," I say, and cross my arms over my chest. "And I am choosing not to be like her."

Remi opens her mouth to speak again, but I cut her off. "We need to go back."

I turn on my heel and begin to climb the dungeon steps.

# CHAPTER 31

# CADENCE

**WE'RE GREETED BY CHAOS** in the ballroom. Ragged soldiers armed with muskets and swords surround a group of nobles who kneel on the floor. Mages hurl songs in their direction, only to be answered by a volley of bullets. Other singers leave the mages' ranks to side with the common soldiers, projecting their voices over the gunfire and targeting those still loyal to Elene. A few of the nobles have broken off legs of chairs and shards of ice and are using them as weapons in the fray. Blood seeps into the magic snow.

I recognize some of the palace servants among the army. Etienne huddles behind a chair, aiming a hunting rifle at a mage. One of the cooks stands on the gallery above and pours heated oil down onto a singer below.

A young black man dressed in the teal livery of the mason's

guild seems to be rallying them. He uses silent hand signals to convey his commands.

For a moment, all I can do is stand in the doorway in shock. How long has this been brewing? How many rebels have infiltrated the palace and worked right under the queen's nose?

Has Remi known all along?

Then an elemental mage in a justicar's uniform aims a blast of fire at a young man who crouches behind the refreshment table. The fire misses the youth but shatters the ice hummingbirds in the air as they chirp, showering the boy in shards. His face is familiar, and when he spots me, he grins. It's the same boy I healed at Saint Izelea's, cursed with Ren's binding spell.

Before I can react, another mage sings and the justicar falls, the skin of her face ripped off to reveal pink tendons and a glimpse of the yellow-white skull beneath.

With Remi at my side, I lift my chin and force myself to stride into the room. My abilities are known throughout the queendom, and in Elene's absence, they confer a kind of status. The other mages will listen to me if I speak boldly, with Elene's authority.

"Nolan!" Remi shouts at the young commander.

He starts and whirls around at the sound of her voice. Seeing us together, he signals to his fighters to stand down.

Everyone goes silent as we walk to the queen's dais. My wet

shoes leave a trail of water behind us. Raquelle has vanished, leaving three seats vacant. For a second, I consider sitting on Elene's throne, but I arrange my skirt and sit in my own chair.

The commander approaches, winking at Remi before he sinks into Elene's throne. He has a handsome face and a roguish glimmer in his eyes that makes me like him immediately. He braces a musket across his knees. The rebel forces stand at attention, but although they don't attack, Elene's mages keep their focus on their targets. If I don't say the right words now, they will slaughter the rebels before they can pick up their weapons.

"The queen has been arrested. She is now in custody," I say. The other mages stare openly, some with joy, others with reproach.

"Arrested? How?" intones an elderly black noblewoman. She wears a fine gray silk gown that has been torn across the shoulder. There are spatters of blood on the dress's hem, but something in her fearless expression makes me doubt it is hers. She takes a step forward, balancing on a cane. She points the cane at me accusingly. The tapered end is coated with slick blood. "We're supposed to believe the word of her pet singer? The queen is playing us all for fools, hoping we'll speak against her and incriminate ourselves when we have done nothing but defend ourselves from attack. We all know you. If she has been arrested, *you* should be in prison beside her."

I flinch, but Remi comes to my defense. "Queen Elene has been taken into custody to face trial. I am Remi de Bordelain, daughter of Claude and Laurel. If you won't take her word, then take mine."

The old woman scowls, and her deep brown eyes narrow. "And let her crown herself as the new queen? We should kill her and the queen she serves."

Slowly, the other guests rise. But despite my words, they still regard me with open hostility. Some look ready to strangle me where I sit. I take a deep breath and reach for Remi's hand.

The old woman plants her hands on her hips and says, "Elene was a usurper. If she is gone, her power should pass to the next of the old queen's line. My great-niece."

"The old queen's line?" one of the mages demands. He opens his arms and turns to the other mages huddled beside the throne. "The quartet gave us magic. We were meant to rule.

Cadence is the most powerful in the academy, so she should have guardianship of the throne, to appoint someone else if she chooses. Or we could even have a king."

"A king?" the noblewoman spits. "We haven't had a king in five hundred years! Everyone knows men aren't fit to rule."

The singer turns to the woman and begins to hum. But before his song can take effect, another mage summons a cyclone that sweeps him up and spits him out across the room.

Nolan flashes the defender a grin. "With the queen deposed, we will have a chance to start over," he says. "Queen Celeste died without producing any direct heirs. Your niece, madam, is only a distant cousin. As I see it, we have a chance to create something else, for all of us."

A murmur of ascent goes up from the commoners in the room. Some of the nobles and mages look skeptical, but they hold their peace.

And then the ballroom doors fly open.

Elene stumbles inside with her mask back in place. Ren follows, dragging an unconscious form behind him. Beside me, Remi gasps.

Ren hauls Remi's father into the center of the room as dazed nobles part to allow them passage.

"I am going to gut him with my magic. I will make all his

bones disintegrate and crush the breath from his body," Ren pants.

Elene points a long finger at me. "You little fool. I have been on the throne since you were a child. I have bled for it. Did you think I would go quietly? After you conspired to poison me?"

Fury glimmers in Elene's eyes. If I want to get any of us out of the ballroom alive, I have to see this through.

I have to be willing to kill.

Elene utters a shrill note, her voice straining to hit the pitch, and Remi's father is propelled upright. He sags in the air as if held by puppet strings, and his body jerks violently. His left arm pops from its socket.

"Cadence," Remi whispers. "Please."

Elene's voice echoes around the ballroom. She sings the words to a song I don't know, and as she does, blood begins to pour from the viscount's nose and eyes. Without thinking, I begin the defensive song I learned for myself, but instead of directing the magic inward, I throw it out wide. I force as much magic as I can into the song. A sapphire shield breaks through the floor and encases Remi's father.

Ren steps in front of Elene. I don't hesitate this time. He has bullied me—hurt me—all my life, and today, it finally stops. I project my voice so that my spell hits him in full. The crunch of bone rings in my ears as his back breaks and his severed spine is pulled through his skin. A snarl of pain and rage erupts from his throat, drowned by the gurgle of blood. His rib cage cracks and splays like wings. The anger in his eyes dims and fades.

I don't notice that the other mages are singing until Ren collapses. Elene is on the floor, lulled into a stupor by their powerful sleeping song. With so much magic directed against her, there was no defense she could sing to deflect.

Blood pools under Ren's body. He looks small like this, folded in on himself with his knees drawn to his broken chest. I expect to feel guilt, but it doesn't come. Instead, I feel so light I could laugh.

I lower the magic shield and Remi runs to her father. They embrace, and the viscount begins to sob. I hum a few notes to check his status. Though his heartbeat is wild and his shoulder is torn, he will survive.

Madam Guillard peers out from behind a curtain at the rear of the ballroom. She walks to the dais, hands clenched at her sides. She curtsies nervously to Nolan, then produces a small pouch from her cloak pocket.

"If you want to detain her," she says quietly, "you will need this."

She pulls a small gold knife from the pouch. I recognize it immediately as the knife she hid on her bookshelf, the one she so ardently forbade me to touch.

When I look at it, the same uneasy feeling I had in her room crawls down my spine. The same smell of slaughter emanates from the blade.

"This is entrusted to all the headmistresses of the academy," she says warily. "Our position requires more than watching over the school, and our duty of discipline extends to all mages we have trained. This is an enchanted blade, created by a priest in the fourth century. A small nick across the throat, just deep enough to draw blood, will activate a spell that will sever her vocal cords."

Suddenly I can't breathe. I look at Madam Guillard.

"Is it the only one of its kind?"

Madam Guillard bows her head. "Yes."

I think about Anette. Her only crime was not having enough magic to satisfy Elene. The Expelled settlement is filled with people whose stories are just like hers. I always thought the ceremony to be a brutal thing, done at the hands of the justicars. Never had I imagined that the weapon used to strip so many innocent people of their song and speech has been sitting on my beloved tutor's shelf all along.

Tears flow down Madam's cheeks, but she meets my eyes. "You have your shame to bear," she says, and holds up the knife. "This is mine."

She walks over to where Elene lies. She crouches down and

presses the knife to Elene's throat. "This was my mistake," she says. "I should have done this the night of Queen Celeste's murder, when you first came to me with blood on your hands."

I take a deep breath then rise. My legs shake with each step, but I walk over to my tutor and hold out my hand for the dagger. Tonight, while others fought, she again chose to hide, to stay neutral. Perhaps she sees this as her moment to prove her worth to the resistance leaders, to the nobles assembled, to Remi, to me.

I won't give her the chance.

Madam sighs then hesitantly passes the blade to me.

I kneel on the floor beside Elene and take her head in my lap. I remove her mask and toss it across the room. Then, in a smooth motion, I cut a faint line across her throat. Bright blood drips from the cut onto the lace collar of her dress. She doesn't stir.

CHAPTER 32

# CADENCE

**THE TRIAL TAKES PLACE** a few weeks later. Folk from all over the country travel to Cannis to present evidence against Elene. Even some of Elene's most trusted mages have agreed to give testimony against her in exchange for lesser sentences. Stacks of letters are presented, secret correspondence between Lacerde and the leaders of the rebellion, detailing all of Elene's crimes within the palace. The sodden note given to Remi during the ball and concealed within her bodice is pressed and dried out, the smeared ink magically restored so it can be read aloud.

A jury comprising singers, nobles, and common folk listens to the proceedings. Remi's mother takes on the role of judge. Elene doesn't try to defend herself at the trial. She wears a red scarf around her throat, her face maskless. When the court scribes offer her a pen and paper to write her testimony, she refuses.

The jury sentences the former queen to death, but Remi's mother commutes it to life in a mageglass cell. Even if she rediscovers how to access her powers, as the mages in the Expelled colony have done, she will not be able to escape. Most of the nobles of the jury fight the outcome, but in the end they concede that the divisions between mage, commoner, and noble are deep enough that the country should focus on moving forward, on coming together. For the first time, we are to have a president, not a queen. Whoever wins the elections will need support from all three factions.

Other than when I am summoned to give testimony, I am not allowed to attend the trial. My own sentence has been commuted. In exchange for saving Remi, and incapacitating Elene, I will not stand trial. For now. I have been moved out of the palace and installed in an old town house a stone's throw from Saint Izelea's, where am I guarded day and night. Lacerde has opted to stay with me.

Still, in the new Bordea, even monsters like me can be put to use. Though I am not allowed to leave the confines of the town house, I spend my days writing new, more versatile healing songs and tending to the patients Saint Izelea's sends my way.

The final evening of Elene's trial, Remi comes to the town

house to visit. Lacerde lets her in, but I don't go downstairs to greet her. Instead, I sit on my bed, surrounded by my music sheets and ink, and just listen to the merry patter of her footsteps as she bounds up the rickety old stairs.

She knocks hesitantly on my bedroom door, then pushes it open. She gathers my papers into a neat pile and plucks the inkwell from its rest in the crook of my knee. She plops down on the bed beside me with a tired sigh.

Her mother is running in the open election, and we haven't had much time alone. Remi has been spreading flyers and speaking to the people her mother may one day rule. If Laurel of Bordelain becomes president, I hope that whatever is between Remi and me won't have to end. A leader may want to cement her alliances. Remi may well face even more pressure to marry.

It's looking likely that her mother will win. Lacerde brings me the papers daily, and Laurel's actions as one of the secret leaders of the resistance are featured in nearly every headline. The letters she wrote and sent to all corners of the country, containing coded plans, have all been printed. The commoners love Laurel for her progressive views, and her title gives her credibility among the still unsure nobility. We mages respect her for her fairmindedness at Elene's trial.

"What would your parents think?" I murmur as Remi maneuvers to sit behind me. She begins to kiss the side of my neck.

"About what?" she asks, nuzzling my hair and nibbling my earlobe.

"What we're doing." I turn to face her. "If you're going to have to marry soon, maybe it's time to accept—"

Remi rolls her eyes. She takes both of my hands. "Oh, we're the talk of the court already. *All* of them saw us dance at the ball." She cups her mouth and shouts, mimicking the news criers in the square. "Future president's daughter embroiled with former principal!"

"And your parents don't care?"

She shrugs. "Before we were arrested, they were doing everything they could to marry me to a commoner. I was afraid to tell them that I didn't want to marry a man, but after everything that has happened, they're just happy I'm alive. They don't care who I love."

"*Love?*" I say, my voice rising an octave too high. "And if your mother becomes president? Won't you need a political marriage?"

Even knowing Elene's prejudices, after everything she's told me about nobles, it's hard to imagine Remi's parents just accepting it. Us.

"The country is changing," Remi insists. She tugs a lock of my hair. "Mama wishes you had a different past, but she accepts me. She doesn't care that you're a woman. Give her time to get to know you."

I smile at that and push the last of my papers off the bed. They land in a flurry.

"There's going to be chaos," Remi says as she wraps her legs around my waist and pulls me backward into a sea of white pillows. "With all the new systems Mama wants to put in place. She wants to break down all the barriers between nobles, mages, and commoners. Some share her vision, but it's not going to be easy. You were the most powerful of the queen's singers, so I'm sure she'll be knocking on your door before long, trying to get your endorsement."

"Then she can't very well separate us, can she?" A fragile hope takes root inside me. The mages all respect me, for my magic if nothing else. I can bring them around for the viscountess.

Before I can think anymore about it, I lean in and brush my lips over hers. Her grip on my chin tightens, and she pulls me against her. We fall back against the pillows, a tangle of limbs and soft kisses.

Every nerve inside me sings. It feels as though my lips have waited a lifetime for this, as if I had known when we met at six years old that we'd be together like this one day, and everything we did in between would just be wasted time.

Much later, we break apart, and Remi bounces off the bed. "I have to meet with my father, but have dinner with us tomorrow night. Mama will give you a pass to leave the town house. She really does want to meet you."

"Of course," I whisper.

When she leaves, I gather my papers again, but I can't banish the smile from my lips.

Another knock sounds on the door. I glance up, expecting Remi to come bounding back in, for a final kiss, or because she forgot her purse. But when no one enters, I call, "Come in."

One of my new guards opens the door and tips his hat to me. He carries a long white box under his arm. "A present," he says.

I sit up straighter and motion to my dressing table. "Put it down over there."

The guard nods. He places the box in front of the mirror and then scrambles out the door again. Pulling the stool from under my table, I sit beside the package. The box is simple, without decoration. There is no ribbon or card tied to the outside. I ease off the lid and peer inside.

The box contains a lone tulip. It's a pale pink, with bright red stains on the edge of each petal. Drops of water still cling to the stem, and when I lift the flower, they remain frozen in place. I lift it to my nose and inhale. The aroma is crisp, and slightly too sweet. A light perfume of familiar magic still lingers.

# ACKNOWLEDGMENTS

First and foremost, I want to thank my family. My wife, Sophie, who is the stable rock of our relationship in the face of my chaos. Thank you for supporting my dreams and for all those morning cups of tea. Thank you also to my parents for nurturing a lifelong love of reading and always encouraging me to pursue writing. Though they will never read this and their helpfulness is questionable, thank you to my two cats for being my daily writing buddies.

Secondly, I want to thank all the people who made *Ruinsong* into a book! My agent, Eric Smith, who, when I first described the book to him, literally said, "You have my sword!" and has been its champion ever since. *Ruinsong* could not have found a home without you. My amazing editor at FSG, Trisha de Guzman, who believed in this book and whose feedback, notes, and encouragement have been truly instrumental in shaping *Ruinsong* into the story it is now. To the fantastic team at FSG and Macmillan Kids, especially Cassie Gonzales, Taylor Pitts, Celeste

Cass, Jill Freshney, Elizabeth Clark, Jessica Warren, Nancee Adams-Taylor, Mandy Veloso, and Brian Luster. To Rebecca Schaeffer, who stepped up into the thankless role of Chief CP and Publishing Therapist, and who I am thankful for every single time I plow into her DMs. To Katherine Locke, whose help was significant in shaping *Ruinsong* from its early drafts. To Jenn, Chasia, Suzanne, Sangu, Erica, CM, and Gabe for offering invaluable feedback on *Ruinsong* along the way.

I also want to thank the amazing writing friends who have supported me during my writing journey. To C. B. Lee, who always knows what to say to make me feel better and who has included me in so many of her conference adventures. To Laura Lam and Kaite Welsh, and the rest of the Edinburgh Monday writers: Thank you for your support while I was writing this book and on submission! Seattle is great, but I miss you. To my newfound Seattle writing crew—Rachel Lynn Solomon, Rachel Griffin, Margaret Owen, Jennifer Mace, Alix Kaye, and A. J. Hackwith—thank you for welcoming me to your city and being ready with coffee and cocktails when I have needed you! To Team Rocks and all the Fight Me crew—thank you for being fountains of knowledge and unending support over the last few years.

Finally, thank you to my readers, for taking a chance on this book and embarking on this journey with me!

# GOFISH

## JULIA EMBER

**What did you want to be when you grew up?**
In grade school, I really wanted to be an equine veterinarian! I've always loved and ridden horses, and it seemed like the ideal job to me! Unfortunately, science and math were not my best subjects at school, so in middle school, my focus turned toward being a lawyer because I was good at arguing with people (or so my mom said frequently). I never pursued either of those career paths as an adult!

**When did you realize you wanted to be a writer?**
I think I always had some sense that I wanted to write a novel, but I didn't have a good grasp of what it might mean to have a career in writing or be an author until much later. I was always a huge reader—I have a lot of middle school memories of my parents leaving me in bookstore cafés with stacks of books to keep me occupied while they went shopping for clothes.

I also wrote literally millions of words of fan fiction in high school and, in tenth grade, wrote my first original novel because our school required us to do a yearlong substantial personal project. I tried unsuccessfully to query it with agents. This was back in the days of snail mail queries, and, after more rejections than I could handle, I stopped opening them and just kept the sealed envelopes in a box. I opened the last of them live on a panel where several YA authors read from their teen writing at RTCon in 2017, after the publication of my first novel, which has always felt right, exactly the kind of "See, I *could* do it!" moment my teen self would have relished.

**What sparked your imagination for** *Ruinsong*?
I grew up absolutely loving musical theater. My family moved to London when I was nine, and we frequently went to see plays on the West End. I felt then, and still do, that there was something really magical about old Victorian- and Regency-era theaters with their frescoes, marble floors, and rows of perfect velvet seats. In high school, I would frequently take the train into the city with friends, and we would visit the last-minute-ticket booth to get the cheapest tickets they had—which often involved sitting behind pillars or being squashed in the back row.

Writing a book with a musical magic system was always on my radar to some extent, because I wanted to capture the feeling of awe that I experienced in London theaters in a fantasy setting. Then, a few years ago, I reread the classical *Phantom of the Opera*, and the idea started taking a firmer hold as a retelling.

**What were your hobbies as a kid? What are your hobbies now?**
Horseback riding, gaming, and reading—and I really have not changed! I still ride horses multiple times a week and am currently playing my way through *Assassin's Creed Valhalla* for the second run. I still adore reading, but it can at

times be a little more complicated for me as a writer than it was when I was kid, since there is quite a bit of pressure to keep up with books being recently published in your genre.

I also cycle and go for long walks, which I find really inspiring for writing. I love to be outdoors and don't mind poor weather!

## What book is on your nightstand now?

My nightstand is always extremely chaotic, and right now I have seven books on it! *Wilder Girls* by Rory Power, which I just finished, and it was incredible—so visceral and creepy! My current read, *Deathless Divide* by Justina Ireland, the sequel to *Dread Nation*, which was one of my favorite books of 2018. I have my semi-permanent stack of three writing-craft books I keep meaning to read and haven't yet, though sometimes I trick myself into believing just looking at them counts as productivity. Then I have two new books (at the time of writing) that I just bought: *We Are the Fire* by Sam Taylor and *A Dark and Hollow Star* by Ashley Shuttleworth!

## Where do you write your books?

Where I work is dependent on where I am in the writing process. I need to be alone to draft, so I usually work on new projects in my office. This is partly because I talk to myself and read phrases out loud while writing a first draft, and partly that my first drafts are so chaotic, raw, and personal to me that I can't handle other people looking at me while I work on them! (Or even worse, trying to read them over my shoulder!)

Most of *Ruinsong* was written at my kitchen table in

Scotland because I didn't have a home office before we moved back to the United States. For editing, I love to work in coffee shops and cafés with writer friends! Long-distance flights or train rides are also especially productive spaces for me, because there is no internet and I can't sleep at all while flying.

**Cadence can come across as pretty unsympathetic at times. Why did you decide to write a POV character who lives in more shades of gray?**
As readers now know, the world of *Ruinsong* is a brutal place. Queen Elene sees people starkly as either with her or against her, and missteps can get you killed or worse. In developing Cadence, I wanted to create a character who was very anxious and aware of the danger she was immersed in, but who had a good heart underneath her cowardice. All of her life, Cadence has been raised to be one thing: a weapon of torture for the queen. She has been taught that is her purpose and been ruthlessly shown what will happen to her if she doesn't comply, both through being shown the expelled settlement and through Ren's direct physical abuse of her. Yet she doesn't want to be a weapon at all. She wants the opposite: to be a healer.

At the start of the book, I saw Cadence as a character trying to perform a balancing act. She knows that what she does for the queen is awful, but she hopes she can wipe her slate clean in a way by healing patients in the hospital. It's only after her atrocities become more personal to her, when she realizes what she has done to Remi, that she starts to understand her balancing act has never been enough.

I think very few people are born as brave as Remi and

many other YA heroines, so I wanted to create a character who remains essentially fearful but is able to work through her terror to do what is right.

## What challenges do you face in the writing process, and how do you overcome them?

I think a lot of writers struggle with the often-joked-about "thirty-thousand-word hump," and I am certainly one of them! I find it easier to write openings, because I spend quite a long time ruminating on new ideas and plotting them, but by the time I get to the novel's second act (which is usually around thirty to forty thousand words in), I have to start thinking about bringing together all the plot threads I introduced and how I might conclude. It can be overwhelming and is also the point where I experience the most self-doubt—wondering if I have the skills to finish, whether anyone will like the manuscript, etc.

I cope with this in one of two ways. If my schedule allows, I'll take a break and let myself ruminate all over again on the middle and end sections of the book. I'm not the kind of writer who believes you have to write every day to be successful, so I do build breaks into my drafting process. If I'm on a deadline, I will write up a very detailed outline—so detailed it's almost a draft but not quite, so that I can trick my brain into figuring the plot out without worry that anyone will read the sentences I'm writing!

## How did you celebrate publishing your first book?

When *The Seafarer's Kiss* came out in 2017, I went to Atlanta for a book convention. It was a great experience for me because I got to meet that book's publishing team in person for the first time. On the actual release day, my girlfriend (now my wife) and I slipped away from the convention for a while and went to the Georgia Aquarium, where we hung out with beluga whales! The whales were a huge part of the book and are my favorite animals, so it was a special day.

**What was your favorite book when you were a kid? Do you have a favorite book now?**
I had a few favorite series as a kid: Artemis Fowl by Eoin Colfer and all the books of Tamora Pierce's expansive Tortall Universe, especially her Protector of the Small quartet. For me, Keladry was such a selfless and inspiring protagonist, and I was obsessed with her grumpy horse, Peachblossom. (I really think Tamora Pierce can take credit for inspiring an entire legion of millennial YA authors! So many authors I know and love reference her works as being foundational for them.)

Now my favorites tend to change all the time. I'm constantly reading and discovering new voices!

**What do you want readers to remember about your books?**
I think my books share a common theme of protagonists discovering the power of their voices. In *Ruinsong*, this is not subtle through the explosive magic that Cadence works, but it is a shared theme across my work. I hope that readers will be inspired by this and realize that yes, your voice does matter and can make an impact!

My books tend to be pretty dark, but I hope for my queer readers that they will find comfort and hope in the happy endings my girls find even in the bleakest of worlds.

## What's the best advice you have ever received about writing?

Your first draft is about path finding and only for you! I used to get very stressed out trying to perfect my first draft and would edit the opening scenes over and over until I was satisfied with them before moving on. But it's not really a manuscript yet at that stage, and therefore, not something I would show even my gentlest critique partners. Another piece of great advice I received, which goes along with this, is that you can't edit what you haven't written yet, so you have to focus on finishing first. Writing is a lot like sculpting, constantly reshaping a rough ball of clay. You can only really see where the flaws are once you have a manuscript nearing completion!

For emerging writers with a completed manuscript, I can't recommend mentorship programs like Pitch Wars or Author Mentor Match strongly enough. I think a lot of writers hold back from entering these contests because they see them as all about querying or finding an agent, but the real purpose is to form communities and ensure new writers are getting the best possible support and guidance. There is so much community building leading up to entering that, whether your work is accepted or not for the program, you meet other writers and potential critique partners. I would be very lost without writer friends on my own journey!

## Do you have favorite music to listen to while writing?

It really depends on the manuscript and what stage I'm at in the writing process! While I'm still outlining, I like to listen to music that captures the mood of the project I'm working on. With *Ruinsong*, unsurprisingly, I listened to a lot of songs from the *Phantom of the Opera* soundtrack, and also *Symphony* by Clean Bandit pretty much on repeat! However, once I start drafting, I have to listen to music without lyrics. I love to listen to game music because the soundtracks are often hours long and have an epic-fantasy feel to them. My all-time favorite game music is from *The Witcher III: The Wild Hunt*, from the islands of Skellige! More recently, since I got a puppy, I've been listening to a lot of soft, classical cello music because it puts him to sleep so I can write.

**What draws you to retelling fairy tales and classic stories? What are some of your favorite YA retellings other than your own?**

One of my favorite things to play with as a writer is reader expectation. With retellings, readers generally come to the story with ideas about what the characters, the narrative arc, or the setting will be like, linked to their previous experiences of an original tale or a movie version. I love to begin my books with something that feels familiar, but then swiftly diverge from the known. *Ruinsong* opens with a scene that would be instantly recognizable to *Phantom of the Opera* lovers—an audition for a potential patron—but then quickly takes a very dark turn when we realize that Cadence is being asked to kill a child with her magic to avoid a terrible fate herself. With my duology, which is a *Little Mermaid* retelling, I opened with a shipwreck and a drowning man, whom readers might expect to be the "Prince Eric" figure, but the main character lets him die because their love interest is a woman who has already saved herself from the wreckage. As a queer writer, there is also something powerful for me in reinterpreting beloved stories that have historically been very heterosexual.

I really loved Leigh Bardugo's entire *Language of Thorns* short story collection because the stories are such original retellings. With a few of them, it took me a while to even realize which classic they were based on, and I adored that because it was like solving a puzzle. Some of my other favorites are *Girls Made of Snow and Glass* by Melissa Barshardoust, *A Clash of Steel* by C. B. Lee, *Peter Darling* by Austin Chant, *Forest of a Thousand Lanterns* by Julie C. Dao, and *The Wrath and the Dawn* by Renée Ahdieh.

## What is your favorite part of the writing process?

I love writing the second draft! My first drafts are usually pretty lean, sometimes not even half of the book's finished length, and they're exploratory—I'm still figuring out a lot of the plot elements as I go. By the second draft, I know where I'm going, I know the characters, and I understand the book's themes. In the second draft, I'm adding layers, writing secondary plots, fleshing out characters without the stress of navigating the unknown . . . and without pressure to make it perfect because I know the book will still go through many more drafts in the future. It's a very relaxed and happy writing stage for me!

## What is the first thing you would do if you had Cadence's magical powers?

If I had Cadence's corporeal magical abilities, I would probably risk dangerous self-magic to cure myself of back pain like she does for Remi in the book! I hunch over my keyboard when I work, and it causes all kinds of issues! After that, I might turn my attention to destroying my enemies or pursuing my childhood dream job as a horse veterinarian after all; good at math and science or not, they would have to accept a candidate who could magically cure tumors and difficult-to-treat suspensory ligament injuries.